KATLYN DUNCAN grew up in a small town in Massachusetts with her head always in the clouds. Working as a scientist for most of her adult life, she enjoyed breaking down the hows and whys of life. This translated into her love of stories and getting into the minds of her characters. Currently, she has published twelve books with HQ Digital and has ghostwritten over forty novels.

When she's not writing, she's obsessing over many (many) television series. She currently resides in Connecticut with her husband, kiddo, and adorable senior citizen dog (who will forever be a puppy at heart!).

Also by Katlyn Duncan

Wrapped Up for Christmas

KATLYN DUNCAN

ONE PLACE. MANY STORIES

HQ
An imprint of HarperCollins*Publishers* Ltd
1 London Bridge Street
London SE1 9GF

This paperback edition 2019

1

First published in Great Britain by
HQ, an imprint of HarperCollins*Publishers* Ltd 2019

ISBN: 9780008405205

MIX
Paper from
responsible sources
FSC
www.fsc.org   FSC® C007454

This book is produced from independently certified FSC™ paper
to ensure responsible forest management.

For more information visit: www.harpercollins.co.uk/green

Printed and bound in Great Britain by
CPI Group (UK) Ltd, Croydon CR0 4YY

For anyone who can get the Christmas feels no matter what time of year or how hot it is outside. This book is for you.

Chapter 1

The Christmas song blaring from the pocket of the man in front of Angie was the last straw. He turned off the ringer of his phone, but that was it for her. She hadn't even reached the end of the jet bridge before heat surged behind her eyes for the dozenth time that afternoon.

Don't you dare cry, Angie Martinelli.

At least not until she'd buried herself under the covers in the room she hadn't slept in since high school.

A day ago, she had lain in her queen-sized bed with eight hundred thread count sheets. When she wasn't in her apartment, she was in Brett's California king, treating it like a twin. She recalled the firmness of his body, snuggling up against him—

'No,' she hissed, startling the family of four next to her. The parents tucked their children closer to them, away from the crazy woman talking to herself. 'Sorry.'

The mother grabbed onto her daughter's backpack and steered her into the airport.

Angie tried to take a calming breath, wanting to push Brett and his cheating self to the farthest reaches of her mind. She gripped her rolling carry-on bag and adjusted her handbag on her shoulder.

With her belongings accounted for, she swiped away a stray tear threatening to fall and dipped her chin against her chest as she made her way through the waiting area toward baggage claim. Angie was determined to keep everyone out of her business – even strangers. She was adamant that they weren't going to see the tortured expression she wore on her face. As an only child, she prided herself on being a strong and independent woman.

Or at least, she used to.

Once she reached the food court, the scent of greasy cuisine filled her nose. Her stomach ached for something to eat; she had waited too long on the flight to get one of the prepared meals and they were sold out. Nothing on the plane went her way. She sat behind someone who reclined their chair the entire time and the three complimentary bags of chips did nothing to ease her emotions as her mind and stomach churned across the country.

Angie stopped in front of a pub and hesitated, thinking of her bank account. Dollar signs filled her vision for the charges she'd had to pay for the three extra suitcases she'd brought with her. Only one more deposit would come through her account for her severance pay and then nothing. She shook her head, her long dark hair swooping across her face. It clung to her damp cheeks as she tucked the stray strands behind her ears before heading to baggage claim. She could wait to eat until she arrived at home. No doubt her mom would have prepared a feast for her already.

As she followed the signs toward the first level of the airport, she managed to hold back the dam of tears that threatened to break. She was doing well until she saw a handwritten sign on lined paper which read 'Aunty' taped to the huge belly of her best friend standing next to the unmoving carousel.

Tears burst from her eyes as Angie sagged into Reese's arms and sobbed against her shoulder. The ugly, snotty cry that only a best friend or mother could take without feeling utterly disgusted.

Reese patted Angie's back. 'Let it all out, girl.'

'How was the flight?' her husband, Jeremy, asked.

Angie choked out a laugh and wiped her nose with the sleeve of her shirt. 'Hi, Jer.'

The tall and still handsome high school football champion of their day stood a few feet away, clearly freaked out by the tears coursing down her face. Ten years after graduating, he had aged well. His mother always said youthful genes were a blessing in their family despite the lighter strands now peppered throughout his jet-black hair.

Men had it so easy.

A flash of Brett's blond locks and million-watt smile threatened to crumple Angie's composure.

Reese flipped her caramel hair over her shoulder. It seemed smoother than ever. Reese had been over the moon when she found out what pregnancy hormones did to her body. Her warm brown eyes peered down at Angie, filled with concern and warmth.

Angie couldn't imagine starting a family, never mind getting married, since her life was already over. The dramatics were unnecessary, but it was hard to think of anyone but Brett at the moment. He had been the vision of her future. Now what?

'Why don't you grab Angie's bags?' Reese said to Jeremy.

He backed away as if Angie was a bomb ready to go off.

Angie stood straighter and wiped her face with her sleeve again. 'Do I look okay?'

Reese raised an eyebrow. 'I mean, I could lie and say you look great.'

Angie snorted a laugh, and more tears streamed down her face.

Reese folded her arms over her chest. 'There are only two ways that dating your boss could go. Unfortunately, you got the short end of that deal.'

'I never thought it would end like this.'

Reese patted Angie's back before pulling her as close as she could, avoiding the basketball-sized lump under her shirt. 'Love is a funny thing. Sometimes it blinds you.'

Angie wrinkled her nose at her friend. 'That still doesn't make me feel any better.'

Reese gently scratched the side of her belly. 'It's not supposed to. You're hurting, and nothing I say is going to help until you start to heal. Right now, you can't do anything about it. Brent—'

'*Brett*,' Angie corrected, even though the sour taste of his name made her already sensitive stomach quiver.

Reese waved her hands dismissively. '*Brett* lied to you. Now you need to learn from it and move on. You've been on the go since you graduated from college. Take some time for yourself. Slow down and appreciate life.'

'I can't,' Angie said.

'Why not?'

'Keeping busy is going to help me forget about him.'

'Why not enjoy the time off and a chance to have a break? It's Christmas, and you haven't been home in forever.'

Angie shouldered her overpacked handbag she'd dropped at Reese's feet. 'Is any part of this conversation going to be helpful?'

Reese's smile fell. 'Were there any signs?'

Angie considered that question. It was all she had thought about when he informed her the day before Thanksgiving that they weren't going to work out because of his fiancée. Fiancée!

The return to work was incredibly awkward. Angie didn't flatter herself to think that every employee knew about her breakup, but all she could think about was where Brett was in the building and how she could avoid him. There was no way that she could watch Brett and his fiancée – soon, wife – strut around the hotel in front of her. Determined for them both not to get the better of her, she decided to quit and demanded proper severance pay to tide her over the Christmas period.

The signs, though? Angie spotted them immediately after coming out of her love cloud to stare them in the face.

Brett was away at least two weeks a month on business. She had made excuses for him, putting it down to work since he had a hotel to run. It had worked out well for her as she was busy planning events. Her work had started to pick up as Thanksgiving approached; everyone wanted a holiday party in the hotel during December. Every night she had passed out fast asleep well before ten to get up and do it all over again the next day. But that had been their routine.

'He wasn't around much lately,' Angie admitted.

'I guess absence didn't make the heart grow fonder.'

Angie shot her a look.

'Sorry,' Reese said. 'I can't control it sometimes.'

When Reese's family moved to Brookside, Connecticut when they were in the second grade, Angie liked her plucky attitude immediately. Her best friend's sarcasm didn't earn her many friends in high school or beyond. But Reese's bluntness kept Angie down to earth, giving her a reality check as her mind tended to float up to the clouds. Even though it hurt to realize how idiotic she had been with Brett, she needed the truth now. It was the only way she could move on.

They walked over to Jeremy as he searched through every bag that passed him on the baggage carousel, much to the annoyance of the other travelers.

'What color are your bags, Angie?' Jeremy asked over his shoulder.

Angie wiped the residue streaks of tears from her face. 'Green.' When she had left for college, her dad insisted she had a set of suitcases for coming home. Even though they were a hideous shade, it was his way of helping her out when she traveled.

Jeremy rocked on his heels. 'How festive.'

Reese lifted a small bag of trail mix from her back pocket. She ripped it open and started to snack. 'I bet your mom is thrilled you're coming home for Christmas. What did she say when you told her?'

Angie chewed on her lip. For the past five years, Angie had flown her mom out to visit her in San Diego for Christmas. It wasn't the white Christmas they were used to at home, but for Angie, it was better than returning to a place which reminded her of her dad's absence. Her mother didn't complain too much when she sat on the terrace of Angie's apartment, soaking in the sun. If all had gone well with Brett this year, everything would have been the same. It would have been the first time that Brett had been able to meet her mom.

'Considering she hates flying, she was thrilled,' Angie said, picking up one of her bags as it came by. Jeremy took another. 'It finally gave her a chance to decorate the house. The Thompsons next door helped her with the tree and lights.'

'The Thompsons?' Reese asked with a snort. 'I bet that was a struggle.'

Angie laughed and lunged for another of her bags.

'I've got it!' Jeremy appeared beside her and grabbed the handle before she could.

Angie stepped back and glanced down at Reese, licking her fingers for the last morsels of salt. 'How are you feeling? Are you ready for the baby?'

Reese answered without looking up. 'As ready as we'll ever be.' Reese snaked a hand around Angie's waist. 'I'm glad you'll be here to meet her first.'

'Wouldn't miss it for the world.'

Reese raised an eyebrow.

Angie sighed. 'It was going to be a surprise, but I did book a flight home after New Year's.' Another plan in her life she had to cancel.

Reese snorted. 'You better have. Or else I would have kicked Brett's butt for keeping you across the country.'

A break from California would get Angie's head on straight again. Her life couldn't get much worse, and she was determined to break her unlucky streak as soon as possible.

***

'They've outdone themselves this year.' Reese craned her neck to peer around the driver's seat. The Thompsons next door spared no expense to make their house light up like a Christmas tree from December 1st through mid-January every single year.

Angie had forgotten how brightly their house shone and the memory caught her by surprise. Each polished ornament from her childhood stood in the same place as if they were stored in a snow globe. Though there were a few new ones, including the six – no seven – elves appearing to prance along the sidewalk. She didn't need to roll down her window to hear the joyous 'ho ho ho!' from the mechanical Santa surrounded by his famous reindeer.

Angie's mom had always tried to keep her dad away from accepting Mr Thompson's annual request for assistance with their display for fear of him breaking his neck falling from the roof. Her mom had aligned their Christmas tree shopping that same weekend for many years to avoid the argument. As a child, Angie had sometimes woken weeks after Christmas, hearing the sound from the Santa on the neighbor's roof.

As they drove by, Angie smiled, fondly thinking about her dad grumbling to himself for the entire month and a half about the outrageous display. The image of his face burned into her eyes, imprinting on her memory as Jeremy pulled into the driveway of her childhood home.

Colored lights climbed the highest peaks of the house and sloped toward the ground. A swooping sensation filled her, stealing her breath. Coming home was what she needed. She knew that now more than ever.

A familiar station wagon sat in her old spot on the driveway. The rusted edges of the wheel wells had extended to the back bumper. She was surprised it still ran. Angie's mom must have invited her nonni over for dinner, knowing Angie was coming home. She braced herself for tight embraces and sloppy cheek kisses, but couldn't help smiling. Her home had been a place to run away from for years. Now she wanted nothing more than the familiar.

Reese yawned and turned in her seat as much as she could. 'We would love to visit, but I'm exhausted. This little angel sucks up all my energy. Let's meet up tomorrow?'

Angie leaned over and kissed her friend on the cheek. 'Definitely.' She opened the door and hopped out of the car. 'Thanks for picking me up.'

Jeremy grabbed two of her bags before they walked together to the porch with Angie rolling the last, and her carry on. She wasn't sure where she was going to put everything.

'How is she doing?' Angie asked as they approached the house, out of Reese's earshot.

'She's having trouble sleeping,' Jeremy said, massaging the back of his neck. 'I've been on the sofa.'

Angie spotted movement from behind the living room curtains. 'Let me know if you need help with anything.' *Not like I have much to do anymore. I'm jobless, homeless, hopeless ...* She shook the negative thoughts from her mind.

'Sure thing,' he said. 'It's nice to have you back. Reese will never say it, but she misses you. Even more now with the baby on the way.'

'Hormones?' Angie tried to make light of the conversation. She hadn't been the best best-friend since moving to California.

'She's become more emotional. It's an adjustment for everyone.'

Angie sighed. So much had gone on the last few days, she wasn't sure if she could handle more emotion from herself or her friends. 'Thanks again for the ride. I'll come by the house soon.'

'No problem.'

Jeremy leaned forward, and they awkwardly hugged. Even though Jeremy and Reese had been together for years, he and Angie had never quite mastered the closeness either of them had with Reese. She was their glue.

The front door opened just as she reached for the knob. Donato grabbed his chest as if she'd knocked the wind out of him. His wheezing breath billowed above them. 'Jesus, Mary, and Joseph, you scared me. I thought you were a damned ghost.'

Angie smirked. 'I'm not a ghost, Nonno.' She took the cigarette and lighter from his hand and put them in the pocket of his thick knitted sweater. 'Those things are going to kill you, you know?'

'That's what your nonna says, but my ticker is as strong as it was when I was fifteen!'

Angie steered him inside and closed the door behind her, taking in the blazing heat of her home. It was worse in the summer as her mom insisted on cooking the same amount of food all year round. At least since Dad died. He had always been the grill-master, and after he had passed away, her mother saw no reason to change her cooking habits away from the kitchen. She hugged Nonno, sturdy as ever.

A loud cackle caught her attention.

Angie's nonna, Emilia, held her hands in front of her, gesturing for Angie to come closer. As if she hadn't been the one creeping behind the curtain. 'Angela! Angela!' The thick Brooklyn accent filled Angie with a warmth she hadn't expected. The round woman pressed herself against Angie's middle and squeezed. Even now, in the later end of her seventies, she still made Angie breathless with her hugs.

Angie leaned her cheek against the top of Emilia's head. Her gray-streaked hair was shorter than she remembered.

'I think you've shrunk.'

Emilia pressed her hands against Angie's waist. 'You too.'

'It was so nice of you two to come and visit me,' Angie said. 'I missed you.'

Emilia stiffened and took a step back, keeping her hands on Angie's waist. A version of the terrible stink-eye that could send any man in a ten-foot radius skittering away had befallen Angie.

'What's with the face?' Angie looked at Donato who suddenly found his hands fascinating.

'Maria!' Emilia barked, making both Angie and Donato jump.

'You've done it now.' Donato rubbed a hand over his stubbled cheek.

'What did I do?' Angie asked.

Emilia darted from the room, and Angie followed her toward the kitchen. She barely had a moment to take in the boxes of Christmas decorations on the floor before approaching the raised voices of her mother and her nonna going at it.

Angie peered into the kitchen, not wanting to get in the middle of whatever was happening. 'Ma?'

Emilia placed her hands firmly on her hips, and her bottom lip jutted out. 'Tell her.'

Angie's heart warmed when she saw her mom, pear-shaped as ever, holding a wooden spoon tipped with gravy. Her mouth watered thinking of a home-cooked meal for once instead of take-out or airplane food.

'Tell me what?' Angie thought of all the possibilities of horrible situations. Was one of them sick? Dying? Did it have something to do with her coming home?

Maria rolled her eyes. 'Mom, can you give me a minute to say hello to my daughter?' She darted across the room and kissed Angie on the cheek. Her skin was softer than Angie remembered. 'Welcome home, Angela.'

No one could stop Emilia when she was about to scold someone. 'You had plenty of time to tell her, now you're going to disappoint your only daughter.'

Angie huffed. 'Can someone fill me in?'

Emilia crossed her arms and avoided eye contact by staring at the ceiling.

Maria took Angie's hands in hers. They were warm. 'I told Nonna it wouldn't be a big deal to you.'

Angie's gaze darted between her mom and Emilia. 'What wouldn't be a big deal?'

'Nonno and Nonna had to leave their apartment.'

'Rodents!' Donato said from the doorway.

'Disgusting,' Emilia spat.

'So, they're staying with us for a little while.'

Angie waited yet no one else spoke. 'Is that all?'

'Well,' Maria said, dragging the word out longer than necessary. 'They're staying in your room. It's bigger and more comfortable for them.'

'I told Maria we could stay in the guest room,' Emilia offered. Maria glared at her mother.

Angie mustered a smile to appease her family. 'I'll stay in the guest room while I'm home.' She had no intention of staying longer than necessary and moving her nonni out of the room for a week or so didn't make any sense.

'See!' Maria shrieked and pointed the spoon at Emilia. 'I told you it was fine.'

Emilia grunted and sat at the table set for four.

Maria led Angie to the chair she had sat on since she was a kid, gesturing her to sit. 'Tell us all about your trip. I'm almost finished with dinner. I made your favorite.'

Angie sat at the table, allowing the warmth of the house to envelop her into a tight hug. She was used to the wide-open space of her and Brett's apartments. The house where she grew up felt smaller than it had the last time. But the laughter and happiness shining in her family's eyes lulled her into a sense of security she hadn't realized she had missed.

***

Angie could barely keep her eyes open during dinner, even though her brain was three hours behind. She guessed the exhaustion from moving her life across the country and breaking up with the man she had expected to marry had finally caught up with her. At least she would soar over the potential jet lag.

After saying goodnight to everyone, Angie headed upstairs to the guest room. She wearily carried her heavy feet down the long hallway toward the last door, lugging her suitcase behind her.

Angie had slept in smaller confines in college, so she didn't mind the change in her plan. The moment she pushed open the door, it rebounded back, smacking against her arm. Pain zipped through her elbow and she frantically rubbed the spot to make the radiating ache stop.

Angie pushed the door open again, slower this time, and flicked the light switch. Against the back of the door, a folded-up treadmill blocked her way. She squeezed into the room, turning her suitcase to pull in behind her.

In the far corner was a table, covered with scrapbooking supplies, and on the floor were about twenty photo albums. Next to that were even more Christmas decoration boxes, which her mom usually stored in the attic. Angie guessed that she hadn't dared to pack them away since her dad had died. The rickety pull-down ladder to the storage space always terrified her mother.

A headache formed behind Angie's eyes and she rubbed the side of her temple, willing for it to go away. Adding physical pain to her mental anguish wasn't going to help her get any sleep. She abandoned her other suitcases in the hallway, turned the light off, and flopped onto the bed. Moonlight poured into the room, throwing shadows across the walls.

It wasn't long before a single tear slipped down her cheek. Even in her own home, she couldn't help but feel cast off. Days ago, she was a successful event planner for one of the most prestigious hotel chains in the country with a sexy, wealthy boyfriend and a fantastic apartment. Now she was back at home, in the town she had always wanted to escape from.

Angie thought of the giant rock on Brett's fiancée's finger, and her skin prickled. Hot tears coursed down her face and she tightened her grip on the blanket around her as the memories of her relationship with Brett flooded her mind. He was the perfect boyfriend. When they were out together, he never seemed interested in other women. Though, they did keep their relationship a secret since he was her boss. Was that the appeal for him?

Angie wasn't the type to throw herself pity parties, but her chest had felt empty from the moment she boarded the plane in California.

Gathering all the memories of Brett, she mashed them into an ugly ball and shoved them into the darkest reaches of her mind. Her breathing slowed as her eyes became heavy.

Angie was a list-maker, which was a big part of her job. If there was ever a time to make one, this was it. Her eyes squeezed shut as she worked out the next step of her plan. She was on the other side of the country, so she doubted she would see Brett again. Not that she ever wanted to. Before she left, she had demanded a glowing recommendation letter to help in her new job search. It was part of her request in the severance package.

Her job had been a coveted position at the company, and she knew the vultures would be there after the holidays picking up the pieces of her previous life. This was a tough time of year to search for another job. But, with the New Year on the horizon, there wasn't a better time to start over.

First, she would update her resume and scour job openings in New York City and surrounding areas.

Angie never intended to stay on the East Coast, but it would have to do while she could get back on her feet. After bouncing back from this, she would leave again on a new adventure.

This was all temporary, and with a plan in mind, she snuggled under the covers with visions of job offers dancing in her head.

Chapter 2

The pounding of Nick Bower's feet against the ground and the tinkling of dog tags next to him created a monotonous sound in his head. It was the perfect rhythm to help him free his mind and think more clearly. The temperatures had dipped over the last week, and it was almost cold enough outside to decide against taking his morning run. But he couldn't disappoint the most important girl in his life, Charlie. At least that was what he told himself. Running cleared his head and helped untangle any family or work issues and working with his father led to a lot of those. It also helped ease his guilt during his busiest season when he couldn't be there for Charlie as much as he wanted.

After his second lap around the park, he headed home. Charlie trotted next to him, her tongue lolling to the side.

Nick had found the golden retriever at a dog rescue event three years ago during one of his solo runs. She'd howled for him, louder than the others in her litter, until he'd walked over. The moment he'd looked into those brown eyes, it was love at first sight.

The duo came to an abrupt stop at the front door to Nick's apartment building, where the doorman, Frederick, stood between the outer and inner doors rubbing his gloved hands together.

'Good morning,' Nick said, pausing to stretch his hamstrings.

'Getting a little cold out,' Frederick said, blowing air into his fists.

'Not for this girl,' Nick said, scratching Charlie's head. She pushed her nose into his hand, demanding more love. 'She's the only one who matters.'

'Until you find a lucky woman.' Frederick winked.

Nick smiled, tighter this time, and walked inside. Frederick wasn't the only person in his life pushing for him to meet someone else. Heat clung to the sweat on his forehead. The uncomfortable change in his temperature wasn't all from the exercise.

As he trudged over to the elevator, thoughts of his ex, Molly, filled his mind.

The doors opened, and he stepped inside, trying to shake her out of his head. The 'lucky woman' Frederick described was a myth. At least based on his most recent history. Charlie was non-negotiable in his life. Even with the sweetest dog on the planet, Molly somehow couldn't stand the hair on her clothes and Charlie's kisses were as horrifying to her as dunking her face in a toilet. For a while, he chose to ignore her many ultimatums. But with his work schedule taking over his life, he didn't quite understand Molly's real disgust until he came home to a half-empty closet and a confirmation of their breakup via text.

It wasn't much after nearly a year of dating. But when Molly wanted something, she went after it. Molly didn't shy away from letting everyone know how much 'better' she had done lately. She had filled her newsfeeds with vacations and events with her new boyfriend.

Eventually, Nick deleted his social media accounts to keep his head in the game and from falling through the black hole beckoning him to search through more of Molly's pictures.

No one had been more excited about the breakup than his dad. He didn't appreciate distractions from work, and according to him, Nick's girlfriends were the biggest. He'd been out on dates a few times since their breakup, but he wasn't interested in any of the women long-term. Thirty-two was young enough to make these mistakes, and he was going to be more careful this time.

When Nick opened the door to his apartment, Charlie pulled away from him and took off toward her water bowl. She stood by the bay windows which overlooked the city he'd lived his entire life.

Charlie padded over to Nick with dripping jowls as he headed for the coffee maker, nudging his knee with her snout. He scratched her head and reached for the container on the counter.

Nick scooped kibble into her bowl. He knelt, offering the perfect opportunity for a quick lick on the cheek. 'You must be hungry, girl.'

The scent of percolating coffee moved through the apartment and snapped Nick back to reality. Molly was five months ago. He had moved on, and he tried to forget the memories as quickly as they had appeared.

Nick sat on the couch glancing out at the city waking up around him and sipped from the steaming mug of coffee. His phone buzzed from the table next to him – six-thirty on the dot. His dad was already at the office. Work didn't start until eight, but his father liked to make a point of showing up before everyone. It was a mix between wanting to show off and proving that he was worthy of being the boss. Not that anyone ever challenged him.

When Charlie finished her food, she hopped onto the couch and curled her body around herself, bumping Nick's arm. He absently rubbed her head while admiring several of the apartment buildings across the way that had already decorated their windows and trees with twinkling colored lights.

It was the second day of December and people were ready for Christmas. Last year, Molly had hired a company to decorate the apartment for the holiday. The fake fir tree and poinsettias didn't bring him the Christmas spirit at all. He preferred the scents and warmth of the season surrounding him. The only time he experienced a sliver of that was at his parents' house, or his brother David's, around Christmas.

Nick leaned over to grab his phone. Charlie lifted her head and plopped it down on his lap, looking for more scratches. He couldn't help but laugh; she knew he was leaving soon and wanted to get as much time with him as possible before Mrs Wilson arrived to take Charlie to her apartment for the day.

He scrolled through his phone until David's name came up in his messages. The last discussion they'd had was about the timing for Thanksgiving dinner. His parents always hosted the holidays, so David scheduled his dinner later to make sure Nick wouldn't have to choose between his parents and brother.

The rift between his father and David had gone on too long, but their dad would never concede. When David chose to leave the company to pursue his passion, it severed the ties between their family. Well, mostly because their dad couldn't let go of the fact that David no longer wanted to work for the family business. Nick was never going to abandon his older brother, his wife, and two nephews, but their father made every holiday more complicated than it needed to be.

Their mother met with David and the kids often, but no one talked about it. To his father, it was as if David never existed. When Nick had tried to bring it up with his dad, he'd attempted to convince him many a time to build bridges, but the results were always the same – stern glares and long strings of uncomfortable silences. David had contested it wasn't worth making Nick's work-life a living hell, so the silent barrier carried on.

An alarm blared from Nick's phone, catapulting him back to the present.

Charlie looked up at him with wide dark eyes.

'Don't look at me like that.' Nick got up and walked toward the bathroom while Charlie plodded over to her bed to wait for him to get ready.

***

On the way to work, Nick's shoulders lifted slightly. He tried to hold onto the loose feeling in his body from the run, but it proved to be a challenging task. His fingers tensed around the steering wheel of his Lexus as lyrics of a magical snowman floated from his speakers. The town had started its transformation into the holiday season. Workers stood on cherry pickers, placing lit snowflakes against tall poles. Wreaths hung from most of the business doors while artificial snow collected at the corners of the windows.

A text came through on the console in his car, and Nick glanced at the name.

'I'm on my way,' he said into the speaker before the phone sent the text off to his dad. He'd never been late for work but always had to be on his toes.

The mall loomed next to him as he drove past the entrance toward corporate parking. Knowing he had a meeting with his father in about a half hour, Nick needed more coffee to lubricate the conversation. A pastry would help too.

The valet lot was in the back of the mall. Nick stepped out of his car and straightened his tie. A young guy dressed in a puffy vest and hat branded with the Westford Mall logo walked over to him.

'Good morning, Mr Bower,' he said, as a white cloud billowed from his mouth. It seemed to be colder than earlier that morning during his run.

'Morning,' Nick said, handing over his keys before rounding the lot toward the street.

The sign for Kevin's Café beckoned Nick to pick up his pace.

Years ago, Nick had negotiated the contract for the café. At the time, his father took a lot of convincing that the café wouldn't take money away from the food court, and that it would be a draw for the mall instead. Patrons loved the coffee, so they tended to stick around to shop while sipping from their lattes.

Entering the café, the strong scent of freshly ground coffee filled his nose. The light from the hazy December sun cascaded down through the front windows. Nick unzipped his coat and stepped into the line already six people deep.

While waiting, he scrolled through several emails to get a head start on work.

'Two everything bagels with extra cream cheese,' the woman in front of him ordered.

While Nick only really wanted to order for his dad, the thought of a bagel made his stomach growl.

Vickie, the twenty-something barista, caught his eye as she started on the food. She winked her false eyelashes at him. 'The usual?'

'Yes,' Nick said. 'Also, a scone and a wheat bagel with lite vegetable cream cheese.'

'Toasted?' she asked.

'No,' Nick said, checking the time on his platinum watch.

The woman in front of him glanced over. She did a double take and her eyebrows arched before she turned back to Vickie.

Nick had no idea what that look was for, but he couldn't help moving closer to explain himself. 'Your order sounded good.'

'I can't stand wheat bagels. I mean, what's the point if you're not going all in?' she said.

Nick smiled at her. 'Should I change my order?'

The woman smiled, and her light green eyes crinkled at the corners before she turned back to her phone. 'Do whatever you want.' She was several inches shorter than him, wearing workout gear and a puffy red jacket. Under a knitted gray hat, her shiny dark brown hair almost reached the middle of her back. The same style of gloves peeked out from her pockets.

'Are you starting your Christmas shopping early this year?' Nick couldn't help himself. He wanted to think it was more because of his line of work than wanting to talk to her.

'Already done,' she said. 'I'm an online shopper.'

Nick winced. Not what he expected, but at least she was honest. She also had no idea what he did for a living. 'Are you from around here?'

The woman cut a look his way. 'I grew up in Brookside.'

'A local?'

'Does that surprise you?' she asked, finally putting down her phone.

He cleared his throat, lifting his hands in surrender. 'You have enough outerwear for a trip to Alaska.'

Vickie came back with her order and rang her up. The woman handed over her card to pay.

The woman pulled the hat from her head, smoothing her hair back. 'I've lived in California for years. I'm *so* not used to the cold anymore.' She unzipped her jacket, revealing another layer.

Nick wanted to ask her where in California, but Vickie spoke first. 'It's not working.' She held the card between them.

The woman wrinkled the paper bag of bagels she held close to her chest as if she wasn't willing to let it go without a fight. 'Please try again.'

The door opened, letting another gust of cold air into the café, and three more people joined the already growing line.

Vickie shrugged, holding the card between two fingers. 'I've tried it twice, and it's not going through.'

The woman lowered her voice. 'Please try it one more time.'

Vickie sighed and tried again.

The same double beep sounded from the machine.

Vickie raised her thick eyebrows at the woman. 'Do you have cash?'

The woman blew out a breath. 'I can't believe this.'

'Do you have another card?' Vickie made a point to examine the line behind them. It was almost to the door now.

'What's the hold-up?' someone behind them asked.

Nick glared at the guy.

The woman at the counter looked as if she wanted to crawl into the bag she gripped in her hands.

'Here,' Nick said, handing his card to Vickie.

The woman scowled at him. This time her eyes held an edge of skepticism. 'You don't have to do that.'

'It's fine,' he said.

Her eyes narrowed as she looked him up and down. 'No, really.'

'You need to pay for your stuff,' Vickie said.

'Just take the card,' Nick said, handing it over. 'It's no big deal.'

Vickie swiped the card and handed it to him.

'I'm paying it forward—' Nick's words dried on his tongue as the woman was already halfway to the door.

Vicki turned to the next customer as she slid Nick's bag across the counter. 'See you tomorrow.'

The woman was already at the door before Nick caught up with her. Couldn't she even thank him? He misjudged the distance between himself and the door as two teens rushed inside. The door swung so quickly that the collision was inevitable. He braced himself as he gripped his coffee. The door nailed the lid, and the flimsy cup buckled under the weight. The searing hot liquid splashed his shirt, coursing down his chest.

The two teens linked hands and joined the line as if they had no idea what they had done. Apparently, it was a day for rude people.

The woman whipped around, and her jaw dropped at the sight of him. She gave an apologetic smile and wave before taking off across the street. The countdown of the walk signal at the traffic lights wasn't enough for him to safely catch up to her.

Nick wasn't about to get into another accident on her account. He curled his lip and sidestepped the door, grabbing several napkins from the nearby dispenser. He could go home and change, but his dad would never forgive his tardiness. There was no separation between family-dad and professional-dad. He was all in, all the time, and held Nick to a higher standard.

It was a good thing Nick liked to be prepared and had backup clothes at the office. All he had to do was make it there without his dad spotting him.

***

21

Nick trudged through the office, holding his coat against his sopping wet shirt.

'What happened to you?' Maya asked, sipping from her snowman-shaped mug.

Nick turned toward the head of Human Resources. Her cubicle was across the hall from his office. He didn't have a lot of time to delay before the morning meeting with his father. 'Someone rushed the door as I was leaving the café.'

'People are insane around the holidays. Do you have an extra shirt?' she asked.

'In my office.' He didn't want to talk about the mishap anymore – though he had a few words for the woman who left him dripping wet. 'How are the Christmas hires going?'

Maya smoothed a chunk of black hair from her face. 'Only a few more spots to fill.' Maya had come in as an assistant right out of high school and made her way up the ladder quickly.

Nick's dad, Quinn Bower, popped his head out of his corner office and spotted him.

Nick's entire body tensed as Quinn's eyes met his. 'I should go. Have Carrie send me the numbers at the end of the day.'

'I know how to handle my assistant, thank you,' Maya said to his back.

Nick smirked. Maya never let him get away with anything. After David left his position, Nick was there to swoop in. As the son his dad had never intended on working with, Nick's first year was harder than all the rest. With David as a manager, Nick had passively sat by while his father and brother ran the corporation. Nick had proved himself over the years, but Maya never gave him any slack and kept him grounded when he needed it.

Nick opened the thin closet at the back of his office and changed his shirt. As he walked toward his dad's office, he plastered on a confident smile while his fingers gathered the top of the paper bag in his hands.

'Nice of you to join us,' Quinn said, gesturing at Nick to close the door behind him.

Nick lifted the pastry from the bag in his hands. 'It's five of eight, and I picked this up for you.'

Quinn's eyes sparkled for a moment before darkening again. 'I need to speak with you about something important.'

'Okay,' Nick said, handing over the bag.

Quinn placed it on his desk before shoving his hands into his pockets. 'You're coming up in the business, which is great. But I want to discuss a move forward.'

'What did you have in mind?'

'You remember Jared Kent.' Not a question.

'Sure,' Nick said, racking his brain to place the name. 'He was into real estate. You went to business school together.'

Quinn nodded. 'We've stayed connected over the years and are going to dinner this week. We're discussing a new project, and I would like for you to attend.'

'Really?' Other than holidays or business lunches, his dad rarely wanted to share a meal.

'I'll have Rachel put the details in your calendar.' Also, not a question. His dad already knew Nick's schedule, especially during this time of the year. Maybe the Christmas spirit had affected him as well? Whatever the reason, after the morning Nick had had, his mood improved slightly. The moment with the rude woman faded into the background as he considered what his father had in mind for him.

Chapter 3

Angie bolted across the street, holding the paper bag against her chest. She didn't dare look behind her until she walked through the entrance of the mall. She couldn't believe she had embarrassed herself like that. The first cute guy in a suit she saw brought her back to the foolish woman she had been with Brett. Then, her card was denied.

The reminder that things like food and clothing cost money reeled in her head. She didn't think she had spent that much in her move back home, but last-minute plane tickets after Thanksgiving were expensive, along with moving her furniture into storage until she had found a permanent place to live. The severance check should have been enough to cover all her budgeted expenses.

Heat seared her cheeks as she glanced over her shoulder. From the furious expression on that guy's face, she fully expected him to come after her. Thankfully, he was nowhere in sight. It wasn't her fault those kids had knocked the door into him. She supposed he was upset she hadn't thanked him for paying, but she was too embarrassed to stick around. Reese's voice screamed in the back of her mind to run away. This was her chance to get a break from men like Brett, and she had failed her first test.

While the guy was attractive, their short conversation reminded her so much of Brett – the suit, the slick-backed hair, and throwing money around like it wasn't a big deal. While it was nice of him, the fact that she had no money to pay for bagels loomed over her like a thick cloud.

Brett had said she would get a severance check. She hadn't bothered to review her bank account; she had simply assumed the money would be there. He couldn't have lied about that too. It was a silent deal they had made. She didn't want to make a big deal of their breakup, and she got what she needed to get out of there.

With two bagels in her hands and Reese waiting for her, Angie would have to wait to find out what was going on with her finances. She located Reese outside of Bloomfield's department store. Somehow, her friend appeared even more tired than when she had seen her last. As she neared, the bags around Reese's eyes darkened.

'Finally,' Reese said. 'I'm starving.'

'Sorry. Did you eat breakfast?' Angie asked, sitting next to her on the bench.

Reese cut a look at her. 'If I say yes, don't judge me.'

'I won't,' Angie said, grinning.

They were the type of friends who could pick up where they left off every time they met. Reese dug into the bag and pulled out a bagel.

'I've been dreaming about this,' Reese said, admiring the food from all angles.

'Really?'

'It's my favorite place to eat down here. I needed some fuel this morning. I hate coming to the mall after Thanksgiving, though.' Reese narrowed her eyes at the people walking past them. 'Especially this year. I've realized how many shoppers don't care about mowing down a pregnant woman as long as it means they get their cheap television.'

'Turning a little green there,' Angie said.

Reese tilted her bagel toward Angie. 'Don't you dare call me the Grinch.'

Angie laughed. 'You said it!'

'What's on your list?'

'I can't get anything today,' Angie said.

'Why not? Don't tell me you're Scrooging it.'

'I couldn't even pay for the bagels this morning.'

Reese stopped chewing and stared at her bagel. 'You didn't get these out of the trash, did you?'

Angie groaned. 'No, some guy paid for them.' She drifted into her thoughts, thinking of him. She started to regret her reaction of fleeing the scene.

'What happened?'

Angie told her every agonizing detail of the story. Reese's expression went from pity to confusion.

'What?'

Reese grabbed her arm, smearing cream cheese on Angie's coat. 'Sorry.' She licked the remaining cream cheese from her fingers before continuing. 'Why are you smiling like that? Was the guy hot?'

She almost wished her best friend didn't know her that well. Angie knew where Reese would go with the information and besides that, she didn't want to be interested in any guy. 'He was attractive, I guess.'

'No way, Ang. You need to back up.'

'I know! I'm horrible. He swooped in like some prince charming and I fell for it! He reminded me so much of Brett and the way he used to flaunt his cash.'

'Well, as long as you're aware of it. Don't you want a little time to be single and recalibrate your life?'

'Yes.' Angie shoved her hair away from her face, stuffing a piece of bagel into her mouth. She needed a minute to think. This was typical behavior for her. Angie had only been single for a few days before she met Brett. And before that with Jonathon. There wasn't much of a break between men in her past, and she needed to change her pattern, give herself the time and space to heal.

Reese eyed her friend but gestured for her to continue. 'So, let's get back to why you don't have money. Did Brett do something else to screw you?'

Angie put her food down and grabbed her phone. 'I was supposed to get the severance already. Do you mind if I check my account?'

Reese waved a hand at her to go ahead, while she started on the second half of her bagel.

Angie plugged her mobile banking data into the app. In the few seconds it took for the website to load, her stomach clenched. Then it plummeted when she saw the overdraft notice.

'I'm assuming it didn't go through?' Reese asked.

Angie shook her head, willing away the sting in her eyes as she moved money over from her savings to account for the overdraft. She tried not to dip into that account often, but in this instance she had no choice. Her job had been enough to keep her afloat while she saved as much as she could. Angie never counted on Brett dumping her, in a way forcing her to leave her job. 'I don't want to call them. It's so mortifying.'

'You did nothing wrong. He made you uproot your life. I'll call them if you want.'

'No,' Angie said, protecting her phone. Reese had always been like a big, scary older sister to anyone who messed with her. Angie had to do this on her own.

'Do you need a loan?' Reese asked.

'No.' Angie had created this mess, and she was going to fix it.

'Well, the offer stands. Whenever you need it.'

Angie nodded and drafted an email to Melissa from the hotel. She handled all the employee paychecks and would be discreet in Angie's hour of need. She wanted to avoid contacting Brett if she could help it. It would only prove that he had made a better choice with whatever woman he thought was worthier than Angie of his grandmother's diamond ring. Though she had some choice words she wished she could give him.

She had only just put her phone in her bag when her email pinged.

'That was fast,' Reese said.

'They owe me,' Angie said, checking the message. It was from Melissa, but her hopes disappeared as she read the out of office reply.

'She's not in the office today,' Angie said, reading the email three times, hoping it would change into a message more in her favor.

'Is there anyone else you can talk to?' Reese asked.

'No,' she said, even though it wasn't true. Today wasn't about her old life. She had enough savings to get her through as long as she kept to a tight budget.

Angie couldn't help the sinking feeling that her pride was getting in the way of reaching out to Brett about her paycheck, despite it being what she was owed. Her heart was heavy in her chest, and she was considering that it might be better to go without than confronting Brett again. Her cheeks burned with anger and frustration. Shaking Brett from her mind she glanced up at her friend.

'So, what are you looking for?' Angie needed to change the subject. 'I'm your bag carrier for the entire day.'

Reese ticked names off her fingers. 'Jeremy, his parents, our niece and nephew, his coworkers too. Are you sure you're not going to do any shopping?'

Angie knew Reese was fishing to find out about her gift. She was awful at accepting surprises. When they were kids, Reese used to come over even more than usual around her birthday and Christmas to try and find presents in Angie's house. Little did she know Angie's hiding spot was behind her dad's toolbox in his basement workshop.

Reese pushed off the bench. 'Well, let's get going then. I might fall asleep here if we stay any longer.'

***

As they walked through the department store, Angie continued eating her breakfast. Her stomach was a jumble of nerves, but she tried to savor each bite. There was no way she was eating lunch out. She was looking forward to her mother's home-cooked meals, and there was no way her bank account would allow too many frivolous purchases until she was sure of the extra money. Sneaking small pieces of bagel out of the bag at a time, Angie remembered how food wasn't allowed in the store. It didn't stop her keeping candy in her pocket when she worked there all those years ago, and it certainly wouldn't stop her now.

'Bringing back memories for you?' Reese asked.

'It's like stepping into another time,' Angie said. The harsh lighting was still the same, and the warmth inside the store was unmistakable. It was a simpler time and place in her mind, yet it had a substantial impact on her life. Starting work young had helped her understand the importance of responsibility. It helped that Dad was proud of her for accepting the important responsibility of work. Paychecks funded her trips to the movies and new clothes for school.

'Have you thought about what you're going to do moving forward?' Reese asked.

'I sent a bunch of resumes before I left California. It's a good thing since the Wi-Fi is spotty at home.'

'You can always come over to my place to do that stuff. You know Jeremy and his gaming. We have the highest tier of internet we can afford. Which still seems not enough for him.' She made no effort to hide an eye roll.

'Thanks,' Angie said, unsure of why she didn't think of that before. 'Hopefully I'll hear back soon.'

'Are you considering staying local?' Reese asked.

Angie remembered what Jeremy told her the other day about Reese missing her. She missed her best friend too, but soon a baby would distract her. Though, Angie wouldn't mind being closer to home for visits. Anything to be as far from Brett and his fiancée as possible.

'I'll take anything I can right now but most of the bigger jobs are in cities, and I feel like I can't stay at home with everyone there. Mom is already driving me crazy and I've only been back for two days!'

'How so?'

Angie rarely complained about her mother around Reese since her friend's parents had died in a car accident not long after their high school graduation. 'It's just a lot. I went from being on my own to a house full of relatives. Nonna and Nonno are at each other's throats most of the time. It's all innocent, but loud. Since they came to stay with us, Mom is working less, so I think things are a little hectic for everyone.'

'Well, you know my house is always open to a little company. We have a sweet couch bed. Jeremy says it's comfortable.'

'Do you really make him sleep out there?'

She shook her head. 'He chooses to. I can't get comfortable lately, and this prevents him from shuffling around like a zombie at work after I toss and turn all night.'

Angie wished there was someone in the world who was that selfless for her. With the ghost of Brett looming over her, she doubted that would ever be the case. She didn't deserve that kind of love if she couldn't tell that someone wasn't single while she dated them.

Angie followed Reese around, while her thoughts drifted. They were different shoppers. Angie liked to browse while Reese always went straight to where she needed to be. Within an hour, she already had all but one gift.

Angie wished there were carts in the store. The box holding a large decorative bowl for Jeremy's mother-in-law dug into her side, and she started to regret the offer to hold everything for Reese.

'I'm done here,' Reese said, topping the pile with several shirts for her niece and nephew.

Angie adjusted her grip. 'We're going to your car after this.'

'Can you go? I need to put my feet up. Then, we can shop for Jer.'

At the checkout, a bright red sign with NOW HIRING in bold letters stood out to her. Angie loved Christmas season at the mall. There were always interesting people shopping for their loved ones. As a teen, she worked at numerous places around the mall. When she worked at the information booth her senior of high school, she had been a big people-watcher. During Christmas, there were even more crowds, and it had entertained her to no end. It distracted her from the long hours during the holiday season.

Reese noticed the sign too, tapping the top with her finger. 'Why don't you work temporarily over your break? There are always places hiring here in December.'

'At the mall? No way.'

The older woman behind the desk eyed her.

Angie avoided looking at the woman. She didn't mean to offend her but working at the mall had been a high school job, not a career choice for her.

'Well, it might get you out of the house,' Reese said. 'Isn't that what you wanted?'

'Not at all,' Angie said under her breath as Reese paid. 'Besides, I don't want to start something new for just a few weeks. When someone calls me back for a job, I'll have to quit. In any case, what is it going to look like on my resume?'

Reese took the receipt from the woman and slipped it into the bag on Angie's shoulder. 'I'm sure they need supervisors or something. That never looks bad on a job application.'

'I guess. But I'm hoping one of these offers comes through first.'

'Do you want me to look over your resume?'

Reese was top of their English class and always used to correct people's grammar, which thoroughly annoyed everyone. It took years to break her of that habit.

'I would love that,' Angie said, slightly regretting that she had already sent it to prospective job opportunities already. But there was always room for improvement.

'Email it to me, and I'll review it,' Reese said.

'Thank you.'

Reese looped her arm in Angie's. 'After you get back from the car, we need to get a snack.'

'We just ate,' Angie said.

Reese rolled her eyes. 'Do you even know me at all?' She made a show of thinking about her food choices. 'How about we share a pretzel?'

'As long as you're paying,' Angie said.

'Deal.'

Chapter 4

Nick pulled onto the gravel driveway toward David's house. It wasn't even six, and the sun was already across the horizon. A brightly lit Christmas tree glistened through the front windows. It seemed as if everyone was ready for the holidays except for him. He had no idea where to start, or if he wanted to bother this year. It wasn't as if anyone was coming over his place to celebrate.

Charlie started whining from the backseat, and her tail swished against Nick's face as she paced between the two windows. Nick was lucky to have the type of dog who didn't need to be on a leash. City ordinances required it for their runs, but she liked coming to David's house as much as he did. The three acres of land away from the road allowed her to roam without restriction.

Nick parked next to the shared family silver SUV as David appeared from around the corner of the house.

Charlie's whines escalated until Nick opened her door. She bounded onto the front seat and hopped onto the ground. She sniffed around David's feet before taking off toward the back of the house.

'You're late,' David said, tucking his hand into the pocket of his jeans. With his flannel shirt, he looked more like a cowboy than an ex-corporate type.

33

Nick was late by almost an hour. He couldn't help but wonder if his dad had seen his meeting with David in his calendar and added more to his workload on purpose. The truth was, Nick wasn't on anyone's side. He loved them both and couldn't imagine choosing between his brother and father. Nick wished his dad would stop being so stubborn.

'Might want to put a jacket on.' Nick shivered at the chilly night air.

'I'm hot-blooded, remember?' David said, clapping a hand on Nick's back.

Nick tugged the collar of his pea coat tighter around his neck.

'You've spent too much time in a heated office,' David said, inspecting Nick's suit. 'You need to get outside more often. You're pale as hell.'

'Look who's talking,' Nick said, shoving away David's hand. David pushed away a chunk of light brown hair from his face. It was much longer and freer than it had been when he worked for their father.

David chuckled and turned around. 'I'm almost done in the workshop. Come back with me for a minute.'

As they walked over, Charlie galloped across the lawn, sniffing everything along the trail toward the doggy door at the back of the house, leading into the kitchen. David had made it for her before she had turned one. They didn't have a pet, but David's handiwork gave his sons, Evan and James, enough of an excuse to ask their parents for a dog around any major holiday. Nick suspected it was part of the reason David allowed Charlie to visit since it allowed the kids to play with a dog without long-term commitments.

Inside David's workshop, the air was almost as cold as outside. A small heater chugged in the corner of the room, but only blasted enough warmth at a small radius.

Various unfinished projects sat around the room, while tools hung from hooks on the walls. Nick leaned against one of the wood beams, looking up at the ceiling. The second-floor loft was for storage, the compromise between David and Theresa for her permission to build the shed in the backyard.

David walked over to a wooden chair sitting atop a table he had crafted himself. He picked up a piece of sanding paper and started to smooth one of the legs. 'What's going on with you lately? Dad driving you crazy?'

'It's Christmas, what do you think?'

'I think he needs to retire.'

'Mom wouldn't be able to stand it if he did.'

'I get it. I wouldn't want to subject her to that.'

David worked in silence for a minute, a consistent reaction any time their father came into the conversation, even though he was the one to bring him up.

'Everything good with business?' Nick asked.

'It's better around this season, but the hustle never goes away. Especially when I have a family to support.'

Nick nodded in agreement. David hadn't taken the easy route when he started his woodworking business from scratch, but he continued to surprise his little brother with his determination.

'Are you just going to stare at me or help?' David tossed his piece of sandpaper to Nick.

Nick missed the paper, and it fell to the ground.

'Too much time in the office,' David muttered.

They sanded for a while, staying on neutral topics. Smoothing his hand against the wood cleared Nick's mind as much as running did. No wonder David liked his job.

David's cell phone rang. He sat up, placing the paper on the table. 'Time to eat.'

'Is that how Theresa lets you know?' Nick asked, grinning. As much as Nick teased his brother about his love life, he was incredibly jealous of what he had.

'It's better than the bell she suggested hanging outside the porch.'

'No way,' Nick said.

David pulled a face. 'Don't remind her about it. I still don't think she was kidding.'

They were only a few feet from the shed when the back door burst open. 'Uncle Nick!'

Evan and James, six-year-old twins, raced over to him, their arms pumping as they neared. Charlie was on their heels before she overtook them and ran ahead.

The boys favored their mother with their pale blond locks and freckled cheeks.

'Come here, guys.' Nick knelt, ready to hug his nephews.

Between Charlie's licks and the boys pummeling into him, the weight overpowered him, and he plopped onto the wet ground.

Nick ruffled Evan's hair while James tried to tickle Nick under his shirt.

'Come on, boys,' Theresa said from the doorway. 'Give Uncle Nick a chance to get inside. Go wash your hands.'

David laughed so hard his eyes teared up.

The boys shoved each other as they fought to be the first one inside with Charlie in tow.

'Hilarious,' Nick said, trying to get up without ruining the rest of his pants. The cold liquid seeping against his skin reminded him of the coffee spilled all over him at the café yesterday morning. This wasn't his week.

Theresa grinned from the doorway. Her hair was twisted in a bun on top of her head, a style she'd preferred ever since he had known her. 'Hey, Nick. Come inside, and I'll put those in the wash for you.'

David held out a hand to help his brother up. 'It's a good thing we're still the same size. That says a lot for me being older. I picture a pot-belly in your future.'

'You're only two years older and I'm never getting a pot-belly,' Nick said.

'Sitting around on that desk chair in your fancy office will get you there soon enough.'

'I bet you'll be the first, old man,' Nick said.

'Do you want to put money on that?' David asked, leading Nick into the house.

***

After Nick had changed into a pair of David's jeans, he headed into the kitchen. The square footage of the house was around the same size as Nick's apartment, yet he always felt it held more warmth.

From Nick's perspective, David had the life. He had a good family and a job he loved. After quitting, David had relied heavily on Theresa for money and insurance. The Bower men were hard-working, no matter what they did. David built his business from the ground up and proved himself again at each milestone. Too bad his dad wanted nothing to do with it.

Theresa walked over to Nick and hugged him. 'Good to see you clean. How's work?'

Evan and James sat quietly in their chairs, but from Charlie's tail sticking out from under the table, Nick knew they were petting her. She was spoiled here even more than she was at home.

'Busy,' Nick said. 'How about you?'

'The laboratory slows down around this time every year. We shut down for cleaning in two weeks,' she said. 'It couldn't come any faster. Sit, let's eat.'

Nick wondered how much David's passion affected their family. But they were able to see each other more than Nick and Molly had. And they were still happily married. David had somehow found the magic formula to love.

'I'm starving,' James said.

Steam swirled around the lasagna at the center of the table. The boys reached for the homemade bread first, but Nick was right behind them. Theresa was the most intelligent person Nick knew *and* could make an incredible meal. Once again showing off his brother's luck.

'How's your love life?' Theresa asked before Nick cut a piece for himself.

Nick looked at David. His brother could hardly mask the smile on his face.

'David can ask me whatever he likes.'

David lifted a piece of lasagna from the plate. 'I know you'll answer her.'

'I want you to be happy,' Theresa said.

Nick dipped his bread in the sauce. 'I can be happy without a girlfriend.'

'That's true, but all you do is work. It's not good for you,' Theresa said, sliding a glance at David.

That had been a taboo subject at their home, growing up. Their dad had always said that hard work was everything, which was why David gave up that life when he met Theresa. She had good intentions, but Nick didn't appreciate them discussing his life behind his back.

'We know another person isn't the secret ingredient to a happy life, but it helps.' David gave Nick a look of understanding.

'I met a woman yesterday,' Nick said, without thinking. The unsure stare of the woman from the café leaped into his mind. He wasn't convinced that he would want to see her again, but making up a story about the first woman who had showed interest in him – at least for a few minutes – might get them off his back for a while.

Theresa's eyes lit up and David tilted his head to the side.

'Did you kiss her?' Evan asked, then James let out an 'Eww!'

'You don't kiss girls you've just met,' Theresa said to the boys and then raised her eyebrows at Nick. 'And you always ask first.'

'You talked to a woman. That's progress,' David said around a large piece of lasagna.

David and Theresa continued their own conversation about

Nick's love life as if he were steps away from the altar. He wasn't even sure why he bothered to try to tell them otherwise. Those two could be such gossips at times.

But Nick didn't mind being the center of their conversation. He liked the banter and the way his shoulders relaxed around his family. David's house was much different from their parents'. Dad didn't talk about much other than work. Nick could be himself with his brother and family. It was all he needed after the start to the week he'd had so far.

Chapter 5

Angie woke early the next morning, the sound of her mother's voice and the banging of kitchen cabinets reverberating in her head. Managing to make her excuses to avoid her mother's annual cookie baking session, Angie grabbed the keys to Donato's rusty old wagon and nearly sprinted out the door to leave for Reese's house.

As she climbed into the driver's seat, she couldn't help but feel a small pang of guilt in her chest. Her mother had been so excited to have Angie home, she knew that she just wanted to enjoy all the festive activities that the season allowed while Angie was around. But Angie was all too aware that she wasn't going to find her next job from sitting around all day in her mum's kitchen. None of the hotels called her back, and each time she tried to follow up, one of the assistants blocked her, saying that they would be in touch if they were interested. Angie wanted to see if Reese had reviewed her resume for changes. Making a mental note to set aside some baking time to appease her mother, she dialed Reese's number in her cellphone, started the ignition and set off to her friend's house.

***

'Can I pay you to move back home for good and make my food every day?' Reese said as she shoveled the last bit of Belgium waffle into her mouth. She licked the syrup from the fork. Angie barely ate two bites in the time Reese had finished hers.

'You can't afford me,' Angie said, unsure that she wouldn't take any job offered to her. 'Besides, this is temporary. You'll have a baby soon.'

'I'll need more help than ever.' Reese walked into the living room and Angie followed with her plate. 'Everyone keeps telling me how tired I'll be in the first few months. You know me. I love to sleep.'

'Is Jer taking any time off?'

'A little.' Reese sat on the couch with a little groan. 'But it's not going to be enough.'

'What about his parents?'

'I'm sure they'll help.'

Angie sat next to her friend, placing the plate on the table. She propped pillows around Reese. With her hands busy she thought again of what Jeremy said. Reese missed her and she couldn't help feeling guilty that she didn't have roots here so that she could be around for her friends. They were happy, but Reese seemed overwhelmed.

'It will be fine. I don't think I'm going to the West Coast again, so I'll be home more often.'

'That would be nice. Aunty Angie can't stay away too long.'

Angie didn't want to get into her next move with Reese quite yet. Especially because she had no plan in mind. 'Did you look at my resume?'

'I did. Looks good. No notes from me.'

Angie sensed there was something else Reese wanted to say. But if her resume was flawless and she still didn't receive any phone calls, maybe the problem was her.

'I think your luck will turn around soon,' Reese said.

'When did you become so wise?'

'Don't you know all pregnant women are clairvoyant?'

Angie's phone rang with an unknown number on the screen. She flipped the phone to show Reese.

'Who is it?' Reese asked, leaning over.

'A job?' Angie's heart leaped in her chest. *Merry Christmas to me.*

'Answer it,' Reese said with a huge grin on her face.

Angie picked up the call. 'This is Angie.'

'Hi, Angela Martinelli?' a woman said on the other line.

'Yes.' Her heart fluttered in her chest. She wondered which hotel was calling her back. Though it didn't matter. She was ready to restart her life.

'This is Carrie from Westford Malls, we received your resume and wanted to have you come in for an interview.'

Reese's eyes widened before she stood from the couch, faster than Angie had seen her move lately.

Angie shook her head. 'I'm sorry, I don't—' Realization flooded through her. Reese pushing Angie to get a job. Asking to see her resume.

'You didn't,' Angie hissed at her best friend.

'Excuse me?' Carrie asked from the other line.

Reese shook her head, but even she couldn't hide the mischievous grin from her face.

'I, um …' Angie's mind went blank.

'We have a ten-thirty interview slot tomorrow morning. Can you make it into our corporate offices for then?' Carrie asked.

Angie fisted the fabric of the throw pillow next to her.

Reese's gaze wandered around the room.

'Ms Martinelli?' Carrie's voice rang in Angie's ear. 'Do we have a bad connection?'

Angie shook her head, though it wasn't as if Carrie could see her. It was the first job offer she'd received, even though it was unsolicited.

'Yes, I can be there for ten-thirty.' She hadn't interviewed in a while, and this could be a practice round before the interviews for the hotel jobs.

'See you then,' Carrie said before hanging up.

Angie sunk into the silence on the other line before putting her phone down.

'At least you have an interview,' Reese said.

'I can't believe you did that behind my back.'

'You need money. This is your chance at a job. You already have experience there.'

'I told you I don't want to work at the mall, especially around Christmas.'

'What's your alternative? Sitting around, waiting for your phone to ring? That's not the Angie I know. Besides, your severance money will only last so long.'

With an apologetic email back from Melissa, the money had landed in Angie's account later than expected. At least someone from her previous job was on her side. It would last her a little while, but she didn't have a backup plan if no one from the other hotels returned her phone calls. Anxiety filled Angie's chest.

'What if I run into someone I know and have to explain why I'm back home and working there?'

'Who cares what people think?'

Angie cared, but she wasn't going to say that to Reese. Her best friend was right on all accounts. Angie needed money, and no one was calling her with a job offer.

'I didn't apply for any particular position, just at the mall in general,' Reese said. 'I'm sure you will be able to have your pick.'

'Well, thanks for that,' Angie deadpanned.

'What are best friends for?' said Reese, ignoring the sarcasm. 'Now, I'm thinking we can put a good dent in my Christmas romance movie list before you are busy with work!'

Angie sat back against the couch, propping her feet on the coffee table. Work. At the mall? A place she never thought she would return to. She had no idea what to expect tomorrow, but she wasn't going to allow her situation to put her in a mood. This hiccup was temporary. It had to be. Once one of the jobs called back, she would move on. It was the only thought she could have to ease the ache in her chest at her current situation.

Angie would enjoy the movie marathon with Reese and worry about tomorrow when it arrived.

***

On the day of her interview, Angie tried on a few of her more business casual outfits. Most of her suits were a little over the top for the position she was going for, but she wasn't going to dress like a slob.

To delay the inevitable, she checked herself out in the mirror for longer than necessary. Brett would have laughed at her if he saw how she had lost everything.

At the thought of him, she narrowed her eyes, wishing she could show him how much better off she was without him. Or would be when she finally landed another amazing job. He had tended to put others down. Her rose-colored glasses had prevented her from understanding that part of him.

Angie lifted her chin. She wasn't going to let him ruin another part of her life.

***

The closer she got to the mall, the more her stomach churned. She wasn't sure why she was so nervous.

Once she'd parked, she had fifteen minutes until her interview. The corporate offices were at the rear of the mall through a separate entrance. She recalled interviewing there in high school, and all of it looked the same.

Angie took several deep breaths as she rode the elevator. She knew this wasn't her dream job, but the quiver in her stomach was still there, making her legs wobbly as she stepped out onto the floor for the corporate offices.

She headed over to the desk toward a young woman with a headset. There were already several people in the waiting area possibly competing for the same job as her. They ranged from teenagers to a man in his sixties.

'I'm Angie Martinelli. I have an appointment.'

'Have a seat,' the woman said with a broad smile. She seemed closer to Angie's age. Maybe there was an opening in the office? She could see herself temporarily working there.

After sitting in one of the plush chairs, she glanced around the space. If she worked there, at least she wouldn't run into anyone she knew.

A few minutes later, a familiar person darkened the doorway. 'Angie?'

Angie stood and did a double take. She locked eyes with Maya Taylor and froze. Angie and Maya weren't enemies in school, but not exactly friends either. They were in direct competition on the cross-country track team, and Maya never allowed Angie to forget any of her record-breaking times.

'Maya?'

Maya looked at the paper in her hands, then back to Angie. She plastered on a smirk. 'This way.'

Maya led Angie into a small conference room, overlooking the tall buildings surrounding them. On the way, she couldn't help thinking that Maya held her immediate future in her hands. Surely they were both mature enough to not bring their old rivalry into their working worlds.

'When I saw your cover letter and resume come through, I had to see if it was you,' Maya said.

'It's me.' Angie couldn't even look at her. Once again, Maya had the upper hand. So much for not holding on to their high school pasts.

'You were let go from your previous job in California?' Maya asked, placing Angie's resume on the table between them.

It was a standard question, but Maya could make anything sound like an insult. 'It was time for a change. This is only a temporary job.'

'Considering the Christmas season, that's all we have for now,' Maya said as if it were a challenge. 'You *are* coming into the season later than usual. Most holiday jobs become available at the beginning of November. Black Friday and all that.' She lifted a second sheet of paper from behind Angie's resume.

Angie craned her neck to see the paper.

'Are you good with kids?' Maya asked.

'Sure, why?'

'We have one spot open for a photographer at the Santa booth in the food court.'

Angie cleared her throat, unable to fathom wearing whatever costume they required for working with Santa. 'Is there anywhere else?'

Maya sighed as if Angie was wasting her time – but Angie was determined their relationship in high school wasn't going to affect how she spent the next month of her life.

'We have three retail positions,' she said. 'Four in food service. Also, an opening for an information specialist.'

'That was the last job I had when I worked here,' Angie said, jumping at the opportunity. Working at the information booth at the center of the mall would give her a lot of downtime to continue her real job search.

'You're a bit overqualified.'

'I'm interested. I figured there would be a pay cut, but I don't mind.' When she came to the mall, she wasn't thrilled about taking a job, but Angie couldn't stand the pitying looks Maya kept throwing her. She wanted to prove Maya wrong, that she could overcome her situation.

'All right. I have other interviews today. I'll get back to you soon.'

'Thank you,' Angie said, but Maya was out of her seat already.

Angie showed herself out, glancing over her shoulder. Maya was gone, but she hoped their past wouldn't affect her present.

***

As she walked over the bridge linking the offices and the mall, Angie admired the holiday decor. Garlands of red, green, and silver and gold swooped down from the ceiling. The hum of activity from the mall moved over her as she entered the throngs of people shopping for their loved ones. Even close to lunchtime on a Thursday, the place was packed.

It would only get worse as the holiday neared.

Taking a detour, she found the information booth where she remembered. There was a line of people in front of the empty stand. They were clearly short-staffed, and Angie wondered if she should call Maya to confirm her interest.

Choosing to ignore the bustling counter, Angie quickly passed by, leaving Maya to decide her fate.

In the food court, holiday music played from the speakers, barely audible over the conversations around her. The lines at most of the stands were outrageous, but she had nowhere to be. She chose a sandwich wrap place she'd never tried before. While waiting, she scanned the area, fully expecting to run into more people she knew.

What would she say when they asked about her life and her job? She could lie, but Brett was a prime example of lies blowing up in people's faces. She wasn't that person, despite her embarrassment about her desperate need to get work after living in California.

After she paid for her turkey wrap, she waited off to the side for her order.

A guy in a charcoal-grey suit approached the counter. She blinked, immediately recognizing him. If she weren't so concerned with the growling in her stomach, she would have fled the scene.

47

Heat bloomed within her, and she regretted her choice of thick jacket. There was no way she could avoid him.

When the guy from the café turned around and met her eyes, his polite smile fell as recognition flooded his expression. His eyes narrowed slightly as he approached her to wait for his food.

'It's you,' he said.

Angie gave him a shaky smile. There wasn't much else she could do after he called her out like that. She got a better look at him without his jacket on. His tailored suit shaped his fit body. He looked like a runner.

'Oh, hi.'

'Hi.' He smirked, and a chill ran down her spine. It was the same confident grin Brett always had for his employees. It was the same one which helped her fall for him.

Silence stretched between them, making the crowded food court close in around her. 'Thanks again for the other day. I can pay you back for the bagels.'

He waved his hand in front of him as if to say it wasn't a problem. 'You figured it out, then?'

'Yes, thanks.' She wrung her hands in front of her, unsure of what to do with them.

'I hope you enjoyed your breakfast,' he said.

It seemed as if both of them were terrible at small talk. For some reason, it made Angie smile.

'What did I say?' he asked with a hint of a grin.

Angie tucked her hair away from her face, trying to cool off. 'Nothing. So, are you Christmas shopping today?'

'No, I'm on my lunch break.'

It made sense that he worked nearby since she had met him at the café the other morning.

'I'm Nick, by the way,' he said.

'Angie.'

He cleared his throat.

'Angie!' a young man from the food stall called.

'Excuse me.' She sprinted to the counter to get her tray.

'Nick!' the guy called next.

Angie glanced around at the nearby tables and chairs. There were only a few open tables. She could take her food to go.

'Do you want to sit together?' Nick asked.

'Sure.' If he wasn't going to take her money, it was the least she could do to repay him for his kindness.

When they sat, Angie was aware of his movements. His knee brushed against her leg, and he muttered an apology. She sipped from her soda and unwrapped her sandwich, desperate to look anywhere but at him.

'What are you up to today?' he asked. 'I thought you said you said you were an online shopper.'

'Good memory.' Angie hesitated about the real reason for her being there, but she needed to get over herself. 'I applied for a job today.'

'Here?'

She inwardly cringed, unsure about how much she wanted to reveal about her life to this guy. 'Yeah, I'm unemployed right now. I worked at a hotel as an event planner in California. Right now, I need a temporary place to work until I get back on my feet.'

'Well, you came to the right place at the right time. The holiday season is perfect for a temporary job.'

'When I was sixteen, I worked here. I blew all of my paychecks on new clothes.'

'Which store?'

'Oh, everywhere. I started at the Smoothie Shack, then the movie theater as an usher. I worked for a little while at Bloomfield's department store. I was the best bow-tie-er in town.' Angie laughed, and he joined her. 'That was during the break of my freshman year of college. I never came back after that.'

'You got around,' Nick said. His eyebrows rose as if he was impressed. Angie's barometer of men was off lately, and she wasn't sure what to make of him.

49

'Well, I only did one sport, and I loved to shop.'

'I'm sure you have a good shot at getting the job.' He took a bite of his sandwich as the words hung between them.

Angie had the urge to engage him more. The image of the door closing behind her in his face brought another wave of flames over her body. 'For some reason, I was nervous about the interview. To make it even worse, I know the girl who interviewed me. We didn't get along well in high school. I know I'm more than qualified for the position, but I hope she doesn't use that against me.'

'It couldn't have been that bad,' Nick said.

'It wasn't great. It makes me slightly anxious to think that Maya holds my future in her hands.'

'I'm sure it will all turn out as it's supposed to.'

Angie was *supposed* to be in California with her boyfriend and the life she'd spent so many years building. Working at her high school job wasn't exactly her plan.

'Do you come here a lot?' Angie asked him. 'Since you work nearby?'

Nick wiped his mouth with a napkin and smirked. 'I like the food here. I'm not much of a cook. You?'

'I know my way around a kitchen.' Thanks to her mother. 'But the takeout in California was much tastier than what I could cook up with the amount of time I spent at work.'

'Did you go out a lot with friends?'

Angie tried to hide her burning cheeks. 'Sometimes.' She wasn't ready to admit that she had the tendency to get swept up into the life of whoever she dated that she ended up seeing less of her friends than she liked. It was a habit she would make a point not to continue in the future.

'I bet the nightlife is better there than here.'

'I'm sure it's not so bad.'

'I bet you could make a night out here fun for anyone.'

Angie's gaze dipped to the table, as a tingling sensation skittered up her arms.

Nick cleared his throat. 'But I also bet you're leaving town right after the holiday?'

'It depends on if I get a more permanent job nearby.' Would she go out with him regardless? There was no harm in having a little fun for herself. Though that was what got her in trouble with Brett to start.

'I'm sure you'll hear back from someone soon. If it were up to me, I'd hire you.'

'Thanks.'

Nick wasn't as bad as she originally thought. But the last time she fell for a handsome guy in a suit, he uprooted her life and forced her home. He was cute, but she wasn't going to go down that rabbit hole again.

'Well, I should get back,' Nick said, crunching up the wrapper in front of him.

Angie sat up straighter. Seeing Nick twice in one week seemed like a strange twist of fate. 'Maybe we'll run into each other again?'

'I hope so.' He flashed a heart-melting grin. 'See you, Angie.'

'Bye.' She watched him walk away and couldn't help the slump in her shoulders. There was no way she would consider starting a new relationship with someone, never mind a crush. It was better this way.

Chapter 6

On the way back to the office, Nick couldn't believe he had run into Angie again. When he first saw her, he had noticed how she avoided his eyes. After not thanking him for paying for her food, he wanted her to be uncomfortable about the other day. But it seemed that it all was a misunderstanding. The banter they had from their brief encounter had returned, and he found himself wanting to be around her. It was a strange feeling toward someone he barely knew, but a sense of urgency had forced him to invite himself to eat with her.

Nick wasn't happy that Angie lost her job. But with her applying to the mall an opportunity to help her appeared in front of him.

Maya oversaw the interviews, so she would have all the resumes. When he returned to the office, he couldn't help gravitating toward her desk.

'Did you have a good lunch?' he asked, propping his arm on the divider of her cubicle.

'It was fine,' she said, sorting resumes.

Nick peered down, looking for Angie's name at the top of one of them.

No such luck.

Nick couldn't imagine Angie doing anything to have a strained relationship with Maya, but one thing he knew of the HR head was that she didn't care for people who were on her bad side.

'What's going on with you?' she asked.

'What do you mean?'

Maya sat up in her chair. 'This isn't the time of year for you to be so happy. Or lie.'

Nick dragged a finger over the top of the cubicle. 'I'm in a good mood. I had lunch with someone. It was interesting.'

She raised an eyebrow. 'Interesting, how?'

Nick shook his head. 'It's not important. But I have a few minutes. Did you need me to approve anything?'

Maya trapped her bottom lip under her teeth. 'Actually, yes. I wanted your opinion on a potential applicant for the information specialist position. I went to high school with her, and she's a bit overqualified. I'm not sure if I should keep looking or not.'

Nick cleared his throat, leaning closer. 'Who is it?'

Maya handed over a piece of paper.

Nick held the paper in front of him as if it was from any other applicant.

Angela Martinelli.

He pocketed her last name for later. Scanning through, he found out she had worked at a prestigious hotel as an event planner since she'd graduated from college.

Nick was more than impressed.

'I have a few teens looking for work,' Maya said, sifting through the other resumes. 'They're seniors, but all of them brought phones to their interview. They seem more into looking as if they are working than actually doing the work.'

Nick tapped his finger against the EMPLOYMENT HISTORY section of the resume. 'Under relevant work, Angie – Angela, I mean, has worked at the booth. She has training.'

'There isn't much training involved, though. Is it weird if I pick her? She seemed a little desperate and sad. I don't want this to be a conflict of interest. Since I know her.'

'That was years ago. To me, it doesn't seem like a conflict of interest.'

Maya raised a questioning eyebrow. 'At least, I'm assuming, from what you said,' he said quickly. 'You have to trust your judgment.'

Maya swiveled in her chair. 'I'll think about it a little more.'

Nick placed the resume on her desk. 'I know you'll make the right choice, Maya.' He walked into his office, not wanting to interfere with the hiring process. It wasn't his place, but he hoped Maya would give Angie the job, he wanted to get to know her a little better. As he sat down, he woke up his computer. His eyes strained to stay on the screen instead of checking in on Maya.

The front of his office was all glass, giving him a view of Maya's desk. He left his door open to hear her making phone calls to the applicants. After some time, his ears perked up when Maya said Angie's name. She was on the phone, the top of her head barely visible over the cubicle wall.

Nick hadn't expected to hear anything from that distance, but he crossed his fingers that Angie would accept. His water bottle stood empty at the edge of the desk, offering the perfect opportunity to fill it at the water cooler out front.

Nick slipped by Maya's desk, but she wasn't on the phone anymore.

With each desk he passed, his smile widened. A few of the other employees blinked away their surprise. Nick wasn't the grinning type at work, especially with his father around.

With a full bottle, he made his way back to Maya's desk. 'How goes it?'

'Fine.' She lifted a piece of paper in front of her. It wasn't Angie's resume.

'Good. Did everyone accept?'

'I'm still making phone calls, Nick.' She wheeled her chair around. 'What gives? Are you checking up on me?'

'No, not at all.'

'Why don't I believe you?'

'You should because it's the truth.'

'All right,' she said, eyeing him.

When he returned to his desk, Nick let out a sigh. He couldn't let Maya know why he wanted Angie to get the job. But it was the least he could do to help a new acquaintance for the holidays.

***

That night, Nick returned to his apartment much later than usual. When he walked through the door, Charlie popped her head up from the other side of the couch. Her eyes were bleary with sleep.

'Hey, girl.'

She rolled over, exposing her chest for a rub. Charlie's slobbery kiss met his hand. He settled into the couch, running over the day in his head.

Tomorrow, he'd find out if Angie had accepted the job. It seemed an inevitability, unless she had a better offer.

He had wanted to tell her he was the manager for the corporation that ran the mall, but most women only saw dollar signs and a free pass to new clothes when he talked about work. However, there was something in Angie's expression that made him think that she was different to the rest. She had a spark of determination in her eyes that drew him in, and it made him eager to get to know her better.

She had wanted the job so badly, but he knew any favoritism would put him in a bad light. Besides, he didn't know her that well. The opportunity would come if it were meant to be.

A text pinged from his phone on the table by the door, lighting up the wall behind it. He had finished with work for the day, the message could wait until tomorrow.

Nick grabbed the remote and flipped the television on. He needed to distract his mind for a little while and spend time with his girl.

***

The next morning, Nick woke with buzzing energy throughout his body despite sleeping less than usual. He searched for his phone, realizing it hadn't moved from the night before. Nick mentally prepared himself for his dad asking about work or telling Nick he needed to redo something.

Southside Villa, Saturday at 7

Nick couldn't help the flitting excitement moving through him at the prospect of a new venture with his father. It wasn't an option he was given before, but David had had numerous opportunities. Maybe Nick was in his dad's good graces after all.

He mulled it over while running with Charlie. Quinn hadn't prepped him for the meeting at all, but Nick's enthusiasm to push further in his career would have to shine through. He debated asking his father for more information but wasn't sure if this was a test for him to think on his feet.

The plummeting temperatures outside were enough to put him in a sweatshirt and jogging pants, but Nick needed to figure things out in his head before going into work.

Angie's smiling face appeared in his mind. He wanted to help her get a temporary job until she got back on her feet. There was nothing wrong with helping out a new friend. Other than the fact that he hadn't told her his job.

Most of the mall workers only knew him by name, so no one would call him out as one of the corporate bosses. Though, at what point would his omission come out? He wanted Angie to get to know him properly, without his job and position casting a shadow over any relationship they might have, but it wasn't fair that he kept the information to himself.

When he reached his apartment building again, he wasn't any closer to figuring out the questions in his mind surrounding Angie and him.

Chapter 7

The call for the job came quicker than Angie would have thought. Her phone rang before she'd entered her house after coming home from the mall, and Maya wanted her to start Friday morning at ten-thirty.

As she was getting ready for her first day of work, Angie recalled the conversation with Nick from the day before. Who was she kidding? He was all she thought of on the way home yesterday, and he filled her thoughts the moment she had woken up. His confidence in her getting the job was overwhelming, maybe she was too used to conversations with Brett only revolving around himself.

The familiar tingles of interest floated through her, but she tried to crush them before they could take hold. Nick seemed interested, even after their disastrous first meeting but she had only just come out of a relationship and she no longer wanted to be *that* girl, moving from one disastrous relationship straight to the next. Maybe a phone call to Reese would stop her from thinking of Nick in that way.

She took a deep breath and walked into the hallway. Her family was already up and moving around the kitchen. Her mom was going to ask her if she was excited about going to work again.

If Angie was truly honest with herself, her heart felt heavy as though she had backpedaled ten steps from where she wanted to be. But without anyone from the hotels returning her calls, she couldn't turn down a company who wanted her.

Maria was already in the living room, digging through another box of decorations. They were multiplying like snow bunnies. Christmas-themed knick-knacks and houses that her mom had painted in her ceramic classes years ago already covered every surface.

Angie had about an hour before she needed to leave.

'Do you need help?' Angie asked. 'I have some time.'

'Thanks,' Maria said.

Her nonni were in the kitchen having coffee. She kissed them each on the cheeks before coming back into the living room.

'How are you feeling about all this?' Maria asked.

'Okay …' Angie flipped the box open and looked through the contents.

'You don't sound okay about it.'

'I'm grateful for the opportunity, but I wish some of these hotels would call me back.'

Maria lifted a snow globe from the box and turned on her heel. She eyed the room, looking for a place to put it down. 'I'm sure the holidays are busy for these places.'

'They are.' That was an excuse she had repeated to her family all week. At her previous job, she planned parties from Thanksgiving through New Year's at the many event spaces for local corporate businesses. Other than keeping track of her team and subcontractors, she barely had time to breathe never mind look at someone's resume. She wished someone would make the exception for her.

'I just need to keep working. If I don't, I'm afraid I'm going to turn to a ball of mush sitting around eating cookies.'

'Calories don't count around Christmas. Remember that.'

Angie wished that was the case, though her nonna made a point more than once to tell her to eat more.

'How about you open those holiday cards for me?' Maria asked.

An activity that always brought on another blast from the past. When Angie was younger, she would rush to get to the mail after school to see who had sent them. Maria was the traditional type and sent cards filled with glitter. Apparently, she wanted to be remembered by the piles of minuscule sparkles which stuck to every surface through the Christmas season.

Angie held the stack of a dozen cards ready for opening before she plopped onto the couch.

Maria handed over a letter opener with the face of a reindeer at the end.

Angie opened the first card. An unfamiliar family of four stared back at her all wearing matching Santa hats. They smiled at the camera as if preserving their lives in one of Maria's snow globes.

Angie flipped the photo around. 'Who's this?'

'The Richards family. Susan plays bridge with Mom. That's her daughter.'

'She sent *you* a card?'

'I go with her to the community center. We're all close.'

Angie shrugged. Throughout the season, only a handful of people sent her cards. The stack next to her was from one week at Maria's house. She couldn't help the pinch of envy in her chest. Her mom grew up in this town and had so many connections. Angie wondered if that would ever be the case with her.

Maria explained the history of each of the unfamiliar faces on the cards. Several came with letters detailing the lives of a family throughout the year. Maria wrinkled her nose at those, calling them 'braggy', but Angie thought it was a nice touch. Especially because it helped her get to know the families better.

The last card had a familiar face on it. 'This is from Emma.' Her college roommate always sent Angie a card each year.

Maria sat next to Angie, letting out a long sigh. 'Her daughter is the cutest.'

Emma had the most adorable three-year-old girl on the planet. At first, it was a shock when Emma announced her engagement a year after they graduated. But even with Emma's excessive partying, she met a studious guy named Nathan and fell in love.

'What does she do again?' Maria asked.

'She works for a non-profit in the city.'

'Emma always had a good heart. I'm glad her husband calmed her down a bit.'

Angie smiled, thinking of all the good times she'd had with her college friend. 'I should tell her I'm home. She's going to get her card back from my address.'

'It would be nice if you caught up with her more often than over Christmas.'

'Ma,' Angie warned.

'What?'

'It's different with Emma. We text each other sometimes.' Usually when Angie experienced a memory linking to their four years together. They had a similar relationship to Reese and her. When they saw each other, memories flooded their conversations, and they could talk for hours as if no time had passed at all.

'Sometimes isn't going to make your Christmas card pile any bigger.'

Angie waved a card at her mother. 'That's not how I gauge friendships.'

Maria kissed Angie's head, and pulled Angie close. 'I know, but it's nice to know when people are thinking of you.'

Angie didn't want to admit her mother was right. Over the years, she'd allowed her work to get in the way of life. Whenever she had a lousy day, she always texted or called Reese. Most of her nights over the last year involved Brett and only him. They never went out with a group of friends, and now she understood why. Angie had alienated the people in her life because of a guy and that thought made her stomach twist into knots.

Heat seared her eyes, and she stood up from the couch. 'I'm going to hang these.'

When Maria came into the kitchen, Angie was composed

again. She wanted nothing to do with Brett anymore, but he still affected her. What a waste of a year of her life. What would he think if he saw her now? She didn't care. It might take time, but one day, he would regret treating her the way he did. Though would he even care to learn?

'Looks great,' Maria said.

Angie considered her handiwork. She placed the same type of cards together, so they came together artistically. This was her project. It was small, but she was proud.

Emma smiled back at her through her card. Angie lifted her phone from the table and sent a quick text giving vague details about her trip home.

Emma returned her text about a minute later.

Tell me everything!

The words poured out of her as Emma's response threw her into the past. She could almost feel the springs in her twin bed in their dorm room under her as she and Emma gossiped together over microwave mac and cheese.

As she relived each moment between her and Brett and coming home, a sense of relief washed over her. This was her life. He wasn't going to dictate anything anymore.

I have a job at the mall. The same place from high school. I'm waiting to hear about my resume from a few other hotels.

Let me know how I can help. Miss you.

Maybe after the holiday, I'll visit?

Yes, yes, yes! I would love that.

Angie and Maria gathered fixings for omelets and French toast while Donato and Emilia argued about the state of the world as

61

he read the newspaper. Emilia told him he was too sensitive about politics which put him on track for another rant.

While Angie ate, she couldn't stop smiling at her family.

***

Angie arrived at the information booth with ten minutes to spare. A metal shade covered the window in front. Maya had told her a man named Stuart Greene would get her settled. She wasn't sure when Stuart would show up, but she prided herself on being early.

Despite the mall being emptier than she remembered in years, the parking lot was already filling up. This was the first weekend in the busiest month in the year. She walked through the back entrance to reach the booth before anyone came inside. The familiar hallways and the silent mall reminded her of a simpler time in her life. She yearned to keep that in mind while getting over the man who had shattered her heart.

A tall blond guy in a mall security outfit walked toward her. Angie pegged him in his forties. He shoved his glasses up the bridge of his nose. 'Angela?'

'Stuart,' she said. 'It's nice to meet you.'

He let out a guttural smoker's cough and Angie almost gagged. 'Sorry.'

'It's fine,' she said, waving him off.

The information booth was a rectangular structure in the center of the mall. The sign had been updated since she was there last. Apparently, now it doubled as a security office as well.

Using a set of keys, he dug through the choices and shoved one in the back door of the booth. 'Someone will open this for you each morning and lock it after the last shift. You'll share the booth with other security guards. We fill in sometimes, but there are two other specialists on the schedule. Trina is on maternity leave, so you and Gary are splitting shifts.' Stuart looked her up and down. 'I hope you're not as lazy as him.'

62

Angie hoped not too.

'If you ever see one of my guards hanging out too long, feel free to contact me. Sometimes those guys lose track of time on their breaks.'

The door opened, and he stepped inside. 'Mrs Theroux said you worked here before?'

'Who?'

'Maya Theroux. Head of Human Resources. You are Angie Martinelli, right?'

As if someone would pretend to work at the booth. What would they steal? Mall maps? 'Yes. I didn't realize her last name had changed.' There wasn't much time during their interview to catch up on Maya's married life. Not that she would have shared willingly.

The lights flipped on, and once again, Angie walked back in time. The cramped space still looked the same. When she worked there during high school, she and Reese had free rein of the booth during Angie's shifts.

Mall maps were stacked haphazardly to one side of the desk, and food wrappers littered the floor. Stuart stepped on them as if they were carpet. He lifted a walkie talkie from one of the cradles. 'If you need a break, you can use this to call one of us to fill in. Timecards are over here. Santa tickets here.'

'Santa tickets?'

'Yes, you're in charge of the sales for Breakfast with Santa each Sunday through Christmas. There's an information sheet here. The cap is twenty-five kids per session.'

'Wow, there are a lot more events here than I remember.'

Stuart nodded. 'We're competing with the online market, so we are trying to attract more people to the mall.'

Angie doubted the events would change many people's minds, but she kept her mouth shut.

Stuart explained about the coupon books for customers, the Lost and Found bin, and the app for the mall toting discounts as well. 'There might be more interest when the Christmas scavenger hunt comes along. That's next Friday. We're supposed to double the numbers from last year.'

'What is that?'

'All of the stores will have a theme, and those participating will stop at each location based on the clues and take proof to the final event. The theme for our booth is Santa's Workshop and we're handing out paper presents.' Stuart smiled as if the idea would win him a promotion.

Angie glanced around the space. 'Where are we getting these paper presents?'

Stuart nodded to a stack of construction paper. 'You'll work on that first.'

'I have to make them?'

Someone rapped on the metal covering, and Angie jumped.

'It's time to open.' Stuart showed Angie where to hold to get the shade to move upward. 'Make sure you lock it into these holes here.'

An older woman stood outside. Her poof of white hair appeared freshly styled, and a small Yorkie peeked out of her handbag. Angie knew dogs outside of service ones weren't allowed, but Stuart didn't even notice.

'How can I help you?' Angie asked.

'I need a map. I have no idea where any store is,' the woman said. 'Don't you have one of those big electronic ones?'

Stuart started to answer, but Angie spoke first. 'Those maps are on the far ends of each level of the mall near the elevators. I do have paper ones right here if you prefer.'

'That would be lovely, dear,' the old woman said, accepting the folded map.

After the woman left, Angie sat in the chair with her arms over her chest.

Stuart shrugged. 'Looks like you have everything covered here. I'll leave you to it.'

When she was finally alone, she took in the state of the booth. She had work to do to make her area more conducive to getting her job done.

Angie started by cleaning the floor. A broom and dustpan leaned against the far corner. Within minutes she could walk around without crunching over leftovers. Stacking the maps was easy enough, and she managed to change a light bulb above the desk which had been out for who knew how long.

In no time, the booth felt like hers again. With the feeling of nostalgia in her heart, she helped everyone who came to the booth with a smile. The pressure of the season weighed on them as much as their packages and Angie didn't want to add to that.

After a few hours, she fell into a groove close to where she had been at her previous job. It wasn't anything grand like a party for hundreds of hotel guests, but she enjoyed leading people to where they wanted to be.

In her few minutes of downtime between customers, Angie pulled out the instructions for the paper presents. Stuart had said they were expecting at least a hundred, if not more. That was a lot of cutting she'd have to do on her own. Angie debated bringing home the tracing outline she had created to make the job easier, but she wanted to see how the rest of the week went. Her job wasn't difficult, so she had to appear as busy as possible in case Maya came down to check on her.

The thought of Maya's scrutinizing expression sent a jolt of fear through her. She glanced at the wandering crowds around her. Maya wouldn't stroll up to the booth. She would sneakily watch from afar to make sure Angie wasn't slacking off.

But, instead of meeting Maya's hard gaze, Angie spotted another familiar face. Nick's friendly smile struck her as he approached the booth.

Chapter 8

Nick wasn't sure if stopping by the booth put him too close to the metaphorical flame. Angie had no idea he worked so close to her. All he knew was the draw in her direction was strong, and he had to figure out why.

'Hi,' he said when he was close enough to glimpse her unmistakable smile.

'Hello again,' Angie said. 'Are you here for lunch?'

The truth rested on the tip of his tongue. He made a non-committal sound. 'What are you up to?' He gestured at the construction paper spread across the desk.

'There's a scavenger hunt next week. These presents are the clue for the booth. Apparently, I have to wear an elf hat. Can you tell how happy I am?' She gave him a deadpan look.

'I'll be sure to stop by,' he said smiling.

Angie laughed and the sound struck him. 'Well, you're going to have a lot of competition. I hear the event is big.'

One of the biggest of the season. The marketing team had come up with it the year before to bring more crowds to the mall closer to Christmas. They went all in with the advertising this year with newspaper articles and on the online forums for families. The prizes were even better with the donations coming from local businesses in the community.

Nick didn't tell Angie any of this. For some reason, his mouth couldn't form the words.

Angie leaned against the edge of the desk. 'Did you get your Christmas shopping done?'

'Not yet. I don't even have a tree.'

'Your girlfriend hasn't pushed you to get one?'

'My girlfriend?'

Angie's lips twisted and her gaze fell to her hands. 'I wasn't sure.'

She wanted to know if he was single. Did that mean she was interested? If so, that had to mean she didn't have a boyfriend. At least he hoped.

'Real or fake?' she asked, meeting his eyes again.

'Girlfriend?'

Laughter burst through her, and she shook her head, curling a chunk of hair around her ear. 'I mean real or fake Christmas tree.'

He matched her smile. 'In the past, I've had a real one.' It was the only way to go as far as he was concerned. He could forget about the fake ones from his more recent past as he had a feeling Angie was the traditional type.

'Where I used to work, we filled the lobby and spaces with real trees. It helped put me in the spirit since there was no snow.'

'Do you miss California?'

'Not right now,' she said, holding his gaze. 'I prefer having seasons. As cold as it gets here, it's nice to have a white Christmas.'

'That would involve snow, which we seriously lack this year.'

'Have some faith.'

Nick's phone buzzed from his pocket. He had to get back to work, but all he wanted to do was talk with Angie in the booth for the rest of the day. Her interest in him had changed their dynamic completely.

'Did you want to have lunch together again?' he asked. 'Or dinner. Breakfast, even. I'm not picky.' Desperation dripped from his words and he clamped his lips together before he said anything else to embarrass himself. Nick wasn't sure what reaction he expected, but it wasn't her stepping away with a frown tugging at her lips. 'Or not? Sorry, did I say something wrong?'

Angie glanced at her desk, tucking her hair behind her ears. While he thought it was a flirtatious gesture, she looked nervous. The silky ends brushed over her shoulders. 'I want to be honest with you. I just got out of a bad breakup.'

'Oh,' Nick said.

'I'm not ready for anything more.'

'I wasn't implying …' he said, even though that was exactly what he had been doing.

'But if you need help finding a Christmas tree, I can help you out.'

Nick understood bad breakups. He wouldn't push, but he still wanted to get to know her. If she wanted a friend, he would be that. 'That would be great. When are you free?'

Angie reached over to the clipboard hanging from the wall. 'Looks like I'm working the afternoon shift Sunday. How about we go that morning when the nursery opens?'

'That would be great. Send me the address.'

Angie reached into her pocket for her phone. 'Don't tell my boss I'm on my phone.'

'Your secret's safe with me.'

Angie added Nick's number into her phone and then texted him her address and the one for the nursery.

'See you around ten?' she said. 'I should probably get back to work on these presents.'

'I'm looking forward to it,' Nick said before turning away from her.

David was right. Getting out of the office did do him good.

He had an excuse to see Angie again outside of the sticky situation around his work.

***

On Saturday night, Nick arrived at the restaurant for the business meeting five minutes before he was supposed to.

Even though his father was rarely late, Nick didn't want to entertain his father's college friend on his own. It was freezing outside and he hoped Quinn wouldn't run too much later.

The Christmas season touched every corner of the waiting area. Red and gold ribbons wrapped around the potted trees, while several tall decorated Christmas trees stood among the tables in the dining area.

'Are you Nick Bower?' a woman said from next to him. The blonde stood from the bench seat. Her fur coat surrounded her neck as if it were a pet.

'Yes,' he said, not recognizing her at all.

Relief flashed across her face. 'Good, you're the third person I've asked so far. I'm Ivy. Jared Kent's daughter.'

Nick took her hand, still confused. 'Is he running late?' But why would he send his daughter instead of calling his father and postponing the dinner?

Ivy tugged at the silky strands of hair cascading down one shoulder. 'It took me a minute to figure it out, too.' She lifted her phone from the pocket of her jacket. 'I tried calling and texting my dad, but he hasn't answered yet.'

Ivy glanced to the side toward the dining area as realization flooded Nick's body.

'This is a setup,' he said.

Ivy sighed and lifted her eyes to the ceiling. 'This isn't the first time he's tried this. I wondered if your dad would have told you.'

'He didn't,' Nick said.

Her cheeks flushed pink and anxiety flashed across her blue

eyes. She seemed as embarrassed by the set up as he was. 'We don't have to do this.'

Nick sighed. Quinn hadn't ever set Nick up on a blind date before. It seemed strange that his dad would be on the same page as David in wanting to interfere with his love life. 'Are you hungry? We're already here.'

'Are you sure?' Ivy asked, tilting her head to the side.

'I am.' Nick walked over to the host station. They learned the reservation was under Nick's name.

The host escorted them to a seat against the back window, overlooking the water's edge. It was too dark to see much other than the reflections of the city lights. Behind them stood one of the taller decorated trees in the restaurant. Ivy pinched one of the needles between her manicured fingers.

'Is it real or fake?' Nick asked.

'Fake,' she said.

'I doubt they want to send any allergic customers home in an ambulance.'

'I prefer the fake ones too,' Ivy said. 'I can't stand all those needles everywhere. My mother has been pestering me to put up my tree, but I can't seem to find the time.'

'The real ones smell nice, though.' Nick thought of Angie and their conversation from earlier. He could have told Ivy that he hadn't ever put up a real tree at his place on his own, but he hoped that would change when he and Angie went to the nursery together.

'It does. But there is a spray for that,' she said laughing. Nick couldn't help but think about the way that Angie had laughed earlier. He wished it was her sitting across from him. There was no reason to make a big deal about the setup tonight and ruin a connection with his father's friend, but he felt that he should try and let her know that he wasn't romantically interested.

'What do you do, Ivy?'

'I work with my father, at his real estate firm,' she said.

'How is it working with him?'

'How is it working with any father from his generation?'

Nick smirked. He knew better than anyone what that felt like.

Ivy sucked in a breath as if she wanted to say more. Nick waited for her to speak. 'I'm not the type to overly apologize for anyone's behavior, but I hate how my dad involved you in this. He's not fond of my dating choices, and he's always interfering. I suppose he thought by making it seem like a business dinner, that it would fool me. I honestly don't want to waste your time. You seem great, but I'm still working it out with my ex. He's across the country now, but I'm hoping things will change soon.'

Nick let out a relieved breath. He didn't know what Angie wanted, but he didn't want anything to get in the middle of a possibility.

Ivy reached across the table to shake his hand. 'Friends?'

From then on, conversation flowed with Ivy. But as much as Nick enjoyed getting to know her, neither lingered after the check came.

'I'll pay,' Ivy said, reaching for it.

'No way,' Nick said, sliding the small tray closer to him.

Ivy pinched the side of the tray. Her grip was strong. 'It's the least I could do.'

'It wasn't your fault and I had a nice time,' Nick said.

'How about we split it?'

Nick sighed. 'Okay.'

Ivy smiled again. She had seemed a little stiff at first, but they had fallen into a groove which he was grateful for.

Once the check was paid, they walked to the coat check together. 'Well, I hope you have a nice holiday. If I don't see you.'

'You as well.' Nick waited a few seconds before heading out after her. Without Ivy around, a spike of anger rushed through him. He couldn't believe his dad had set him up like that. His father had a lot of explaining to do the next time he spoke with him.

***

Sunday morning, Nick stood in front of the bathroom mirror, fixing the collar of his sweater. With each passing day, the temperature dipped, yet there was still no snow in sight. At least Angie couldn't cancel their trip because of bad weather.

The nursery was about a half hour away, and he offered to drive. It would give him more of an opportunity to talk to her on the way there and back. Even though she wasn't interested in dating, there were other ways to get to know someone.

The afternoon before, Nick had swapped his car for David's truck so he could bring the tree to his apartment without strapping it to the roof of his car.

Nick didn't give David any other information, as he was determined to avoid an over the top interrogation. His chance with Angie stood before him, but he didn't want to jinx anything. She wanted to be friends, and that was what she was going to get from him.

Charlie whined from the doorway. Nick patted his leg to call her over. She trotted next to him and plopped her butt on the tile floor. She leaned her head against his leg, and he scratched her favorite spot.

'I'm not going all day, Char,' he said. 'I'll be back this afternoon.' Nick almost wished he could have swapped Angie's shift, but that would have crossed the blurry gray line between boss and employee. Besides, he wasn't going to deny her a paycheck for his benefit.

Nick gave Charlie a few more scratches before texting Angie to let her know that he was on his way.

***

Angie's home was in the suburbs, outside of the busy downtown. It seemed as if almost all the houses showed off their own personal spin on Christmas with lights, garlands on the windows, and wreaths on the doors. It was a stark contrast to his apartment

72

building where maybe a few on each floor had some decoration.

Nick did a double take at the address when he came across one house without an inch of free space in the front yard or on the roof. It was a Christmas wonderland. It wasn't Angie's house, but it certainly made a statement among the other houses in the neighborhood.

Angie walked out of the house next door, the blue one with a Christmas tree in the front window and a modest number of lights hanging from the porch. She waved him over, and he pulled into the driveway.

Nick wanted to help her with the door, but she was already outside the truck by the time he stopped.

Angie hopped inside, 'Good morning,' she chimed, rubbing her gloved hands together in front of the vents. The fluffy pom-pom on top of her gray knitted hat fluttered as the warm air blasted in her direction. Today, her hair was wavy, different than the smooth, straight style she usually wore.

'Hey,' he said. 'I could have come to the door.'

'No,' Angie said with a laugh. 'Have you ever been interviewed by a family before?'

'Can't say I have.'

'Let's keep it that way.'

Nick pulled out of the driveway and in the direction of the Christmas house next door. 'Your neighbors go all out, huh?'

'Oh yeah,' she said. 'When my dad was alive, there was a friendly competition but not anymore.'

'I'm sorry to hear about your dad. I didn't know.'

Angie shrugged. 'Thanks. It was a while ago, though.' She cleared her throat. Nick wanted to say more, but she spoke first. 'I didn't picture you as the truck kind of guy.'

Nick stiffened in his seat. Had David left something of his nearby? 'Why not?'

'All the suits.'

'Don't judge a book by its cover,' he said.

'I'm learning not to,' she said.

'This is my brother's truck.'

Her jaw dropped in mock surprise. 'So what was with the speech about judging a book by its cover?'

He chuckled.

'So what do you drive?'

He stiffened again. Was outer appearance the only reason she agreed to come with him? A lot of women he dated did that. They cared about the name brands on cars and when they saw a suit and a high paying job, they also saw money. Working at the mall afforded him discounts. He couldn't help but wonder if he saw dollar signs flashing in Molly's eyes on their first date. A passing thought he had chosen to ignore at the time.

'A sedan,' he said, not naming the brand.

'Practical,' she said. 'I had to sell my car when I left. I'm driving my nonno's car around. I feel like I've been transported back in time.'

Nick ignored the sinking feeling of guilt in his stomach. She was just making conversation, so why did he feel the need to put up his walls? He hadn't told her about his job or lifestyle. The truth rested on the tip of his tongue, but he didn't correct whatever judgment she made of him.

'Did you get your tree from this place?' he asked. 'I saw it in the window.'

'My mom did. She's neurotic about getting her tree the moment Thanksgiving is over. She had a family friend go with her since I hadn't come back home yet. My grandparents live with us now, so she is with them most of the time.'

'That must be nice.'

'It can be, but my family is a handful. I'm living in the guest room. It's a lot different than California.'

'Did you have a house out there?'

'No, but a nice two-bedroom apartment.'

'This must be a change.'

'Oh yeah. Though I never thought I'd admit I like being home.

74

After everything that happened, it's comforting to have everything here not change much.'

'Mind if I ask you what made you come back home?'

Angie sucked in her breath through her teeth. 'I was dating this guy. It turned out he was engaged. I had no idea, of course,' she said the last part quickly. 'After Thanksgiving, he told me. Then my life snowballed from there. He happened to be my boss, as well. It was too awkward, so I left.'

A rock lodged in Nick's throat. His instinct to keep his mouth shut was a good one. He wasn't engaged or even in a relationship with someone else, but he could see how she would shy away from him if she knew he was technically her boss.

'I picked up my life and came home,' she continued. 'It wasn't how I imagined my holidays, but I've come to terms with my life. As you can see, that's why I'm not so much into dating.'

'I get it,' Nick said.

'What about you?' she asked.

'What about me?'

'Where do you live? What do you do? My mom asked about you, and I was shocked to realize I don't know all the details. I feel like a lousy person for being so self-absorbed every time we meet. I'm a mess.'

'I don't believe that. But I do live downtown with a wonderful girl named Charlie.'

'You have a roommate?' she hedged.

Nick smirked. 'Sort of. She's a golden retriever.'

Angie put her hand to her mouth. 'Aw, that's adorable. Do you have a picture of her?'

Nick handed over his phone. Their hands brushed, and Angie flicked a glance at him. Charlie's face appeared on the background of the screen.

'She's beautiful,' Angie said. 'Growing up, I had a yellow Lab, Dawson. He was already older when I was born, so I didn't have many years with him, but I've always wanted another dog.'

'Your California lifestyle didn't allow you to have pets?'

'No way. I was too busy. It wouldn't have been fair.'

Nick understood that. For months out of the year, he wasn't fair to Charlie either. Mrs Wilson was his saving grace.

'Eventually, though,' she said. 'I'm jealous of you. You seem to have it all together.'

Nick wasn't sure about that. But before she could press about his job again, he pulled into the lot. There were already several cars parked and people milled around the designated Christmas tree area.

'You have to try their hot chocolate. It's amazing. At least, as I remember.'

'Hot chocolate it is,' Nick said, getting out of the car. He wanted to hold the door for her, but once again, Angie was already out. Her gloves were back on, and she zipped her coat to her chin as her breath fogged around her.

Angie brushed her hand over Nick's. 'You're going to die when you drink this stuff.'

In the short conversations that they had shared, Angie had never seemed so excited about something before. It was as if the Christmas season had inspired her, and in turn, him. He'd never felt so alive until this moment. It both scared and thrilled him. He wanted to see the season through her eyes. For once, not worrying about monthly reports and numbers on how well the mall performed during the time. Wasn't Christmas about loved ones and enjoying the holiday spirit?

Nick caught up with Angie, who waited in line for the hot chocolate. The cart boasted several types of desserts: cookies decorated as snowmen, Santas, and his reindeer; cupcakes, and various assorted pastries.

Excitement rolled off her in waves, and Nick couldn't help his own buzzing energy.

When they reached the top of the line, Angie ordered two hot chocolates.

'One of those snowmen cookies, too,' Nick said.

The woman poured the hot chocolate and grabbed the cookie with a small slice of wax paper, handing it over with the cups. Nick grabbed them, but then realized he didn't have enough hands to pay.

'Here,' Angie said, giving the woman money.

'I was going to get that,' Nick said as they walked away.

'I owe you, remember?'

At that moment, Kevin's Café seemed so long ago. 'Fair enough.'

They wandered closer to the trees. 'What kind are you looking for?'

'Green,' he said.

She lifted her gaze. 'You're hilarious.'

He dodged a swat from her. 'I'm out of my element. I trust your opinion. Treat it as it's your own.'

'How tall are your ceilings?' she asked.

'Nine feet.'

'Perfect.'

Nick watched Angie move through the trees as if she were about to pluck one of them for Santa's house. More than once, she had the nursery worker pull a tree out for an inspection. Some were too thin, others too lopsided. They must have looked at more than a dozen. It might have been tedious work, but he enjoyed every minute. With his schedule, Christmas tended to pass quickly without him. The magic of the season was lost while he worked.

Angie made it come alive. All these years, he'd missed out this major decision of the holiday season. If his dad were there, he'd say Nick was getting a little too nostalgic. He didn't think so. Not when Angie turned to him with the biggest grin he'd ever seen.

'What do you think?' she asked, tilting her cup of hot chocolate in the direction of the tree in front of them before sipping from it.

'It's perfect,' Nick said, looking at Angie.

'We'll take it,' Angie said to the teen boy wearing a tattered knitted hat.

'Your name?' the teen asked.

'Nick,' he said.

'You can pay and pick it up over there.' He gestured toward a growing stack of wrapped trees closer to the main building and then shuffled away.

With the tree already wrapped in netting and closer to the checkout area, they could have left. Nick waited for Angie to suggest it since it was possible she didn't want to spend too much time with him. She didn't have to get to work for a while yet, but he expected her to want to go home as soon as they chose a tree.

'Let's split this,' he said, cutting the snowman cookie in half.

'Thank you.' She bit into the cookie and closed her eyes while chewing. 'So good.'

Nick took a bite too. He had avoided the platters of cookies and desserts which came through the break room since Thanksgiving. Today, he wanted to experience the Christmas season the way Angie did.

'If I could ever eat my past, this is what it would taste like,' Angie said. 'My dad and I used to bring these cookies home after getting a tree. My mom would always get upset since she bakes like crazy around this time. It's different here, though. It's as if the atmosphere adds to the taste.'

She finished her cookie in two more bites, then sipped from the hot chocolate. 'I wish I didn't have to go to work today. I almost feel like sitting at home with a fire going and listening to Christmas music.'

Nick turned, wondering if she could see the lie in his eyes. Would a friend tell her to skip work, or let it slide as her not being serious?

'Do you have ornaments?' Angie asked, eyeing the small store across the lot.

'I think so,' Nick said, wondering if he'd need to take a trip to his mom's house to check. When he moved into his apartment, he'd left a lot of his memories in boxes in the attic.

Old yearbooks, photographs, and clothes collected dust up there. Since Molly hired people to decorate, Nick wondered if she had taken everything with her in the breakup.

Angie snorted a laugh. 'How do you not know?'

'Work is busy around this time of year,' he admitted. 'I needed help finding a tree, remember?'

'That's true.'

'I'm sure my mother will let me borrow some,' Nick said.

'We have extras too — a whole untouched box. My mom goes crazy at the end of holiday sales every year. You can borrow some if you'd like.'

'Are you sure?'

'Absolutely,' she said. 'But I think you should get at least one to start your own collection.'

Angie took his hand and pulled him toward the store. Inside, several families and couples moved between the narrow aisles, admiring the hand-crafted ornaments and decorations hanging from the walls and resting on carved wooden shelves. Nick admired the design as something that could have come from David's workshop.

'Do you like anything here?' She stood close enough to him that her hair spilled over his arm.

'This one,' Nick said, pulling a carved teddy bear ornament from the shelf. 'I think my nephews would like this.'

'Those are adorable,' Angie said, picking up a matching one. 'How old are your nephews?'

'Six. Twins.'

'I bet they love their Uncle Nick.'

'I think they like Charlie more than me.'

'Well, this is incredibly thoughtful. How about something for *your* tree?'

Nick wandered the aisles behind Angie. She pointed out several items for Nick, but none of them were quite right. Between his mother's collection and Angie's, he could fill the branches of the trees. But now he was on a mission to find a piece of his own. In a way, he wanted to break off from his normal routine. His dad had stopped decorating for Christmas when Nick and David were young. Now, his mother did it all on her own. It wasn't fair to her.

'I love this one,' Angie said, holding up a glass snowflake.

'That's pretty.'

'It reminds me of the ornaments my nonna used to have on her tree. I was the only one allowed to touch them since they were all so delicate.'

Angie's expression was wistful, and the world fell away for a moment. She set it down and shuffled to the next shelf. Nick glanced at the snowflake before following her. He wasn't going to go all out with decorations, but he wanted to experience more of the season which joined families and new friends together.

'This is the perfect one.' Angie rushed toward the other side of the aisle. When she turned around, she held a string pinched between her fingers. A replica of a golden retriever slowly turned in the air between them. The figure looked like Charlie did during their runs. The pleased expression on the dog's face warmed Nick's heart.

He took it in his hands. 'This is perfect. Thank you, Angie.'

They locked eyes, and for a moment, the entire world disappeared around him – until a young boy thundered down the aisle, pushing against Nick's legs. He pitched forward, bumping into Angie. Her mouth fell open with surprise as the dog ornament fell from her hands.

Nick caught it and used his other hand to balance himself before he could take her down.

'Good catch,' Angie said, drawing in a deep breath.

'So sorry,' a woman said as she chased after her son.

Nick didn't mind the intrusion, as it revealed a little more about Angie in the process. It seemed as if she didn't mind being closer to him, and neither did he.

Chapter 9

The ride home from the nursery seemed quicker than the trip there. While Angie had been apprehensive about going out with a stranger, there was something about Nick that seemed familiar and comfortable. Their time together passed so quickly, and in a way, she hoped he would ask to see her again. Angie wasn't ready to date, but she wanted to spend time with him.

On the way home, Angie texted her mom to ask if she was okay to let Nick borrow the decorations. She didn't want the Charlie-ornament to be the only one on the tree. As apprehensive as she was this morning, there was no avoiding her mother meeting Nick.

When they arrived in the driveway, the front door opened, revealing Maria holding a box in front of her.

'I'm going to apologize in advance,' Angie said. 'She can be a little much.'

'I'm sure it's not that bad. Besides, you're doing me a favor.'

Angie wondered whether to tell Nick to stay in the car, but she didn't want him to think she was hiding anything from him. However, she wasn't ready to face her mom's conclusion about Angie going out with a man on any sort of date.

'You've been warned.' Angie trudged up the driveway with

Nick on her heels. She was aware of him next to her and how it must look to her mother.

Maria placed the box on the small table next to the rocking chairs and leaned against the door frame.

The curtains behind the front window moved, and Angie spied Emilia's curious gaze before they moved again to conceal her. At that moment, she regretted so many life choices.

'Mom, this is Nick,' Angie said.

'Come in, come in,' Maria said, waving them inside.

'Ma, I need to get ready for work.'

'You can wait five minutes,' Maria said. 'You don't need to be there for another hour.'

Angie shot Nick an apologetic look, but his smile remained. She hoped he wasn't ready to flee as well. As much as her family embarrassed her, she loved them dearly and protected them fiercely.

The shower ran from the bathroom, so at least Nick only had to deal with her Mom and Emilia.

'Nonna, this is Nick. I helped him pick out a Christmas tree this morning,' Angie said.

'Sit,' Maria demanded with a smile.

Angie and Nick sat on the couch, bumping elbows.

'Did you get the hot chocolate?' Emilia asked. 'That was always little Angela's favorite part. She used to have the cutest chocolate mustache when she finished. And the cookies. This girl was a chubby one.'

Angie squeezed her eyes shut, wondering when it would be over.

'We did,' Nick said. 'She also helped me pick out an ornament for the tree. I hate to admit I haven't done much decorating this year. Unlike you.' He peered around the room.

Angie felt the room close in around her as they talked. The clutter seemed too much and over the top.

'Thanks for letting me borrow some decorations. I'll treat them as my own,' Nick said.

Maria walked from the kitchen with a wrapped plate of cookies. Her mother handed them out to everyone she met. 'Speaking of cookies. I know you'll want to take some home to your family. Do you have your own place?'

'Ma,' Angie warned.

Nick chuckled, leaning back against the couch as if he could stay there forever. 'Yes, it's just me and Charlie, my dog.'

'Single, huh?' Maria said, winking at Angie.

There was no way Nick missed that look. Angie tried to develop telepathy at that moment to tell her mother to rein it back.

'Better get that tree home and into some water,' Angie said to Nick.

'You're right.' Nick reached for the cookie tray. 'Thanks so much Mrs. Martinelli. I appreciate the ornaments and cookies.'

'Hopefully, we'll see you again soon,' Maria said.

Angie shuffled Nick from the room and onto the porch.

'Let me take those,' Angie said.

Nick handed over the cookies and lifted the box. 'This is heavier than I expected.'

'We have enough decorations to fill Bloomfield's,' Angie said, laughing. 'Sorry about that in there.'

'About what? Your family is nice.'

'And a little preoccupied with my life,' she muttered under her breath. She didn't want Nick to think she had spoken to her family about him. She wanted to be friends but knew he was interested. The morning washed over her, and she started to picture what future outings would be like with him.

Quickly, Angie caught herself. Nick was a kind and handsome man, but staying home was only temporary. What if a job opportunity came from a different state? It was similar to how she had felt about working at the mall. What was the point in starting a new job as she hoped for another one? Though, no one had called her back about any job other than the mall. Comparing Nick to a job seemed strange, but could she be as open to something new with him as well?

Nick placed the box on the front seat, and she snuggled the cookie plate next to it.

'Which one of these is your favorite?' he asked.

Angie glanced at the house. The curtain moved again. 'Those. Butterballs. I always leave those to Mom to make.'

'Which ones did you make?'

'The sugar cookies with red and green sprinkles.'

He lifted the plastic and picked one of the sugar cookies, biting into it. 'This is good.'

Angie pressed her lips, holding back a smile. 'Two cookies in one morning? You're going to be on a sugar high all day.'

Nick chuckled. A warm sound. 'Probably.'

'I want to see the tree when it's finished,' Angie said, then realized she was inviting herself over to his place. 'I mean, you can text me a picture.'

'I'll text you regardless,' Nick said.

Angie couldn't think of anything else to say. The logical response would be to tell him goodbye so that they could get on with their day. But the silence between them stretched on.

'I don't want you to be late for work,' he said after a beat.

Angie snapped to the present. 'Right. See you later.'

'Definitely,' he said.

As he drove down the street, Angie held onto that promise tight against her as if it would disappear into the wintry morning air.

***

That afternoon at lunch, Angie's fingers trembled as she twirled the lo mein around her fork. During her shift, she had cut out almost fifty present silhouettes. She couldn't wait for that task to be over.

Edward, one of the other security guards, offered to help her. But she didn't think that was part of his job. Angie didn't want Stuart to think she was slacking off. Besides, she wasn't sure she

84

appreciated the older gentleman's wandering gaze each time they had a conversation.

Angie lifted another forkful of food into her mouth as she scanned the area. Nick knew she had work today, but would he come to the mall on his day off? She doubted it. They'd seen each other that morning, and he had a tree to decorate. There was no reason to think about him anyway. They were just friends.

With her fork, she stabbed a piece of chicken and shoved it into her mouth. She wished she didn't think about Nick as much as she did. Next to Brett, Nick was such a breath of fresh air. He didn't mind being in public with her for a start. Though, she wasn't sure why she never thought that was a problem. When she and Brett were together, he had refused to allow her to post pictures of them together, claiming he was camera shy. Another red flag she had completely ignored.

With Nick, she hadn't found anything suspicious. He was honest with her from the start and even agreed to be friends with her. Guys didn't do that. Well, not the guys she dated. It was all in or nothing for them. It was nice not to have pressure with Nick, but she couldn't help imagining spending Christmas dinner together. Her family already liked him, and that was a good sign.

'Hey!' Edward called out across the way. He charged over to a woman digging through the trash can. 'You can't be here.' He spoke loud enough for people in the immediate area to turn to watch the confrontation.

The woman wore stained clothes with several holes and patches stitched into them. Her gray-streaked hair frizzed out under her hat, framing her pale, thin face.

Angie watched the exchange and had no idea why she slipped out of her chair and walked over to them.

'I'm just looking for something I dropped,' the woman said, avoiding his eyes. She shied away from his scowl.

'You can't hang around here unless you're shopping,' he said. 'No loitering.'

'She's not loitering,' Angie said, hearing the echo of her voice in her head.

'Angie, let me handle this,' he said.

'No, Edward. I, uh, asked her to meet me here.'

He eyed the woman and then Angie. 'You know her?'

'Yes.' The word came out before she could stop it. She had no business butting into the conversation, but a more protective side of her took over.

The woman tilted her head with as much confusion as Edward.

'We're having lunch together. I told her I dropped my, um, bracelet in the garbage. She was helping.'

'I don't know what's happening here,' Edward said, his gaze darting between the two of them.

'Let's go …' Angie said, hoping the woman would help her out.

'Hazel,' the woman said to Angie, catching on.

Angie clapped her hands together. 'Hazel. It's fine. I came over to tell you it was attached to my coat. Silly me.'

'Where is the bracelet?' Edward asked.

'The clasp broke,' Angie said, unwilling to let Edward win this argument. 'It's in my purse.'

Edward chewed on his lip, considering her story. 'Be sure to stop by Hayes Jewelry. They're good. I got my wife's ring from there. On discount.'

'She's a lucky woman,' Hazel said flatly.

'Well, I only have ten minutes left,' Angie said. 'See you later, Edward. Come on, Hazel. Let's finish our conversation.'

Hazel limped behind Angie to the table.

When Angie sat, she waved at Edward who continued to stare after her.

'You're an angel,' Hazel said, glancing at Angie's food.

Angie handed over her extra egg roll. 'Are you hungry? I'm stuffed and I haven't touched it.'

Hazel snatched it from Angie and took a massive bite, the insides spilling from her mouth. 'I appreciate you stepping in. I normally don't come here on Sundays.'

'No problem. But what's wrong with the mall on Sundays?'

'The friendly guy from the corporate office doesn't mind me coming in here when I need a clean place to wash up, but he's not usually here on Sundays. I'll head back to the shelter when it opens around five.'

Angie shook her head. 'You stay in a shelter?'

'Don't you fret over me, child,' she said. 'I'm tougher than I look.'

'I don't doubt that,' Angie said.

'You said you had to get back to work,' Hazel said, licking the remains of the egg roll from her lips.

'I do.' Angie didn't want to be anywhere but with Hazel.

'You should head back then.'

Angie reached into her bag and pulled out a twenty-dollar bill. 'Take this.'

Hazel nodded. 'Thank you, child. I appreciate it.'

'It's all I have. I'm sorry …'

'Don't apologize to me. You're truly kind. Like that young manager who normally keeps those mall cops away from me. Well, most of the time.'

'I'm in the informational booth if you want to come by,' Angie said.

'I would like that, but I try and steer clear of security.'

'I understand. Maybe I'll see you around here again?'

'You will.' Hazel smiled, and Angie tried to. She ended up with a forced smile. Nothing about Hazel's situation was ideal, but the woman seemed to be accustomed to it.

Angie lifted her tray and walked toward the garbage. The remains of lo mein on her plate glared at her as her stomach twisted. She was wasting food while Hazel didn't look as if she had much. She turned around to bring it to her, but Hazel was gone.

The thought of Hazel rummaging around in the trash for food plagued Angie's thoughts for the rest of the day. The conversation hadn't gone on long, but she connected with the woman more than she would have predicted. In the few minutes they spoke, Angie couldn't help but feel her heart extend out to the woman and her situation.

Angie wondered about the corporate manager who helped Hazel by allowing her into the mall. That was someone Angie wanted to thank.

The twenty dollars wouldn't buy Hazel much, and Angie wanted to do more for the woman. She decided that she was going to make it her business to keep an eye out for her and the other security guards. It wasn't Edward's fault about whatever loitering rules they had at the mall, but didn't he see she needed help?

For the rest of her shift, she helped customers while searching on her phone for local homeless shelters. Angie wasn't sure which one Hazel stayed at, but she wanted to donate time or resources. With no idea what they needed, she saved the phone number, unsure of what to do with it. Edward had already given her dirty looks when he came in for his water breaks. She doubted he liked her contradicting him while working.

He would have to deal with it. There were more important things in the world.

***

That night at the dinner table, Angie never felt as much gratitude for her life as she did sitting with a feast in front of her.

'What's on your mind, Angie? Are you thinking about Nick?' her mom asked with a smirk.

'Did he call you today?' Emilia asked.

'It's not about Nick. I met this homeless woman today at the mall.'

Mom tutted. 'I can't imagine being out there in this weather.'

'We were almost homeless,' Donato said.

Maria put her utensils on the table. 'When?'

'So long ago,' Emilia said. 'Not even worth mentioning.'

'It was before you and Gianni were born,' Donato said looking at Maria. Uncle Gianni moved back to Italy years ago with Angie's three cousins after his divorce. Other than Christmas cards and the gossip from her mother, Angie hadn't heard about him for a while. 'We didn't have much money, and our landlord threatened to kick us out. It was a good thing he liked Emilia's cooking.'

Emilia preened. 'I made gravy for him for almost two months until Donato got another job at the factory.'

Maria scowled. 'How did I not know this?'

'Don't get huffy with me,' Emilia said. 'It was a part of our lives we wanted to forget. Aren't you happy you have this house?'

Maria and Emilia spoke over each other until they were a cacophony of frantic speech: her mother in English and Emilia with intermittent Italian.

Donato touched Angie's hand with his thick one. 'It's not easy for those in shelters. I have several veteran friends from the club who were homeless one or more times. God help them.'

Help them.

Those words stuck with Angie as they finished dinner and cleaned up. Emilia and Donato went to their room to change for bed while Angie filled the dishwasher.

'I wish there were something I could do,' Angie said, thinking of her nonni homeless. She put Emilia in Hazel's position, and a sadness swooped through her.

'What are you thinking?'

'I have no idea. I gave her money, but I don't know how long that can last. She needs help, long-term.'

Angie's phone pinged, and a text came through.

'Is that Nick? Maybe he can convince you to stick around longer.'

'Ma, we're friends.'

'It's him,' she said. 'I have a sense about these things.'

In the body of the text, a beautiful tree stared back at her. The white lights looked like miniature stars with the dark windows in the background. A familiar dog sat in front of the tree with her tongue lolling out.

Where are the ornaments?

I thought you could come by and help. I'm afraid of breaking them.

She started to type, 'Don't be' and then hesitated. Nick had offered her the opportunity to see him again. While a part of her didn't want to encourage anything with him, Angie couldn't force her finger to press SEND.

'Looks good,' Maria said over Angie's shoulder.

'It does,' Angie said, tilting her phone toward her so Mom couldn't read his invite.

'You know I tease you about Nick, but I want you to be happy.'

'I'm happy here,' Angie said, though she couldn't imagine Hazel feeling the same way as she shared a room with strangers.

'Let us be grateful for what we have,' Maria said, squeezing Angie's hand. 'You're a good person, Angie. That's why you deserve the world. If you're supposed to help this woman, the answer will come.'

Angie hugged her mother. 'I hope so.'

Maria turned to wash her hands at the sink when Angie looked at her phone again. This time, she didn't hesitate with her response.

Tomorrow night works. Send me your address.

Chapter 10

Before starting work the next morning, Nick stopped at his father's office. Quinn had his tie undone and his glasses on the edge of his nose as he peered at the computer screen.

Quinn glanced at Nick then back to his computer. 'Come in, son. How was your date the other night?'

Nick leaned against the door frame. He wanted the conversation to be quick and to the point. 'The date you tricked us into?'

'You didn't enjoy it?'

'She's nice, but I wish you didn't do it that way.'

'I know you. You wouldn't have gone.'

'Since when have you cared about my love life? Didn't you call Molly a "distraction"?'

Quinn sat back in his chair, crossing his arms. 'Ivy is a smart and successful woman. I thought it would be a positive change for you.'

'It's a little weird to be set up by your dad.'

'It's better than those ridiculous apps.'

'Next time just be honest.'

'Next time? I thought you said you liked her.'

'We're not interested in each other.'

'You can't even give it more than one date?'

'This is a little weird, Dad.'

'Don't miss out on something good because you're scared.'

'I'm not scared. It's our busy season, Dad. You know that.'
Nick hated to use work as an excuse, but it was the only language
Quinn would understand. It might even make him see that it
wasn't going to work out the way he wanted.

'She understands busy. Just give it a shot.'

Nick was done with the conversation. 'Is there anything else?'

'I'm sending over the reports for this week. I need you to
review them.'

'Now?'

Quinn eyed him over the rim of his glasses. 'Unless you have
somewhere else to be? I want these in by the end of the day.'

Nick turned, knowing the conversation was over, but only for
a little while. He trudged to his office and took his jacket off,
preparing to dive into work.

From the detailed notes on the reports, Quinn had put in late
hours over the weekend. Nick's email went off every few minutes
with more to-do's. It was as if he didn't want Nick to have an
opportunity for distraction.

But the scheduled lunch with his dad in the conference room
loomed over him. After the conversation from that morning, he
hoped Quinn wouldn't push the issue with Ivy.

With that in mind, Nick didn't go until the last possible second,
not caring if he was late. Nick waited for the opportunity to
mention the workload he had after just one weekend.

Each year, his father obsessed more about the company, but
this was by far the worst. A widening pit of dread expanded in
Nick's stomach. What was he not telling Nick?

When he reached the conference room, Quinn was already
digging into his salad. He barely looked up as Nick walked in.

'Shut the door,' he said, not looking up from his laptop.

'Is this a working lunch?' Nick asked as he shut the door.

'There's no time for downtime.'

'Is everything all right?' Nick said, flipping the plastic top off his salad. There wasn't as much chicken as Nick had wanted, but he supposed after binging on Mrs Martinelli's cookies his stomach could use some greens.

'Nothing is ever all right. We have to strive for better.'

'There isn't anyone else in the room other than me,' Nick said. 'You don't have to be "on".'

'What are you talking about?'

'Never mind.'

Quinn sighed and closed his laptop. 'Did you talk to Ivy today?'

Apparently, his idea of small talk was pushing his agenda with Ivy. 'No, Dad. Why do you care so much?'

'Because you two are compatible. Aren't you looking for someone to spend the holidays with?'

'I'd like to spend Christmas with my family.'

'You're coming to our house. Feel free to invite her. I can have your mother reach out to Jared.'

'*My* family, Dad.'

Quinn blinked as if not catching on to his meaning.

'David, Theresa, your two grandkids.'

Dad shook his head, stabbing the vegetables in front of him with his fork. 'I don't want to talk about that.'

'Because it makes you uncomfortable. How do you think David feels that you're taking away the opportunity for his family to know you?'

'He betrayed my trust, Nick.'

'By following his heart. You can't fault someone for that.'

Dad's attention snapped to Nick. 'That's enough. I don't want to discuss this.'

'Fine, Dad. But I'm not just going out with Ivy because you want me to. I'm a grown man with my own life.'

'Are you seeing someone else? Is that the problem? Who is she?'

Nick was usually on his game. He could have reacted quicker. Angie didn't want anything more. But the possibility of it made him answer seconds too late. 'No.'

'Who is she?' Quinn pressed.

'You don't know her.' In a way, he wanted to pull back a little from his father and show him up.

Quinn rarely showed an interest in Nick's love life other than to criticize. Nick wanted to keep Angie in a little bubble for as long as possible before his father barged in and burst it.

'Why not?'

'Is there anything else work-related we can do?' Nick asked, piercing his salad with a fork.

Quinn sighed and turned the computer screen around. 'I wanted to go over the reports from this morning. There was an error in your review.'

Nick pulled the laptop closer. 'I checked it twice.'

'Looks like whoever that girl is is no good for you,' Quinn said to his salad. 'Distractions.'

Nick ignored the comment and scanned the screen. Quinn had highlighted the error in red. To sift out the location of the issue, Nick would have to go through the entire spreadsheet. It was as if his dad knew Nick was meeting Angie later.

In any case, Nick wasn't going to allow his father to deter him.

After two hours and a forced apology to his dad for the error, Nick figured out the problem in the reports. He worked on as much as he could on his to-do list and turned off his computer around five. Somehow, he avoided a second confrontation with his father and left the office without delay.

**

Nick picked up a package at the front desk of his building before heading up to his apartment. Once he was on his floor, he called David.

'Thanks for bringing this by,' Nick said, opening the door.

Charlie's black nose pushed through the small crack between

the threshold and door. Her body weaseled through and into the hallway. Her tail thumped against the back of his leg.

'No problem,' David said through the phone. 'It was collecting dust in my workshop anyway. It makes me happy to see it on a tree. No matter whose.'

Nick balanced the wooden box in his hand as he greeted Charlie and pushed through into his apartment. 'Hey Char-Char.'

'Sorry, I couldn't meet you. I had a few deliveries this morning.' David went on about an older client of his who insisted on helping him bring a refurbished armoire into his house to surprise his wife.

While listening, Nick headed toward the focal point of the room. The tree. He flipped on the white lights and they glittered off every surface. He had spent most of Sunday figuring out the perfect spot for the tree after lugging it upstairs and into its brand-new stand. Even though he had been covered in sap and had to clean the trail of pine needles, his accomplishments filled him with a warmth he hadn't experienced for a long time. And that was all to do with Angie.

'Glad to hear business is doing well.'

'You're not the only one who understands the holiday rush.'

Nick gave the tree one more appraising glance before heading into the kitchen to feed Charlie. 'You're the only one who does.'

'Why did you need a tree topper anyway?'

'Remember I told you about that woman I had lunch with the other day, Angie?'

'The one you met at the café?'

'Yeah, she helped me pick out the tree yesterday. I asked her to help me decorate tonight, and she said yes.'

David chuckled. 'Good for you, man.' He paused for a moment. 'Is it serious? The other day it didn't seem like it. Unless you played it down.'

'I asked her out, but she said she didn't want to date right now. Bad breakup, I guess. But there's something about her. She offered to help with the tree, and I couldn't say no.'

'Well, you went tree shopping with a woman. She must be special.'

'She speaks her mind. I like that about her. She grew up in this area too.'

'While I'm happy for you, I don't think you should get your hopes up if she's not interested.'

'I don't have my hopes up. What's wrong with spending time with her?'

'Nothing, but I know you.'

'You do, do you?'

Charlie bumped Nick's hand, her nose searching for a scratch.

'You always jump at the opportunity to date a pretty woman,' David said. 'You go all in too quickly.'

Nick thought of Ivy. 'Not necessarily. I forgot to tell you that Dad set me up on a blind date with one of his college friends' daughters. We've decided to be friends, but Dad is hung up on it for some reason.'

'It wouldn't be the first time he did that.'

'What are you talking about?'

'Dad tried that after I told him about Theresa. Her name was Cait. It didn't work out well for either of them.'

This was news to Nick. It made sense, though, at least in his father's mindset. He had been working Nick harder.

'Do you think Dad thinks I'm going to leave the company too?'

'Who knows, but we both know he's not above doing whatever he wants and pushing others aside.'

Nick swallowed hard. The uncertainty in Dad's relationship with David always kept them walking on eggshells.

'But you like Angie?' David asked in an attempt to change the subject.

'When I'm around her, I don't want to be anywhere else.'

'Sounds like you've got it bad for her.'

As much as he would have loved to start something new with her, an expiration date loomed over them. 'She's only here for a short amount of time. She said she didn't want anything more and I'm okay with that.'

'Are you sure?'

'Considering she's working a temporary job at the mall, yeah.'

'Wait, I thought you met her at the café?'

Nick cleared his throat and explained her situation.

'I'm not sure it's a great idea for you to start something with someone who works for you.'

Nick slid a glance at the tree. 'Not for me, exactly.'

'Did you hire her to work for Westford Malls?'

'Technically, Maya did.'

David paused, and Nick already knew what he was going to ask next. 'Does she know you're her boss?'

'I'm not her boss, David.'

'In a way, you are. You didn't answer my question.'

Nick didn't want to hear his brother as his conscience. 'It hasn't come up.'

'Your job hasn't come up,' David repeated slowly, sounding out each word. The echo boomed in Nick's mind as quickly as his heart raced. 'I thought you two were getting close? What am I missing here?'

'Well, it didn't come up at first. When I met Angie the second time, she mentioned applying for a job at the mall. I didn't want her to think I got the job for her.'

'Did you?'

'Not at all. She interviewed with Maya. It was Maya's choice to fill that position.'

'You said she had a bad breakup. Did this guy lie to her?'

Nick hesitated. 'It's not the same thing.' Though it was. He had been her boss too. A dull ache radiated at the back of his throat.

'I'm not an expert at dating,' David said. 'But you're straddling a fine line. I think you should at least tell her you work in the corporate office. These things always come back. It's better to be honest.'

Nick sighed. 'It's complicated. I know I should say something, but how do I tell her without making it seem as if I lied on purpose?'

'That's up to you. But I would recommend doing it soon. Stretching this out isn't going to end well for you.'

The idea had lingered in Nick's mind since Angie got the job. It was better for her to find out through him than someone else.

'I hate to say it, but Dad might be right about Ivy. She at least knows where you work if Dad set it up. He probably told her all of your accomplishments.'

Nick ignored the sarcasm in his brother's voice. It wasn't his fault since it had happened to him in the past. At every party, Dad boasted about his eldest son's accomplishments. Yet he had never mentioned a word about David's side projects until it became more than a hobby.

'Listen, I need to get this place ready.' Nick wanted to move away from his personal life.

'Fine, little brother. But take my advice.'

'I will,' Nick said, mulling over how it could come up in conversation.

'Have a good time tonight.'

David hung up and Nick opened the wooden box his brother had made for Mom almost three years ago. Nick had tried to deliver the tree topper to her that Christmas. Once Dad found out it was from David, he refused the gift for her. Since then, the box collected dust in the corner of David's workshop as a reminder to him about the jagged rift in their family.

Nick lifted the wooden star from the box. It was light in his hands, with exquisite detailing in the wood. It was one of his favorite pieces from David. Too bad their father had to put a stain on its memory.

Nick stepped onto the chair and reached up. Somehow Angie had picked the perfect height for the tree since the top of the star stood a few inches from the ceiling.

He had an hour until Angie's arrival. Nick had planned it not to be a date since that was what she wanted. But there was no reason he couldn't order food for the two of them while they worked on the Christmas tree.

Nick had asked about her favorite takeout. Angie said she loved sushi, so he ordered a variety of hand rolls for dinner.

Shedding his suit, Nick went for a casual look with jeans and a red sweater. He might as well get into the festive spirit while decorating a tree.

The doorbell rang, and Nick hesitated as Charlie bolted for the door, sniffing at the bottom. He released a breath and walked as slowly as he could to the door. He opened it and came face to face with the delivery guy. Disappointment deflated him, but he didn't have to wait long before Angie arrived.

The next time the doorbell rang, Charlie raced him. But for once, Nick beat her to it.

Chapter 11

Nick's building was a lot nicer than Angie imagined. It was in the center of downtown in one of the older, renovated ones. She hadn't been down that area much since she'd returned home and, if she were honest with herself, she was apprehensive about going to Nick's place. Now, seeing where he lived made her want to fake an illness and postpone indefinitely. It wasn't fair for her to compare him to Brett, but there was something about the way Nick carried himself, with an air of confidence and authority that she couldn't help but associate with her former boyfriend.

Angie wasn't sure what to expect when she checked the address for the tenth time before walking through the opulent lobby, but if she was being frank, she felt intimidated by his wealth, just like she had with Brett. She tried not to judge him for it, but it was hard.

The comparison to Brett skewed her vision of him and it wasn't fair. Nick had been nothing but kind to her, he seemed down to earth and not at all like Brett. Yet as she rode the elevator to the eighth floor, she placed them side by side in her mind. Brett had always been one to flaunt his money while Nick didn't. Money wasn't the root of all evil, but she'd come close enough with Brett to harbor a burning sensation each time she thought of being with another man with any similarities.

When she reached his floor, she wandered to the last door. Nick wasn't Brett, she determined. Besides, they weren't dating.

Angie knocked on the door, and it swung open seconds later. Nick stood there, and a fluttering filled her. A wet, black nose filled the palm of her hand. Her heart swelled, and she knelt to pet Charlie.

'Hi, girl,' she cooed while Charlie sniffed her sweater and jeans. Her mom had cooked up a storm earlier for a holiday party at the club. Charlie seemed to enjoy the menu of scents wafting from her clothes.

'Charlie,' Nick said, with a grin and snap of his fingers. 'Can we let her get through the door?'

Charlie dutifully walked to Nick's side and sat. Her tail swished over the hardwood floors.

'Come on in,' Nick said with a smile. 'Sorry, she gets excited about guests.'

'No need to apologize,' Angie said, walking into his place.

Angie pushed thoughts of Brett aside as she took in the apartment. The lights were dim, forcing the tree to draw her to the center of the room. Behind it was an unobstructed view of downtown and beyond. The ceilings were high, as he had said at the nursery. It made the space seem even bigger. It was an open floor with the living area, kitchen, and dining space all accessible. Down a small hallway to her left were several doors most likely leading to the bedrooms. She wondered how many.

Angie waited for her memory to place Brett there too. But when she was with Nick, no one else entered her mind.

'Nice place,' she said.

'It was one of the only apartment buildings which allowed dogs,' Nick said, scratching Charlie's head. From the upward tilt of her chin, she loved it. 'I think I would have paid anything to make sure she had a home.'

Angie walked into the apartment, taking in the space. She missed having her own place where she could experience peace at the end of the day. She would get there soon enough.

At least she hoped.

'The tree looks great,' she said, inhaling the fresh pine scent.

'The lights took a while.' Nick chuckled, rubbing the back of his neck. 'But I think it came out okay.'

'You don't give yourself enough credit. I think lights are the hardest part.'

'Are you hungry?' Nick asked, heading over to the large dining table. Two paper bags sat on top.

Angie wondered how often he entertained guests. She had the urge to know more about him now that she was in his space. 'Starving.'

***

After eating the most delicious sushi she had in a while, Angie wandered toward the tree and lifted the top of the ornament box. Thin crinkled slices of paper filled the space between the delicate ornaments. Maria and Emilia decorated with the most beautiful pieces, but Angie had forgotten these. They threw her back to the past, a consistent theme in her new life.

'A lot of these are from my nonna's tree,' Angie realized.

'Now I feel a huge responsibility,' Nick said, pulling another one out.

Angie leaned closer with the most serious expression she could muster. 'You should. You don't want her knocking on your door after you return them. She probably has every nook and cranny memorized.'

'Really?'

'Somehow, she always remembers when I screwed up as a kid. I broke one when I was younger, and she still hasn't forgiven me.' She concealed a teasing smile.

Nick hung the ornament on one of the middle branches. It was so lonely that Angie rushed over to add hers.

'You don't seem like the "screw up" type,' he said.

'Not until high school. My friend Reese and I used to do some pretty crazy stuff.'

'Like what?'

Angie shrugged. 'Sneak out. Party.'

Nick raised an eyebrow.

'I'm not saying any more. It might ruin your impression of me. I did calm down quite a bit before college.'

'Who's to say you didn't ruin it already?' Nick asked.

Angie laughed and swatted at him, missing his arm on purpose. 'All right. Enough about me. Tell me more about you. I feel like I've been talking the entire time we met. Forcing you to pick out a Christmas tree and all that.'

'You didn't force me. I needed your help. If you didn't push, then I'd probably have one of those tabletop ones.'

'They're not a bad choice,' she said, hanging another ornament, this one a reindeer. 'But you have enough space for a bigger one, so why not take advantage?'

Charlie walked up to Angie and sniffed her leg before moving on to the tree.

Angie dug into Charlie's fur with her nails. Charlie sat dutifully by her side, her weight resting against her leg. Angie missed having a dog in her life.

'She'll sit there all night if you let her,' Nick said.

'I have two hands,' Angie said, showing Charlie an ornament. 'Where do you think this one should go?'

Charlie sniffed the bauble and then turned her head to the tree and sniffed the nearest branch.

'Good idea,' Angie said, hanging it on the branch Charlie suggested.

They worked in silence for a few moments. Nick grabbed his phone and started scrolling through.

'Bored already?' Angie said teasingly, but she was a little worried. She hadn't wanted anything other than friendship from Nick, but she enjoyed spending time with him. The familiar

103

quiver in her stomach made her want to keep him interested as well.

'Not even close.' The room filled with tinkling piano in the tune of 'Silent Night' and Angie spotted the speaker on the side table. 'I wanted to add some mood music to the place.'

Christmas music floated through the room, and Angie hummed along as she grabbed the next ornament.

Nick had the same idea, and their hands brushed, sending a buzz of electricity through her.

'Where are you spending the holidays?' Angie asked, moving away from him toward the box to pick another ornament.

'I'm split between my brother's and parents.'

'Split?'

'It's complicated.'

Angie waited for an explanation before she asked. Families were complicated, so she wasn't going to push.

Nick stared through the tree as he spoke. 'My father wanted my brother to work with him. But David had other plans. Dad is a stubborn man and broke off the relationship completely. He hasn't even met his grandchildren.'

'That must be hard,' Angie said.

'It's not easy,' Nick said. 'But David has a great life. Dad has his issues, but Mom and David hurt the most.'

'She doesn't see them?'

'She does, but she can't even talk about it with Dad. It complicates things.'

'I'm so sorry. I can't imagine.' She couldn't fathom not speaking to any member of her family for a long period of time. As much as California distanced them, she always sent them texts, cards, or called on holidays and birthdays.

Nick shrugged. 'I think Dad will come around eventually, but I hope it won't be too late.'

Nick tried hard to keep a small smile on his face, lightening the situation, but Angie could see how tough it was for him.

Angie reached out, touching his shoulder. 'I'm sure it feels harder around the holidays.'

Nick stood close to her. 'I appreciate you saying that. This season is busy at work. I'm sure Dad doesn't even notice.'

'You two work together?'

'Didn't I mention that?'

'No, but it adds a whole other level to your family dynamic.'

'Sure does,' Nick said.

Angie sensed he wanted to say more but didn't press him. From his pained expression, as he spoke about his family, she didn't want to add any more sadness to his eyes.

'Can I stand on that chair?' Angie asked. The ornaments were middle and bottom-heavy on the tree and needed some closer to the top.

'Sure,' Nick said, sliding one over. The fabric on the seat cover was a pale cream color. Angie slipped her shoes off before stepping up.

Nick held the box of ornaments for her. They worked around the tree until she was on the final layer of ornaments. She lifted a delicate angel from the table and held it in front of her. Hazel calling her an angel flitted to the front of her mind.

'You look like you're thinking about something,' Nick said. 'You don't need to worry about my family.'

'No, that's not it,' Angie said, thinking of where Hazel was tonight. Where did she sleep in the shelter? Did they even have a tree? 'I'm a little distracted. This ornament made me think of someone.'

'Your ex?'

'No,' Angie said with a laugh. 'A woman I met at work the other day. I'm a little disturbed by the conversation.'

'Do you want to talk about it?' Nick asked.

Angie retold her encounter with Hazel. With Nick staring up at her with hope in his eyes, she considered an idea. 'Are there any charities around here that help shelters?'

'I'm not sure. What did you have in mind?'

Angie pressed her lips together, unable to break from the thought of Hazel on her own. 'I want to do something.' She shook her head, placing the last two ornaments. Without anything in her hands, she snapped her fingers, trying to spark an idea.

Charlie barked and leaped upward at her.

The room tilted as Charlie bumped Angie's legs with her paws. The force of her pushed Angie off the chair. She gasped as her arms shot out to grab onto anything to keep her from falling.

Warm, strong hands wrapped around her waist, holding her in mid-air before slowly lowering her to the ground. Her body pressed close against Nick as she looked up at him. Concern shone in his eyes.

'Are you all right?' Nick asked.

His breath was warm against her cheeks. She swallowed and nodded as words didn't form. She couldn't take her eyes off his lips, fully aware that if she lifted onto her toes, she could kiss him.

Nick's mouth spread into a smile, and Angie was happy he still held her as her legs wobbled. 'One of my commands for her is snapping my fingers,' Nick murmured.

Charlie bumped Angie's leg, and she couldn't help smiling. 'Well, at least I didn't take down the tree.'

Nick's gaze fell to her lips before kissing her. Her body was momentarily paralyzed, but as Nick's mouth moved against hers, she leaned into him. Her eyes fluttered closed as she experienced the first kiss in a long time to set her ablaze. Her insides trembled and she gripped him harder to be closer to him. As if Nick could read her mind, he snaked a hand around her to deepen the kiss.

A flash of the breakup with Brett filled her mind and she jumped away from Nick. So much for him not leaving her alone when she was with Nick.

'Are you okay?' Nick's hand stayed on the small of her back as if he expected her to fall again.

It was a comforting touch. Angie wasn't sure her legs would

have held her up otherwise. She gripped the top of the chair just in case.

'Yes. Of course.' Brett had ruined another thing for her. But the more her lips were away from Nick, the more she realized that it was too soon to fall into this again. Or was it?

Nick smiled, a slow and sexy grin. A delicious swirl of tingles wove through her. Her gut couldn't be so wrong, could it?

Nick stepped back from the tree and admired it. The spot where his arm wrapped around her cooled quicker than she expected. At least he couldn't see the flush in her cheeks.

'Looks good,' Nick said. 'Better than if I tried myself.'

'It's all about teamwork.' Charlie sidled up to her again, waiting for another head scratch. As much as a prickling heat rose from her neck, she couldn't be mad at the dog.

'Now, all I need are some gifts under the tree,' Nick said.

'Do you need help wrapping them as well?' Angie asked.

'Are you offering?'

'Well, not to brag, but I was a gift-wrapper at Bloomfield's years ago. Never a complaint or a paper cut.'

'You should put a website up for all your Christmas season talents. I bet you could pull in a lot of money. Only if you help me first. I mean, I discovered you.'

'Of course.'

'Don't forget the little people when you become a billionaire.'

'For Christmas decorating? Yeah, right.'

'My ex hired people to decorate my place last year,' Nick said.

Angie tried to ignore the sting of jealousy in her chest. Nick lived in a bubble in her mind. She couldn't imagine him with anyone else. It wasn't fair in the slightest, yet it was a reflex she couldn't shake. 'Isn't the fun part doing it yourself?'

'I know that now,' he said. 'But it wasn't cheap. With your event-planning background, I bet you would succeed.'

Ideas flowed through Angie's mind. Nick didn't know her in California, but it was nice to hear him boasting her background.

'I'll think about it,' Angie said and meant it. It seemed as if Nick and Mom were on the same page about her sticking around. But Nick seemed sincere in his compliment. She would have an open mind about her next steps since there was no reason to turn anything down because she had nothing to lose.

Angie wasn't sure about a Christmas decorating job – it would take up a few months out of the year. She knew how to plan an event, though. Instead of committing to one hotel or venue, she wondered if branching out would fulfill her more.

'Looks like you're thinking about it right now,' Nick said with a chuckle.

'I am.' With dinner and tree-decorating done, there were only two options. She could take their kiss further tonight or take some space to make sure it was what she wanted before exploring that another time. She wasn't sure she trusted herself to stay longer. Complicated thoughts flitted through her mind as she slipped her shoes back on.

Nick's phone pinged from the kitchen, and he narrowed his eyes in the direction of the room.

Angie had found her perfect excuse. 'I should get going.'

'You don't have to,' he said, walking closer to her. The more she inhaled the scent of him, the less she wanted to leave.

'I'm working the morning shift tomorrow.'

'I want to see you again.'

Her toes curled in her shoes. She wanted to stay, and the instinct terrified her. Angie was sure that she wanted to be friends with him, and she was determined not to ruin it. Jumping into a rebound relationship with Nick wasn't going to help her move on.

Nick took her hands. 'There's a tree lighting ceremony downtown outside the mall on Wednesday night. Want to come with me?'

'My mom has been trying to get me to go.' The town tree lighting had always been the highlight of Angie's teen holidays.

All the kids in her grade went, and it was the perfect time to celebrate the holiday season with whoever she had a crush on that year.

'Great, so I'll see you then,' Nick said.

His eagerness warmed her insides. 'See you then.'

Chapter 12

With Angie leaving so abruptly, it made Nick rethink kissing her. Angie had seemed happy in his arms and spending time with him, and he couldn't help wanting more. He'd never remembered having so much fun decorating for Christmas with anyone since he was young living at home with his parents and competing with David on who could put up the most decorations the quickest.

He understood her hesitation though. The kiss they shared was amazing, but while he would have loved to test the boundaries of their relationship, they had started with the understanding of her not wanting to date anyone.

Saying goodbye created a heavy sensation in his stomach. But he hadn't completely turned her off. With another date set, he couldn't wait for it to come, even though it worried him that he hadn't mustered the courage to tell her the truth about his job. It had been right there, hanging over him the whole time he talked about the dynamic between Dad and David. But he couldn't do it. He couldn't snuff the sparkle in her eyes when she looked at him, especially with the knowledge that her ex-boyfriend used to be her boss too.

Angie had said she wanted to be friends, but a closeness grew between them which neither of them could ignore anymore.

Nick wasn't sure he could hold up that part of the bargain too much longer. He almost wanted to see where their relationship took them, even if it was doomed from the start. He wanted a long-term partner, but how could they make it work if she moved across the country again for a job? Had the holiday spirit captured them both? He had no idea what was going to happen after the Christmas.

Nick's phone went off again, and he wandered into the kitchen to answer it with Charlie on his heels. He lifted a treat from a small jar on the counter and tossed it to her. She caught it mid-air.

He expected several messages from his dad. After their earlier argument, Nick had no doubt Quinn would continue to pressure him about Ivy.

Instead of his father, there were two messages from Ivy. Their dads must have exchanged their phone numbers.

I need your opinion on something. Are you interested in a platonic non-date our parents haven't set up?

Nick smiled at the screen. Even if his dad wasn't on the same page at least Ivy knew where they stood. It made no sense to him that his father was so interested in pushing him and Ivy together.

I'm free tomorrow. What did you have in mind?

Ice skating?

Nick hadn't been on a rink since senior year of high school when he was on the varsity hockey team. He didn't want to think his father had suggested they go ice skating. But he trusted that Ivy understood wanting to stay friends.

***

Nick met Ivy the next night outside of the entrance to Cove Park. Holiday music poured from the covered pavilion outside

111

of the ice-skating rink. Underneath, a holiday party with dozens of people moved around the space drinking from small plastic cups and eating passed appetizers from waiters moving around the space.

'No skates?' Ivy asked, walking up to Nick. She wore a fur-lined hat and a long thick coat cinched at the waist.

'I haven't been for a while,' he admitted. 'I'm going to have to rent them.'

Ivy's lips quirked, but she said nothing. Nick understood that skaters were protective of the tools of the hobby, but he had hung his up a long time ago. Her worn white skates showed she skated a lot. He couldn't help wanting to know more about that. They had a lot in common, at least where their fathers were concerned.

'It's good to see you again,' Nick said, as they walked over to the rental booth together.

Families crowded the space. Kids tried to tie their skates as soon as possible to get on the ice. Nick avoided a particularly excited group of boys shoving each other to get to the rink first. They reminded him of his nephews. Nick couldn't help smiling.

'I wasn't sure if you would come out,' Ivy said. 'I can imagine how this part of the year is stressful for you.'

'This season doesn't let up.' As much as he was busy at work, he *had* found time for holiday fun with Angie. He wouldn't have done anything if Angie hadn't come into his life.

Nick paid for his rental skates and walked over to a bench. Ivy sat next to him and lifted her boots off her feet. She swapped them for skates, quickly tying them as if she were in a rush.

Or maybe Nick was out of practice. When he stood, he bent his knees to get the feel of the skates. They were a little big in the toes, but they would do.

'Ready?' Nick asked, grabbing onto the bench to steady his shaky legs.

Ivy reached out a hand to him, laughing. 'Are you?'

Nick wasn't sure if he was. Once they were on the rink, it

was as if he was one with the ice. It was like riding a bike. His memory of how to move returned quickly and before he knew it, his cheeks were red from the air pinching his skin.

Ivy moved on the ice like a graceful figure skater.

'I see why you wanted to come here,' Nick said. 'Trying to show me up, huh?'

'A little,' she said. 'My company is investing in this park. I wanted to see it, and I haven't skated in a while.'

'What's the plan?'

Ivy twisted her body until she was in front of him. Her body swayed to keep momentum and held his gaze. 'The plan is always for development.'

It was something his father would say. In her, he saw a mirror image of himself. In years past, Nick hadn't looked at the season as anything other than a money-maker for the company. He celebrated at the office holiday party and during Christmas Eve and Christmas dinners and that was it. He hadn't experienced a holiday like this one since he was a child. Already, Angie changed the way he looked at the holiday. Would she understand that if she knew where he worked? Or would she regret kissing him?

Ivy looped around the ice, faster than they had gone before. She weaved through families and couples. They watched with awed expressions as she passed.

When she returned to his side, she let out a breath creating a swirling cloud around her face. Her cheeks were pink. 'That was fun.'

'Looked like it,' Nick said. 'You can do it again if you want. It was impressive.'

'That's what training for thirteen years looks like.'

'Why did you stop?'

'I wasn't going to the Olympics. I chose to follow in my dad's footsteps. It was a practical choice.'

Nick understood the mentality. Most of the time, when asked about his career choice, his father's words slipped into his mouth, just as Jared's spoke through Ivy.

Practical was the word most used.

Nick wondered if his father had set him up with Ivy because he saw what *he* wanted. Not what Nick wanted.

After skating, Ivy suggested a walk around the park. The trails outlined with lights in the shapes of reindeers, Santas, snowmen, bells, ornaments, and other holiday symbols. The display reminded him of Angie's next-door neighbor. 'Over here is wasted space,' she said.

'It's a park.'

She nudged his arm. 'Hear me out.'

Nick commented on her ideas, but as their time wound down, Ivy seemed distracted. It was a look he knew well enough. In her head, she worked through whatever plan she wanted for the park.

'Would you mind cutting this short?' she asked. 'So many ideas just came to me and I want to get them down.'

'Sure.' As much as he said so, Nick wasn't ready to go yet. He wanted to leave the park with a smile on his face, filling himself up with some holiday cheer. 'I'm going to get some food. I haven't eaten yet.'

'This was fun. Thanks for your help.' She leaned forward, and before he knew it, her lips pressed against the corner of his mouth.

'Sorry,' she said. 'It was meant to be a cheek kiss.'

Nick laughed. 'It's fine.'

Ivy waved before turning toward the parking lot, her skates slung over her shoulder and her steps as light as they were on the rink. He waited until she was in the car before he touched his face to wipe off the dampness from her kiss. A small bit of red lipstick smudged across his fingertips.

Nick walked toward the rink again. The lipstick wasn't coming off, as much as he dragged his fingers across his face.

'Do you need a mirror?' someone asked.

He turned to see a woman standing outside the pavilion. She waggled her fingers at him, beckoning him over.

As he neared, he noticed how she rubbed the side of her round belly absently as she dug into her bag with the other. Her dark hair covered her face as she spoke.

'My husband hates when I get lipstick on him, but I keep telling him I don't wear it for *him*,' she said with a wry smile, handing over a small compact mirror.

'Thanks,' Nick said and glanced at the lively pavilion behind her. 'Your party?'

'No, my holiday party is much more fun. These guys can be a little stiff with conversation.'

Nick nodded as he wiped the remnants of Ivy's kiss from his face. 'Thanks again.' He handed the compact to her.

She slipped it into her bag and sighed. 'I should head inside before my husband realizes I wandered off.'

'Thanks again,' he said.

Nick walked around the rink toward the concessions, appreciating the lights strung on the trees and the festive air. Ivy hadn't seen this place for the feel of it. She only saw it for her purposes. What those purposes were, he had no idea.

Nick couldn't help thinking of Angie and how much fun they would have had tonight. He wouldn't have wiped her lipstick off his mouth. The idea of kissing her again overwhelmed him and the image stuck in his head for the rest of the night.

Chapter 13

Between work and hanging out with Nick, Angie needed some facetime with Reese. They kept up their daily texting, with Reese giving her all the gory details of pregnancy and her food cravings, but Angie wanted to do something special for her friend.

Reese usually worked a few days a week at Jeremy's dental practice at the front desk but found it hard to sit all day. Which made her go a little stir-crazy on the days she stayed home.

Angie woke before her shift to visit with Reese. The night before, she'd made chocolate chip pancake batter, knowing Reese would approve. Dad always thought the pancakes came out better when made the night before. Plus, it saved time in the morning. With Reese's pregnancy cravings, Angie wanted to help out as much as she could. Chocolate seemed to be a recurring theme, and Reese insisted Angie bring crunchy peanut butter and whipped cream too.

When Angie pulled into Reese's driveway, the door swung open, and Jeremy walked out, slinging his bag over his shoulder.

'You're a lifesaver,' he said. 'I have early appointments all week. Reese is convinced I'm leaving her for someone who doesn't hold a bowling ball in her shirt – her words, not mine.'

'What's in it for me?' Angie asked.

'I wish I had the time or energy for a snarky remark,' he said, waving at her as he walked toward his car.

'See you later,' Angie said, lifting the metal bowl from the passenger seat.

As Angie made her way up the driveway, she peered at the sky. There were barely any clouds, but the brilliant sun didn't make much heat. She wished for snow so badly since she missed it all the years she was in California.

Angie approached the door and pushed inside. She peered through the living room toward the kitchen. 'Hello? Reese?'

A spike of panic welled within her.

'In here,' Reese said, calling from the small half-bathroom down the short hallway across the room.

Angie let out a relieved breath. 'You scared me.'

'You're scared? I have no idea when this kid is coming. I'm rolling the dice with every sneeze.'

Reese shuffled into the living room wearing billowy floral pajama pants with an oversized T-shirt. Her fluffy slippers barely lifted from the ground. Angie wished she could have taken a sick day to spend the day with Reese. Her next day off was after Reese's holiday party. Angie knew she could convince Reese to stay in with her before the hectic holidays and baby preparation rolled around.

'I smell chocolate,' Reese said, grabbing the bowl from Angie. She pressed her nose against the plastic wrap and inhaled. 'Jer already preheated the griddle.'

Angie lifted a container of peanut butter and a can of whipped cream from her purse. 'All the toppings too.'

'You're amazing,' Reese said, tugging Angie along with her into the kitchen. She lifted the plastic from the bowl and started mixing the batter. 'How's work going?'

'Good. I still haven't figured out how to help that homeless woman though. I watch out for her when I can, but I haven't seen her.'

'After the way that security guard treated her, I'd make myself scarce too.'

Angie plopped onto one of the stools nestled against the breakfast bar, watching Reese pour the batter onto the hot surface of the skillet. Steam rose from the pancakes as they cooked.

Reese whirled around, pointing the spoon at Angie. 'What's going on with you and Nick?'

Angie focused on the batter Reese flung from the spoon. She grabbed a paper towel and scooped up the mess. 'What do you mean?'

'You didn't give me many details about the tree decorating.'

'I sent you a picture of the tree.' Angie tried to push down the heat in her cheeks as the memory of his kiss flooded her mind. There was no way she could deny the growing feelings she had for him.

'That's a tease, Angie.'

'Why? The tree came out nice.'

'The only picture I wanted was you two kissing,' Reese said, pouting her lips.

Angie balked. 'I'd never send you a picture of that.'

Reese's eyes widened, and she leaned in closer. 'So you kissed?'

Angie picked at her nail.

Reese gasped and pointed the spatula at her. 'Oh my God, you did!'

Angie let out a groan and buried her head in her hands. 'It just happened.' With Reese begging her for details, she wasn't sure what her friend would think. When Nick first asked her out, she wanted to just be friends. But after their night in his apartment with the Christmas music, lights, and the tree, their relationship had changed. Now, she wasn't sure what she wanted.

'You *wanted* him to kiss you.' Reese turned back to the griddle to flip the pancakes. 'Spare no details. I've run out of romance movies to watch on television.'

'I came back to start over.' For the first time, she allowed herself the safe space she needed to sift through her thoughts. If she could tell anyone what was going on in her heart, it was Reese. 'This is starting the same cycle again. What's wrong with me?' Was Nick a coincidence or was she one of those women unable to live her life without a guy?

Reese floated over to Angie and propped her arms on the counter. 'First of all, there's nothing wrong with you. Secondly, if you like this guy then don't let the unfortunate incident with Brett deter you.'

Angie thought of Nick and his hands on her. The warmth of his body created a visceral heat to sear through her in the middle of Reese's kitchen. 'I wanted to be friends with him. But when he kissed me, it made me second guess myself. But I can't fall down this rabbit hole again, so soon. I can't believe I'm even feeling this.'

'You're veering from what I want to know. Tell me about the *moment*.'

Angie set the scene for her friend, knowing she wouldn't stop asking until she gave all the details. Angie recalled the memory as if she were experiencing it for the first time. At the time, she was embarrassed and wanted to be anywhere else. But when she remembered the way Nick's eyes stared down at her, tingles rippled down her arms as she still felt his touch and his lips on hers.

'If you were into it, why are you so worried about this?'

'Because I told you I want to be friends. I don't know where my life is going to go after this week or even this month.'

Reese blew a raspberry. 'Angie, things have changed. I had a feeling there was something more between you two.'

'That's it. There isn't.'

'Kissing changes that.'

Nick knew about her past and that she was out of an unhealthy relationship, and yet it seemed as if he wanted to be with her.

'Did you talk to him about what's going on between you two?'

'Weren't you the one telling me not to get involved?'

'He already asked you out. He kissed you. Ang, he's interested.

No guy spends that much time with a woman unless he wants more. Maybe it started as a new friendship, but from the way you're talking and his insistence on spending so much time with you, things are changing. There's nothing wrong with that. Just as long as you trust him, and this isn't going to break your heart again.'

'What if he's seeing someone else?'

'Unless he's like *he who should not be named*, and a liar, he's not seeing anyone else. Besides, you're going to the tree lighting tonight. You said Brett never took you out publicly. This is a step forward.'

Nick wasn't like Brett. After the tree decorating, she knew that more than ever. 'I'm not sticking around forever. Is it unfair to start something when I'm not staying forever?'

Reese turned toward the pancake and flipped it. She smacked the top of it with a spatula harder than necessary. 'He already knows about Brett, right?'

'Yes,' Angie said.

'And that your stay here might be temporary?'

'Your point?'

'If he's still kissing you after that then it seems as if he likes you regardless. Nothing will change his mind unless you do. You can keep your options open.'

A block formed in her mind around the issue. She had the overwhelming urge to change the subject. 'Do you need any help for the baby shower this weekend?'

'I know what you're doing. I'll go with it for now until you think it over some more. Jer's mom is taking care of everything. Though I wish she would have done it sooner. With my due date next week, all I want to do is sit on the couch.'

'That's all you have to do,' Angie said. 'It's your day and your call. Why did she wait so long?'

'She wanted a belly for the pictures,' Reese rolled her eyes. 'She's also getting pictures filled with pregnancy rosacea and bloat. That's just how I want to remember this time of my life.'

Angie tried not to laugh, but Reese did first.

'Gosh, they don't tell you this stuff in the books,' she said.

'You're glowing,' Angie said.

'Like the sun,' Reese said with tears in her eyes, rubbing her belly slowly as if it were wider. 'I feel as big too.'

Angie and Reese exploded into a fit of giggles.

***

With the scavenger hunt coming up later that week, Angie had an influx of customers wanting to be sure the mall app worked for them. The mall was busier during the afternoon shifts, and she didn't mind keeping busy. The burning desire to figure out how to help Hazel subsided when she had her mind on other tasks. But it returned vigorously during her break.

Angie mulled over the idea even more and couldn't wait to finish her shift in an hour to get home. She was meeting Nick at the tree lighting ceremony and wanted him near her for another possible surge of inspiration.

Reese's teasing tone appeared in Angie's head about Nick becoming something more. If she were honest with herself, she wanted to be near him. It felt more right than wrong, and she would run with the feeling. Maybe this Christmas would be different. Angie had no idea what her future looked like but enjoyed every second with Nick. Maybe it was time to focus on her present than her future. At least for a little while.

A child screamed, snapping Angie back to the present.

'Honey, please stop pulling your sister's hair,' a mother said. She was next in line with one kid strapped to her chest while two young blonde girls ran around her feet as she somehow balanced a stack of bags on a double stroller.

'I can help you,' Angie said, wanting to give the woman what she needed right away.

'Thanks,' the mother said, blowing her brown curls off her face.

Her cheeks were red and splotchy. It was hot in the mall normally. Angie couldn't imagine how this woman felt. 'I'm looking for a candle place. I thought it was on this floor.'

'That store closed last year,' Angie said.

The mother looked as if she were going to burst out crying like her daughter.

'But there is an excellent selection of candles at Bloomfield's. I used to work there too. They make great gifts.'

'Do they wrap presents too?' she asked.

'Not anymore. They have a do-it-yourself station though.'

The mother glanced at her kids. The girls were circling her legs, pinching the other's arms while screeching.

'I would pay good money for someone else to handle that part of Christmas for me,' she said. 'I'll check them out. Thanks.'

The woman shuffled away, dropping to her kid's levels to scold them. The two girls quieted, but Angie wondered for how long. They walked away, and Angie was unable to imagine how much this woman had on her plate for the holidays. She wished she could have helped her with something other than pointing out the store for a gift. The woman probably passed out the moment her kids did, but with the holiday preparations there was extra stress involved. The DIY station at Bloomfield's wasn't that helpful with her kids running around her. She pondered the thought for a moment.

'Gift-wrapping,' Angie said aloud.

'What was that?' Stuart snorted awake. He tended to power-nap through his breaks.

'A charity gift-wrapping station,' Angie said, feeling the idea unfurl in her mind.

Stuart shook his head.

'Never mind.' Angie grabbed her phone, searching for a number on her previous calls list. She had no reason to call anyone but Reese and her mother anymore, so Maya's number was the only one not saved on her phone.

'Maya Theroux,' Maya said on the second ring.

'Hi, Maya. It's Angie.'

A long pause on the other end.

'Angie Martinelli.'

'Oh, hi. What's going on?'

Angie explained her plan to Maya. Maya didn't seem as excited as Angie was, but she didn't tell her it was a horrible idea.

'Ginger Reed is in charge of special events. Let me look at her schedule here.' Clicks sounded from the other end. 'She's free this afternoon if you want me to set something up.'

'Would you?'

'I just said I would.'

Angie bit back a snarky reply and said, 'Yes. Thank you.'

When she hung up the phone, a tingling sensation crept up her neck. This was right. This was how she was going to help Hazel.

***

After getting out of work, Angie rushed to the corporate offices. No doubt Ginger was overwhelmed with holiday activities, but she had to try. It was the only idea she had which immediately excited her. That had to mean something. Hopefully, it would help the homeless shelter as well.

When the elevator opened, Maya was walking down the aisle with a mug of coffee in her hands.

'Maya!' Angie called out.

Maya stiffened and turned around slowly.

'Where is Ginger's office?'

'Down there,' Maya said, motioning toward the hallway next to her.

'Thank you,' Angie said softly.

On the way, Angie passed a conference room filled with serious men in suits. She tried to be as invisible as possible to them. She thought of every possible question Ginger might have. The idea of the event excited her, and she only hoped Ginger felt the same way.

When Angie reached the office with Ginger's placard posted on the wall, she knocked on the door.

A woman in her fifties with short gray-streaked blonde hair and bells dangling from her earlobes glanced at Angie before waving her in. The tinkling sound was loud enough for Angie, so she couldn't imagine what it sounded like all day to Ginger.

'Maya already called and informed me about your idea.' Ginger shuffled through the piles of paperwork on her desk. Angie couldn't imagine working with all that clutter. 'Have a seat. You're not the first person to suggest bringing back a wrapping station, but it doesn't make enough money for it to be worth it with our already busy staff.'

'People are more willing to give during the holidays. I see so many come through the mall who are exhausted and need some help. I think it has the potential to bring in a lot of money for the homeless shelter.'

'It will certainly bring a draw for us. There isn't enough in our budget to pay these people to work the station. I don't think you will be able to do both.'

'That's fine,' Angie said, expecting it. 'I can do it during my shift and recruit volunteers to help out. I already have a few interested.' It was a white lie, but she had met several other retail workers who were excited about the holiday season. If worse came to the worst, she would do it on her own for free outside of her working hours.

'What is your initial budget for supplies?' Ginger asked.

'I thought we could get donations from the stores in the mall. We could display their names on a banner or hand out coupons. I don't want to take money away from the charity. Otherwise, what's the point?'

'Have you spoken to these stores yet?' Ginger asked.

'No,' Angie said, wondering if she should have prepared better. All afternoon she came up with ideas as if her thoughts willed the event into existence. She was a little rusty with her preparation of planning an event. 'I was under the impression I needed approval first.'

'You're right. I'll need to put this through to my manager but wanted to chat with you first. I will let you know if it goes through.'

'Great,' Angie said. 'I'll work on everything else in the meantime.'

'This is a great idea.'

'I think so too.'

'I also could use help around the holidays. It seems to get busier each year.'

That was the attitude Angie was hoping for from all the customers. That way they would have a reason to stop by the booth and, in turn, help the shelter.

'Well, be sure to stop by once it's set up.'

On the way out of the office, Angie grinned madly at her phone, spilling her ideas onto her notes app. She had to prepare for any other questions coming her way.

The meeting in the conference room let out, and she moved to the side to let them through. A familiar face made her stop.

'Nick?' Why was he at the corporate office? Was he looking for her? But he couldn't have known she was there.

One of them, a tall older man in a suit, stopped in his tracks and dug his hands into his pockets. 'Nick, you know this woman?'

Angie stuttered, but no comprehensible words came out. Nick in suits. Nick coming to the mall for his lunch break and the café in the morning. Why hadn't she seen it before?

'Hey, Angie,' Nick asked. 'What are you doing here?'

'I work here. Remember?'

The other men carried on with their conversations, unaware of the throbbing heartbeat rushing in her ears. Angie had the urge to follow them and flee from the situation, but she wouldn't allow another guy she liked to lie to her.

Nick glanced at the older man who was still staring at her. 'Dad, we can meet in your office shortly.'

'Don't be long,' Nick's dad said.

'Can we talk in here?' Nick sidestepped her and gestured toward the conference room.

Angie furiously rubbed her arms, the goose bumps springing up under her hands. She wanted answers so she stormed into the conference room. A long table faced a widescreen television hung against the wall. The remnants of their lunch – wrapped sandwiches and scattered bags of chips – were sprawled across two black trays in the center of the table.

'Why didn't you tell me you worked here?' Angie asked. 'Are you my boss or something?'

'Sort of.' Nick closed the door, but there wasn't much privacy since the room's walls were made of glass. 'Let me explain.'

Angie crossed her arms, now willing to stick around to hear how he had lied to her.

'I am a manager in this office. But Maya was the one who hired you. I had nothing to do with it.'

'Why did you lie to me?'

Nick hesitated and Angie wasn't sure if she was ready for his response.

'When people I'm interested in find out what I do, everything changes.'

'What are you talking about?' Since when had this become about him? The slimy feeling she felt when she thought of Brett slinked through her.

'To some, I look like a walking credit card to the shops. My ex, Molly, she had those tendencies.'

Angie wasn't like that, but clearly for some reason he thought she was. Memories of them together flitted through her mind. They had done normal Christmassy activities together. Had he thought she was so shallow?

'That doesn't make up for the fact that you lied.'

'I know. I was going to tell you. It didn't slip into the conversation easily, and I didn't want to ruin anything between us. You said your ex was your boss. I thought if you knew, you wouldn't be interested in seeing me again. I'm sorry I kept it from you.'

What else had he lied to her about during the course of their relationship? 'I have to go, Nick.'

'Are we still meeting tonight?' His eyes were wide and almost pleading. But even puppy-dog eyes weren't going to change her mind. Angie's head felt scrambled and she needed some time to clear it.

'I don't think so.'

'I said I was sorry.'

'I hear you,' she said.

He let out a small, sharp breath. 'Listen, I have to be there anyway. If you change your mind, let me know.'

Angie nodded and pulled the door open, darting out of the conference room as quickly as possible. Her hands trembled and hot tears sprung in her eyes as she reached for her phone.

In the elevator, Angie was finally able to release a breath. Then, she dialed Reese's number.

'Hey,' Reese said. 'Miss me already?'

'Nick works here.'

A long pause. 'Works where?'

'The mall. I just saw him in his office.'

'Back up. Nick works at the mall?'

'He's one of the corporate people. A manager.'

'So he's your boss?'

'I guess.' How could she have wandered into this situation again? She was a magnet for liars. Reese was right from the start. Angie shouldn't have offered to go Christmas tree shopping with him or gone to his apartment. She wouldn't have gone out with him, had feelings for him? That all seemed to go out the window the moment he appeared in front of her, at her workplace.

'What did he say?'

'Something about people seeing him as a walking credit card and bad relationships in the past.' How could he think she was like that?

'Well, he did pay for you the first time you saw him,' Reese said.

'Because my card was *declined*. I'm not like that.'

'Angie, I know. I'm on your side one hundred per cent, but from his perspective, he seems to have trust issues too. Maybe he wanted to get to know you better before he told you. I'm not making excuses for him, but from the way you described him, he seems like a good guy.'

'I don't have trust issues.'

'You do. I'm saying that in the most loving way possible.'

Angie reached the mall level and strode out of the elevator. 'What should I do? I can't afford to give up another job because of a guy.' She couldn't quit, not after planning for the gift-wrapping station to help Hazel.

'You have to figure out how you feel about him. If you can't stand to be around him like you did in California with Brett, then quit. Otherwise, you have to do what's in your heart.'

'I can't give up on Hazel.'

'Then you know what you have to do.'

'He still wanted to go to the tree lighting, can you believe it?'

There was a long pause on the other end.

'What, Reese?'

'If he still wants to go out with you, even after admitting his issues, I wonder if it would be worth giving him another chance.'

'You can't be serious.'

Angie could almost hear her friend shrugging. 'As much as I want you to myself while you're home, you should consider what not going would mean.'

If she didn't go, that would tell Nick that she was no longer interested in him. But how could she be? Angie swore not to get her heart broken by another liar, and a boss no less. Nick seemed genuinely upset at the situation, and other than the omission about his job, she suspected everything else about his life was the truth.

'I'll have to think about it.'

Chapter 14

Nick stood in the hallway, unsure of what to do next. He couldn't believe he'd run into Angie in the office. He supposed it was inevitable, but it wasn't at all how he wanted to tell her the truth about where he worked. He felt a wrench in his stomach as he wondered if he had completely blown it.

'Nick,' someone said from behind him.

He snapped back to the present and turned to Ginger. The tinkling bells from her earrings followed her as she walked. She'd worn those earrings all week. He wondered if she heard them even after she took them off.

'I didn't mean to startle you,' she said.

He plastered on a smile, determined not to show anyone how much Angie had affected him.

'Did Angie already talk to you?' she asked.

He blinked. Did everyone know about his lie?

'About the gift-wrapping station?' she asked.

'No, she didn't.'

'Oh, in that case, I wanted to run it past you.'

'Sure,' he said.

'Angela Martinelli, the new information specialist, had an idea for a charity gift-wrapping station.'

'She did?'

Ginger nodded. Those bells chimed again. Nick winced, but Ginger seemed deaf to them.

'Maya gave me a heads up, so I did my own research. In past surveys, customers have wanted us to bring back the wrapping booth at Bloomfield's, but it wasn't cost effective. With Angie's idea, we can give them what they want to get more of a draw to our mall without the costs involved. And it will offer us more reach within the community.'

Even without Ginger's pitch, Nick approved Angie's gift-wrapping idea without hesitation. He knew she'd be able to pull it off and he loved how it would help the homeless shelter. He wasn't sure why he hadn't thought of it before.

Nick knew Angie would get a boost of confidence from the idea. He couldn't wait to see her tonight to discuss it. His stomach dropped again. That was, if she showed up.

Ginger handed over the proposal, and he signed off on it.

On the way back to his office, Nick considered the tree lighting ceremony. If he had told Angie about his job from the start, maybe she would have been okay with it. Now, he had no idea what to expect. The unknown worried him more than the secret he had kept from her.

Nick couldn't ignore the memory of her in his arms the other night. In the time they spent together, he knew she'd started to have feelings for him too. He felt it in every fiber of his being. Had he ruined any chance with her?

A ping from his computer broke Nick away from his thoughts. He had five minutes until his next meeting. His day was packed with them. At least he hoped they would distract him from his racing thoughts.

***

Due to the tree lighting ceremony, the office closed promptly at five. City Hall planned the event, but it was close enough to the mall that most employees attended. There were food vendors and crafts available to buy before and after the ceremony. It was one of the local family events which drew in most of the town and surrounding areas.

Nick left work earlier than his dad would have liked to change into more comfortable clothes for the event. The temperatures dipped at night, and he wanted to be warm. Many of the office employees would be there, but he wasn't going to risk getting pegged as their workaholic boss.

On the way over, he practiced what he would say to Angie if she showed up. For some reason, the words came out robotic and without feeling. Heat licked at his skin, and his hands slid along the steering wheel as he drove.

After parking, he approached the thirty-foot tree centered in the outdoor courtyard a block away from the mall. The smaller trees outlining the sidewalks had twinkled since the first of December. But the larger tree lighting signaled the official start of the season. Nick had glimpsed the maintenance staff stringing lights during the day, but there was nothing like seeing it lit up at night.

As a child, Nick had attended the ceremony with David and his mom while his dad worked. In his younger years, Nick would stare at the lit corner office, trying to make believe his dad was with them. His delusions worked until his teenage years when he wanted nothing to do with his parents. Then, after high school, he didn't bother going unless it was in a professional capacity. He would have continued that way if David had stayed at the company. Since then, he had avoided eye contact with employees or given a curt nod – something he'd unconsciously learned from his father – but this year, he wanted to be a part of this as much as they were.

Nick walked around the area, stopping to look at the craft tables filled with decorations, ornaments, and jewelry. He spotted several employees and their families, Maya and her husband included. They were in line at the food trucks. There were already droves of people wanting to eat before the lighting. It was a part of the town tradition which he wanted to share with Angie.

Within fifteen minutes, the press of people around him started to grow. He wouldn't blame Angie for standing him up, but he hoped he'd have the chance to explain himself further. What he told her before was the truth, but he hadn't given her context of his worry. He wanted to share his entire self, only if she gave him a chance.

Nick spotted a familiar splash of coiffed gray hair in the crowd, and his body stiffened. His father had sent a memo to the staff to attend the event, but Nick hadn't expected to see him right away. Quinn weaved through the people with his eyes trained on Nick. His mother, Jared, Ivy, and another older woman accompanied him.

For once that day, Nick was glad Angie wasn't there.

Nick's mother, Yvette, wore black pants and heels as if she were going to church. She always dressed up whenever she left the house, and tonight was no exception.

'Hey, Mom,' Nick said, kissing her cheek.

'Are you here alone?' she asked.

'I'm waiting for someone,' he said, giving a pointed glance at his father. They hadn't discussed Angie's arrival in the office earlier that day. Nick intended for it to stay that way.

'Nicholas, I didn't realize you left early,' Quinn asked. 'I was looking for you. I thought we could come together.'

No doubt, his dad invited Jared's family to surprise him again.

Nick shook hands with Jared and introduced himself to Ivy's mother. Fiona Kent was an elegant woman like her daughter. She was taller than her husband and dressed as formal as Ivy.

'Hi, Ivy.'

Ivy kissed Nick's cheek again, this time it was farther away from his lips than last time. 'Nice to see you again.'

132

'Nice to meet you,' Nick said to Jared. His cheeks were red, and he was slightly overweight. If someone slapped on a white beard he could have been mistaken for Santa. He looked as if he dipped into all the Christmas cookies this time of year.

'I remember you when you were this tall.' Jared held a hand at his waist.

Quinn nodded at Ivy. 'What have you two been up to on your dates?'

'We went to the park this week as friends, Dad,' Nick said.

Ivy came to his rescue. 'I wanted to ask Nick for his opinion about the project.' She gave her father a shaky smile. She seemed as unnerved by having their fathers around as Nick did. At least he wasn't alone.

'It can't be all work and no play,' Quinn said, chuckling.

Nick had to cover up his scoff with his hand. His father never took that advice.

Ivy rocked on her heels, scanning the area. 'Mom, did you want to check out the craft tables? I think I saw some nice ornaments over there.'

'I'd love to come with you,' Yvette said.

Jared chuckled. 'I'll be along shortly.'

Ivy reached out and squeezed Nick's hand. 'I'll see you around.'

'Good to see you, Ivy,' Nick said, once again scanning the crowd for Angie. The more people came into the area, the less likely he'd be able to spot her.

Quinn clapped a hand on Nick's back. 'Nick, be sure to mingle with the employees. It's good for morale. And make sure to find us before the lighting.'

When they left, Nick was finally able to breathe. He wanted nothing less than to stand awkwardly with his parents while his dad tried to push him and Ivy together. But he'd have no choice if Angie didn't show up.

'Nick.' His name from a familiar voice forced him to turn in Angie's direction.

Angie's gloved hands fisted at her sides as she approached him. The pom-pom on her hat bounced as she walked. A breath stole from his lips at the sight of her.

'You came,' he said. 'Angie, I'm so sorry.'

She held a hand between them. 'I understand what you said before. But that doesn't excuse you lying to me.'

He'd never do it again as long as she would forgive him. 'I know—'

'Can we start over?' She locked eyes with him.

'Yes. Absolutely.' His heart had never been so full before.

'After what happened in California, I don't want to be lied to again.'

'I understand. I never intended to lie to you about it.'

'I also understand your reasoning as well. Just promise we'll be honest with each other from now on.'

'I will.'

'Good.' She grinned.

'Ginger told me about your idea,' he said. 'I approved it immediately.'

Her eyes lit up, and Nick never wanted to see the light removed from them again. 'You did?'

'Of course.'

'It just came to me. I think it will bring in a lot of money for the shelter. Don't you?' Her grin was unmistakable, and his worries fled his mind.

'I told you I would pay you to wrap my gifts,' Nick said.

'There was this mother at the mall who was so overwhelmed. I think you were the initial spark of the idea and she solidified it. So, thank you.'

'You're welcome,' he said.

Angie walked forward and Nick followed her. He wasn't going to leave her side again. They weaved through the craft tables toward the tree.

'I need to find volunteers to fill the spots. But I think I can do it while working at the booth,' she said.

'You could set hours for it,' Nick said, 'depending on how many volunteers you have.'

'That's a great idea. I want to have it all day to appeal to different types of customers. Not everyone can take time during the week to shop.'

Several kids darted past them, pushing them together. 'This event is much bigger than I remember,' Angie said with a laugh.

'Over the years, it's grown. They even have local food trucks and restaurants to extend the event even more. Did you eat?'

'I wanted to have the full experience, even though my mom was upset that I didn't have dinner with them. I can't believe she's missing it this year,' Angie said, staring up at the tree. 'She has to stay home with Nonna and Nonno since they're uncomfortable in the cold.' She took out her phone and snapped a picture of the tree before texting it to her mother.

'Do you see anyone you know?' Now that everything was out in the open, he wanted to get to know more about the people in her life.

Angie peered through as much of the crowd as she could. She lifted onto her toes and pressed her hand against Nick's shoulder. 'Some people from the stores. Reese wasn't feeling up to it tonight. Did I tell you she's due in a week?'

'You didn't,' Nick said.

'Her baby shower is this weekend,' Angie said. 'Sunday.'

Nick couldn't help noticing that Angie wanted him to know her schedule. At least he hoped. He glanced at the four trucks in front of them with different types of food available on their menus. 'Where do you want to eat?'

Angie drifted toward one of the smaller lines. 'I know I should be sick of Italian food, but I want to get my fill while I'm home.' A picture of a giant meatball took up half the side of the truck.

While they waited, the conversation drifted back to the wrapping station. Now that Angie knew about Nick's involvement, she wanted his opinions. It was a new experience talking about work with her. His mind drifted back to Molly, who didn't want to talk about his work outside of corporate functions. He had lucked out with Angie and would do anything to keep her trust.

'The last item on my list is to rent a table,' Angie said. 'I don't want to spend too much money out of my initial budget, but it is necessary. I'm not about to wrap gifts on the floor.' She laughed, a low chuckle in her throat. 'The information booth is too small for multiple people. Ginger said most of the tables are in use for other events.'

Nick recalled the table he'd seen in David's workshop. 'My brother is a craftsman. He has this beautiful table available. I'm sure he'd be happy to let you borrow it.'

'Seriously? That's amazing. Tell him I'll put a covering over the top, so it doesn't get ruined. He can leave his business cards too. I could repay him with potential business.'

'I'll ask him,' Nick said, typing a message to David. He didn't want to forget to ask. 'I'm sure he'd be able to drop it off tomorrow.'

'It would be nice to meet your family.'

Nick glanced at her. Technically, she had met his father earlier in the day. But with Ivy around, Nick wasn't going anywhere near him for fear of scaring Angie away again.

Angie cleared her throat. 'I mean, it's only fair since you met mine.'

'Of course.' Nick reached over and brushed his fingers over the top of her hand. 'I think you'll like David.'

'I think so too,' she said, staring at their hands touching.

Nick wanted to reassure her, but he hadn't expected the tingling in his fingers.

'What can I get ya?' the guy inside the truck asked.

Angie glanced at Nick.

'You choose,' he said.

'Two of the specials,' she said.

They walked over to the teenage girl handling the money. Nick paid and Angie didn't protest. She wouldn't win that argument anyway. He had a lot to make up to her.

'Did you go to events like this in California?' he asked.

'I wish,' she said. 'Work tends to take over around this season.'

'I know how that is.'

The man handed over two paper boats filled with pasta, and the meatball was almost the size of Nick's fist.

Angie grabbed several napkins from the small condiment table off to the side. She dumped grated parmesan cheese on top of her food. 'You want some?'

He held out his food, and she covered it with a thick layer.

'My mom hates when I put cheese all over everything,' she said, grinning as if she were a child pouring sugar over her meal. 'But it adds to the flavor. She doesn't understand me and my relationship with cheese.'

As they made their way back to the tree, they dug into the food. 'I don't think I'm going to make it through this season without sizing up,' she said. 'Between my mom's cooking and Christmas desserts.'

'You can always come jogging with Charlie and me. If you want.'

'I would, but I'm not much of a runner anymore. After all these years, I doubt I could keep up.'

'We can walk,' Nick said.

'I'd like that.' Her smile moved him. She wanted to spend time with him too.

'I like this,' Nick said, savoring the meatball.

'It's pretty good,' Angie said. 'The pasta is incredible, though. My nonna used to make homemade linguini like this.' Her eyes fluttered closed. 'So. Good.'

'Does she not cook now?' Nick asked.

'She does, but her wrists are weaker than they used to be. All the rolling and turning the crank bothers her. Not that she would ever admit it.'

'The lighting ceremony will start in ten minutes,' a voice boomed. It belonged to Ruben Hoyt, one of the local news anchors who always presided events like this one. Nick recalled his voice muffled through his office windows each year before.

'Let's sit over here,' Nick said.

The fountain in front of the mall had a small ledge around it. There was just enough room for them to sit. Nick became aware of how close she was to him. He wanted to get closer, but it wasn't the time or place. He needed Angie to know how much he felt for her, and he'd try hard to keep her with him.

Angie dug her fork into the meatball, making smaller pieces. Nick couldn't take his eyes off her. He thought about the regrets she had mentioned before. He regretted not opening up to her sooner about his job, but with her sitting next to him, there was no reason for it at all. Everything had worked out for them. Now all they needed to do was look toward the future.

'This is a lot messier than I realized,' Angie said with a laugh. She arranged the napkins on her lap and handed one over to him.

A smudge of red sauce appeared at the corner of her lip. Nick lifted his napkin. 'You have a little sauce there.'

Angie licked the wrong side of her mouth. 'Is it gone?'

'Not even close,' he said, feeling a lump in the back of his throat. If he hadn't lied to her, he might have kissed it off again just for an excuse. But he had to build her trust again.

She swallowed and leaned closer. He dabbed the napkin against her cheek.

'There,' he said.

Her gaze fell to his lips and immediately transported him back to his apartment when they were in each other's arms. Even though he was unsure of everything in his life, he was sure he wanted to kiss her again.

'Ladies and gentlemen!' Ruben's voice boomed through the loudspeakers.

Nick jolted, bumping into the woman next to him. She let out a grunt, and he apologized. When he turned back to Angie, her attention was on Ruben. The moment was gone.

'Five minutes until the tree lighting commences!' Ruben's voice echoed over the crowd. A stir of movement from those milling closer to the food trucks brought the crowd closer to the tree.

'Do you want to move up?' Nick asked.

'Sure,' Angie said.

When they abandoned their seats, the woman next to them took it as an opportunity to squeeze her and her kids into the space. With the number of people around, Nick stuck close enough to Angie that her hair brushed over his arm. He didn't move it away. Instead, he left it there, content with the close contact.

'This is so exciting,' Angie said. 'I feel like I'm a kid again.'

Nick took their empty boats and tossed them in the nearby trash can. 'Me too.'

A rush of adrenaline erupted within him. He wasn't sure if it was the excitement feeding from the crowd or being so close to Angie. He guessed it was a bit of both. It was as if he was transported back to when he was a kid and excited about the lights. Or a first crush.

Nick blinked, and the world went dark for a moment until he realized what happened. The lights from the smaller trees turned off to give the best effect of the tree lighting.

Angie bumped into him. 'Sorry.'

'You're fine.' She didn't move, and all Nick could focus on was Angie's body against his.

'Let's start the countdown!' Ruben called. 'Ten, nine, eight—'

The voices of everyone around them filled the air and swelled inside of Nick. He chanted the countdown, hearing Angie's voice in his ears the loudest. He reached out, took her hand. The crowd swallowed her voice as he turned to her. He barely made out her features in the darkness, but when they reached the final number, her face lit up.

They stared at each other for the quiet moment as everyone took in the display. Then, they turned to the brilliantly lit tree.

As if the world exploded around them, everyone cheered, and Angie's hand squeezed around his.

'It's so beautiful,' Angie said.

Nick looked at her. 'Yes, it is.'

Chapter 15

Since the tree lighting event, Angie was unable to get Nick out of her mind. Their momentary argument from the day before was already a distant memory. With their secrets out in the open, she was able to focus on the real task in front of her.

Shortly after she'd arrived at the information booth that morning, Ginger called to give her approval of the station. Ginger had no idea Angie and Nick had spent the night at the lighting ceremony together. The thought of him forced her into a memory of how close they were the night before. The lighting had been magical in many ways.

Reese had gone to bed early the night before. For once, Angie wanted someone to talk to about Nick, but she wasn't going to bother her friend who barely slept. It was only a matter of time before Angie's phone would blow up with texts wanting every detail of her date with Nick. It was because of Reese that Angie had gone to the event at all. Reese deserved the juicy details she craved, and Angie didn't mind reliving them.

Because of the breakup with Brett, Angie had gone to the lighting unsure of Nick's true intentions. Reese was right, she did have trust issues, but she hoped that they had begun to fade away a little, and she wanted to work toward gaining her confidence back.

Angie wasn't sure she could safely say she and Nick were just friends anymore. He'd wanted more from the start, and deep down so had she, but she had been determined to hold back. Brett seemed so long ago now. Angie had embraced the holiday spirit more than previous years, and Nick was a part of that.

With all that behind her, Angie wouldn't have wanted it any other way. There she was, about to spearhead a fantastic event for a worthy cause. In the brief time since coming home, she saw her life through a festive and brighter lens.

A text came in on her phone from Nick.

Sorry, I can't be there. David will head over shortly. x

Angie focused on the X, realizing she was about to go down a rabbit hole. She typed back a quick 'OK' and turned her phone over, sliding it across the desk. It nearly knocked over the pile of the paper presents she had finished during her last shift.

An email came through on the work computer Angie shared with the security guards. It was only for work-related emails with a restrictive internet capability, but the email was all she needed. Ginger had secured donations from the paper goods store and Bloomfield's for wrapping supplies.

Angie lifted the large banner she had made earlier that morning. She had channeled her inner child complete with red and green marker with glittery drawn presents on the bottom. It was big enough to hang from the front of the booth for all passing mall patrons to see. Ginger didn't have much of a budget to advertise, but she did mention she would put it on the website and all their social media accounts. Angie hoped this wasn't for nothing, and the confidence from Nick and the corporate office meant that she didn't want to let them down.

***

As her shift ended, Angie spotted two men wheeling the table towards her. Her heart raced with anticipation. When her dad was alive, he used to love to take her antique shopping. He had said there was nothing better than items crafted by hand. Even from that distance, she could tell it was an exquisite work of craftmanship. It looked like it belonged in Santa's workshop and it certainly fit the theme of the event.

Angie couldn't help feeling a little disappointed that Nick wasn't with his brother, but the table idea had been last minute. He was busy this time of year, and that was something Angie understood. She hoped he would come by at some point.

David and Jesse – a guy from the maintenance team – set the table down as Angie exited the booth. When David turned around, Angie noticed his chiseled features. She wasn't sure what she had expected of Nick's brother. David had the same color hair as Nick, and just then he swiped it off his forehead. His shoulders seemed more relaxed than his younger brother, though the playfulness in his expression matched Nick's. Nick had said David chose a career he loved, and it was clear in how he treated the table as he inspected it.

'This is beautiful,' Angie said, holding her hand out to David. 'I'm Angie.'

David smiled, and a wave of familiarity moved through her. The reminder of how her feelings had shifted for Nick created a swirling sensation in her gut.

'It's nice to meet you. And thank you. The table is one of Nick's favorite pieces. I always wondered how he would get it out of my workshop,' David said. 'It only took you to do it.'

Angie wasn't sure what to make of that. She tried not to overthink it as Jesse gave both of them a wave before driving the skid away. She circled around the table, inspecting it. The top was smooth, even though the deep grooves of the wood were still present. 'I'm not sure if Nick told you, but I'm happy to promote your business too. Do you have cards?'

David handed a stack over. 'Thanks for that. My business relies on word of mouth.'

'Thank you for offering the table.'

'Sorry Nick couldn't come,' David said. 'Work during this season is crazy for him. But I know you two are getting close.'

Angie cleared the catch in her throat. 'He told you about me?'

David chuckled a warm sound which was familiar to her. Even if Nick wasn't there, David kept him firmly in place in her mind. 'I've never seen him go out and get a Christmas tree on his own.'

'The topper,' Angie said, remembering the beautiful wooden star on top of the tree. 'That was you. It's gorgeous. You're incredibly talented.'

David smiled, but it had a hint of a wince. 'Yes, I made that a while ago.'

The heat in her cheeks surged. Had she said something wrong? Was she not supposed to know it was from him? She had the urge to crawl under the table and hide.

'Well, I should get going,' David said. 'I have a few more deliveries today.'

'It was nice to meet you,' Angie said.

'You too. Hopefully I'll see you soon.'

Angie was unable to hide a smile from him. Was he giving a subtle hint of an invite to see him again, or was he just being polite? She couldn't help but wonder how much Nick had told him.

A tall, graying man in an expensive suit walked toward them with the kind of purpose she had seen before in male shoppers. They preferred coming to the mall to get what they needed before fleeing as if the building would swallow them whole. As he neared, she recognized him from the corporate office. He was Nick and David's father.

Her stomach swooped, but she was determined to make a good impression. Nick had done that with her family, and he deserved the same.

'Hi there,' she said, but Mr Bower only had a curt nod and a darting glance for her.

'Dad,' David said, standing up straighter.

Mr Bower's jaw clenched even more, if that was possible. Angie was glad to get his eyes away from her, but she knew neither of them expected to see each other. What a strange coincidence his father would come down while David was at the mall. Had Nick set this up?

Mr Bower glared at the table. 'What is all of this?'

'This is my table, Dad. I'm helping Nick with the gift-wrapping station.'

Mr Bower didn't even glance at the table.

'We don't need your help,' Mr Bower said.

'It's a beautiful piece,' Angie said, hoping to diffuse the situation. Maybe Mr Bower didn't realize David had *made* the table.

'This is none of your concern,' he said to her.

'Dad,' David said in a warning tone.

The relationship between her and Nick was new, but if it were to go anywhere, she didn't want his father to have a negative impression of her.

'I didn't mean to step in,' Angie said. She glanced at David. There was nothing official about their relationship just yet, so she went with the safe option.

Mr Bower turned his steely gaze on her. 'You were in my office yesterday.'

'Yes, I was. Sorry, we didn't get to meet officially. I'm Angie. I know your son. Nick and I are friends.'

Neither David nor Mr Bower spoke.

'I was the one to suggest the gift-wrapping station,' she said.

'I didn't know you were going to be here,' Mr Bower said to David, completely ignoring Angie. 'I came down to check on my employees.'

'Dad, I—' David started.

'This isn't the time. I'm working,' Mr Bower snapped.

'When will it be a good time?' David asked. 'We can get coffee and catch up? I can reschedule my other deliveries.'

'You know the answer to that,' Mr Bower said, glancing at Angie.

Angie had no place standing there, yet she couldn't lift her feet from their spot. If she dared move, she wasn't sure how Mr Bower would react. His neck started to turn red and she tried not to stare at the scarlet creeping across his skin.

Mr Bower's chin lifted at his son as if challenging him to say something.

Angie's heart broke for David. From all the memories Nick had shared about his brother, and in their short meeting, Angie liked him already. Now, he seemed like a younger version of himself as his father reprimanded him. Nick had said his dad was hard to deal with, but Angie couldn't imagine this man raising Nick and David. His cold shoulder was sharper than an icicle.

'I have to go,' Mr Bower said.

'Of course, you do.' David's smile disappeared, replaced with a scowl. At least she saw the family resemblance.

'This isn't the time or place,' Mr Bower said.

'Will there ever be one?' David asked. 'Do you even want to meet your grandkids?'

Mr Bower's lips pinched together but he said nothing as he turned on his heel, walking in the same direction from where he came.

David stood there, staring after him. 'Sorry about that.'

'Don't be,' Angie said.

David turned to her. 'He wanted me to be someone I wasn't, and my family is paying the price.'

Angie opened her mouth to speak, but David shook his head. 'I should get going.'

'Thanks again,' Angie said at a loss for comforting words. David seemed as if he was done talking about it too.

'Have a good Christmas,' David said before walking away. His

146

easygoing smile had disappeared, and he stared in the direction where his father had gone before trudging away.

Angie sagged against the table as the weight of their conversation washed over her. She hadn't been involved but seeing that type of family conflict was enough to exhaust anyone.

***

Setting up the gift-wrapping station distracted her from the awkward conversation she'd had with Mr Bower. She hoped he wouldn't return.

Instead, she focused on preparing for the event. A mall-wide email went out to employees, asking for volunteers. Angie was optimistic about raising as much money as possible, but she still had a job to do and only so many hours in the day. The more people involved, the more likely the word would spread and bring more customers to the booth.

While she waited for responses, she thought of David, which brought a wave of sadness through her. Nick hadn't prepared her for a confrontation between his father and brother. It was unlike anything she expected. Angie had no idea if she should mention it to Nick the next time she saw him. She wouldn't win any points by gossiping to him about his family. David's hurt expression plagued her mind. She hoped Nick would be able to ease the pain for his brother. Ultimately, she decided to stay out of it. When she saw Nick next, she'd see what David had told him first, if anything.

Even though her shift was over, Angie hung around the booth to continue with set up for the wrapping station. She already had about ten volunteers to schedule into the malls' extended holiday hours. From Bloomfield's manager, she borrowed the instructions on how to perfectly wrap a gift. It had been posted in the gift-wrapping section all those years ago, and it was a strange sort of nostalgia to hold it again. Angie encouraged the volunteers to practice at home with their own Christmas gifts and come ready to work and wrap.

A buzzing excitement radiated from the information booth. Angie drew customers in who had come to the booth with questions and made sure they knew where to return with their parcels for wrapping.

While Angie stacked the donated wrapping paper, bags, and tissue paper into the already cramped booth, the other security guards posted flyers throughout the busier areas of the mall. By the time security was on their way to do the last sweep before maintenance came through to clean, Angie was ready to collapse. Any other day she sat for most of her shift, but with preparations for the event to start, she fell back into a rhythm she only had working at the hotel. Her feet ached, but in the best way.

During her walk to the car, Angie checked her phone. Several texts from Nick lit up the screen and her heart. He wanted to see how she was doing. Apparently, he had thought about her a lot during the day, which warmed her as if she sat in front of a roaring fireplace. In his texts, he didn't mention David and his father, so she avoided bringing it up.

Today was busy for us. But I promise I'll stop by the booth tomorrow.

She couldn't help but smile at the thought of him coming by and seeing what she had created. Nick took an interest in her work, and the promise of seeing him again so soon had lit a spark in her heart.

***

The next morning, Angie went into work earlier than scheduled. As she opened the booth, she spotted a familiar person walking toward her.

Maya wore a fitted pantsuit which highlighted her thin frame. She still looked like a runner even after all these years.

'Did I miss some paperwork?' Angie asked, wanting to know why Maya had come down from the offices. Maybe, like Mr Bower, she was there to check on Angie.

Maya raised an eyebrow. 'I'm volunteering at the wrapping station. Corporate suggested a few of us take shifts.'

Did that mean Nick would come by to help too? Angie smiled at the thought, but when she saw Maya's confused expression, she cleared her throat and pushed Nick from her mind for the time being. Angie had made the schedule and emailed it to Ginger the night before. She hadn't a chance to check her email yet, so she assumed there were changes including those from corporate.

If she had to work with Maya, she didn't want to continue the awkwardness between them. Their rivalry had been years ago, the least they could do was work side-by-side for an hour or so without snarky remarks.

'Great,' Angie said. 'I can give you instructions.'

Maya snorted. 'Instructions? It doesn't take a genius to wrap a gift.'

Angie smiled, trying to keep the mood light. 'There is an art to it.' She pulled out an extra sheet from her bag and handed it to Maya.

The skin around Maya's lips tightened into a thin line.

'It's from Bloomfield's. They let us borrow it for the booth.'

Maya snatched it from Angie's hand and stared at it while Angie walked over to the back door of the booth. It was still locked, and Angie reached for her phone to text Stuart. Maya didn't want to be around Angie by choice, so she would give her some space.

A few minutes later, Stuart walked toward them. Angie's leg bounced with anticipation. The mall would open in fifteen minutes, and she couldn't wait for their first customer.

Once they were inside the booth, Maya offered to help bring out all the supplies.

They arranged the table to be the most conducive to wrapping as quickly and efficiently as possible. Angie had high hopes for the station and didn't want anything to get in the way.

Maya made suggestions in her curt tone, which were helpful and unhelpful at the same time. Angie hoped her scowl didn't turn too many people away.

It wasn't until Maya spotted another woman approaching the booth that she showed any semblance of a smile.

'Your coffee,' the woman said, holding two stainless mugs. Her makeup was flawless, and her hair was pulled back in a ponytail that swished as she walked. Her skin was a shade of brown which Angie only achieved in the bright summer sunlight of California. Since she had been home, it faded severely.

'I'm Carrie,' the woman said. 'Maya's assistant.' Her smile was kind and warm, and Angie wished it was contagious, at least in Maya's direction.

'Angie,' Angie said.

Maya reached for the mug before sipping from the top.

'I brought you one too,' Carrie said, offering the other one.

'Thank you.' Angie smiled at the girl's kindness. Etched into the side of the stainless steel was the Westford Mall logo.

'Do you need anything?' Carrie asked Maya.

'Not now. Keep your phone on you in case I do,' Maya said. 'Feel free to sift through my emails when you get back to the office. I want to enjoy myself tonight at the party.'

'Oh, a Christmas party?' Angie asked. 'Where are you going?'

'It's at the office. Nothing fancy but the food is always good.'

'Sounds fun.'

Maya narrowed her eyes. 'It's corporate only.'

Angie ignored Maya's cutting tone and turned to sip from the mug. There was no reason for her to assume that Angie would have invited herself. She briefly considered if Nick would invite her. She tried not to get her hopes up.

Besides, she had enough to do in preparation for Reese's baby shower on Sunday, the thought of tagging along to a Christmas party she wasn't invited to was the last thing on her mind. Tonight, she and her mother were going to make cookies for the shower. Even though Jeremy's mother said she had it under control, Maria rarely went to anyone's house without food for the host.

'I got that,' Angie said.

'I have your Secret Santa gift too,' Carrie said, holding out a book. From the shirtless guy and girl with the wind-swept hair on the cover, it looked like a steamy romance. The not-safe-for-work kind.

Maya picked at the price tag on the back and peeled it off as she spoke. 'Paula will love that. She's always reading those during her lunch break. I mean that's why they made eBooks right?'

'It's one of the newer ones of the author she reads. I checked. Do you think you can wrap it?' Carrie asked, glancing at all the supplies. 'I mean, while we're down here.'

'It will be good practice,' Angie said.

Maya tapped her fingers along the cover of the book. 'I don't need practice. I know how to wrap a gift.'

Carrie gave Angie a secret smile, and Angie knew she liked this girl already.

While Maya wrapped, Angie pretended not to see her checking the instructions she gave her.

Angie looked around, hoping that customers would show up. Now that the time had come, her talents were on display. She had the opportunity to prove her worth to her bosses and herself.

Chapter 16

Nick had planned David's delivery of the table around their dad's schedule so that they could avoid bumping into each other in the same building. But when David called Nick immediately after he left, Nick wasn't sure where he had gone wrong.

'It says he's out of the office,' Nick said, staring at the calendar on his computer.

'I don't know,' David said. 'It was like he had a purpose for coming down there. Like he was looking for a fight with me. It was brutal.' The sound of David's truck roaring to life drowned his words.

'He was supposed to be out for most of the afternoon at meetings,' Nick said. 'It was a perfect time for you to come by.' He hadn't seen his father come back to the office, so maybe he had taken a detour on the way out. Sometimes he liked to surprise the employees by stopping by, but not on a day when his schedule was so packed.

'Angie was there too,' David said.

Nick rubbed a hand over his face. 'I bet she was mortified.'

'It wasn't great. You know Dad.'

When David first called him, Nick had hoped Angie missed the heated conversation. But he wasn't that lucky. She probably thought the worst of his father. He had a rough exterior to those who didn't know him.

'I wish she didn't have to see that,' David continued. 'It's bad enough he directed his anger at me. I'm used to his moods, but she had no idea what was coming.'

Nick hated that Angie's first impression was his father at his worst. Any interaction between David and their father twisted into the wound of their fractured relationships. Deep down, Quinn loved David, but his disappointment trumped any feelings he could show to his eldest son.

'You might want to figure out what you and Angie are,' David said. 'If Dad didn't suspect anything yet, he might now.'

Nick had to keep the two of them apart. He considered the wreckage if she knew his dad didn't approve of anyone but Ivy. He wanted to see her soon to let her know how sorry he was about his father's behavior.

With the plan to see her during their break, he texted Angie to confirm.

Her response came within a few seconds.

I'm going to stay here for my break. I want to make sure everything runs smoothly. Hope you understand?

Nick sighed and typed several responses before he settled on one.

Okay. Will text you later.

He debated inviting Angie to the staff party, but neither of them was ready for another confrontation with his father. Nick hoped she still liked him, even with his family drama.

His father wasn't in the office the rest of the day, as his schedule dictated. And there would be no time to talk to him tonight at the party about it. His father wasn't going to get off that easily, but Nick dreaded their upcoming discussion.

***

Nick pushed through his workload to distract himself. His father arrived at the office in time to inspect the food brought in from a local catering company. Nick happened to be in the hallway at the same time.

Quinn met his eyes, and Nick knew he was in for something.

'My office,' Quinn said and turned on his heel.

Maya let out a low whistle, and Nick brushed her off. She had spent the morning with Angie. Other than asking how the table went – *slow* was her answer – then how Angie was handling it – *fine* – Nick didn't push her any further, but he hoped for Angie to succeed.

When Nick walked inside, Quinn stood by the window staring out. The sun set on the other side of the building, giving enough darkness in the room for Nick to see his dad's reflection.

Nick closed the door without being asked. 'Dad, I talked to David.' He wanted this conversation over as quickly as possible. Since the rest of the staff weren't headed home anytime soon, they would have an audience outside his office.

'Glad to hear you two stay in touch.'

'You know we do.'

'Yes, but I didn't think you would mix him with work.'

'He's helping with an event which will benefit the mall. Why would I turn that down?'

'You could have rented a table.'

'Cutting into the budget.' Quinn was always a stickler for budgeting. He should have been proud that Nick thought about that. 'What were you doing down there anyway?'

'Oh, so you were trying to keep this from me? Sneak around on my out of office day?'

That *was* the plan. 'He donated a table for the event.'

'This is why I tried to bring you and Ivy together.'

'What are you talking about?'

'Don't think I didn't notice you and that woman at the tree lighting ceremony. She works for us too. What are you thinking? You can't date her.'

154

'I'm not dating her.' At least not technically. The moment she was ready to, he would be too.

'I don't know what it is about you two.'

'Me and Angie?'

'No, David.'

They were back to David. His dad must have been upset as he was bouncing between thoughts quicker than Nick could keep up. He wondered if his father saw David in him now that there was a woman in his life who he didn't choose for his son. He wasn't about to quit his job. Unlike David, he liked it.

'Dad, I'm not going to do what he did. But I have to live my own life. Ivy is nice, but she's—'

'She's what? Too successful? Too attractive? What is it, son? What has this other woman done to you?'

'Please leave Angie out of this. This is between you and me.'

'That's the problem, Nicholas. You're always thinking with your heart instead of your head.'

'Is that so bad?'

'Ask David.'

Nick's mouth clamped shut. He wasn't getting anywhere with his dad today. If they kept going, one of them might end up saying words they regretted. They still had to host a Christmas party for the employees. He didn't need the extra awkwardness. 'I'm going out there. It would be nice for company morale if you perked up a bit.'

His dad turned around and flashed a smile. The one that graced his biography on the corporate website. 'I know when to keep up appearances.'

Nick left the office, his mind whirring. Quinn's whole life was an appearance, at least to his employees. Nick wished he could get it through to his father that life was short, and he should try to let go of things that didn't matter. Like his one-sided fight against David. His kids weren't getting any younger, and Nick wouldn't be any happier with the woman his dad chose for him.

155

His effect on his family had far-reaching ripples, and they were only getting bigger.

Nick always liked the Christmas party, but this year he wasn't feeling the spirit as much as he would have liked. Nick wanted to be anywhere but there. Then to make matters worse, ten minutes into the party Ivy and the Kents walked out of the elevator. Nick skirted into one of the cubicles and sat in Maya's chair, taking a moment to himself. Of course, his father had invited them, which made Nick even guiltier. He should have been there with Angie, even if his dad was going to make it awkward. He wanted to be with her and show her off to everyone. But with Angie on his father's radar, Nick had no idea what to expect from him.

'Are you going to hide here all night?' Maya balanced a glass of champagne on the divider.

Nick peered over the top to locate his parents and the Kents. 'Maybe.'

'I don't like to get into people's personal lives, but you *are* sitting at my desk. So, I have a right to ask why you are hiding.'

Nick straightened his tie. 'I needed a break.'

'After that argument with your dad?'

Nick didn't need to ask if she heard. Her office was close enough, and she had an uncanny ability to sneak around. The head of HR knew a lot of secrets and drama from the employees at the mall. Nick didn't like being a part of that group.

'Listen, it's not a big deal. No one else cares. We all know he can be a little over the top with you.'

It wasn't because Nick was his son. Quinn had envisioned David taking over, not Nick. For some reason, his father never wanted Nick to forget that. At least that was what it felt like from the outside.

'Have a good time, Maya,' Nick said, walking away from her. The sooner he talked to Ivy and her family, the sooner he could leave the party.

Nick planned to see Angie tomorrow. Technically, he was off but would come into work for the morning. He wasn't directly involved with the scavenger hunt throughout the mall, but it was the perfect excuse to see her. He knew she was swamped with gift-wrapping and her job, but he also knew she'd do it all with a big smile on her face. Stopping by for a quick hello wouldn't do any harm. If anything, it would bring him the real happiness he found so hard to muster for the party.

***

With Maya's warning that the gift-wrapping booth was slow going, Nick wasn't sure what to expect when he arrived at the mall the next morning. It was late enough into her shift that Angie had been at work for a bit, and the scavenger hunt was in full swing.

Nick held a small paper bag in his hands, unsure of why he was so nervous about giving it to Angie. On the way to Angie, he dodged the more eager participants who sprinted down the walkways toward the next stop on their list.

A crowd stood outside the booth. The line wasn't moving at all as it snaked around the booth.

Angie and two others stood side by side at the table, their hands moving quickly as they cut, folded, and taped presents for the waiting customers. Another volunteer walked down the line, collecting money, and counting presents. Everyone had a smile on their faces.

An employee from the Smoothie Shack handed out small cups of samples and pretzels.

Nick approached the booth and stood at the end of the line, watching Angie work. She hadn't noticed his arrival. Angie's wide smile never left her face as she handed over the presents to those waiting. Some had bags of gifts, and Nick wondered if they should have anticipated a big turnout, especially on the weekend with an event in progress.

As Nick approached, he caught Angie's eye. She smiled, and he was finally able to draw in a breath.

'Do you need that wrapped?' Angie asked as she finished with her customer. She thanked them for coming before starting on the next.

'I do,' he said.

A woman in line cut a look his way.

He held his hands up in surrender. 'I'm going to wait for my turn, though.'

Angie shook her head, laughing. It was impressive to see her under pressure and keeping a smile on her face.

Nick's phone pinged, and he grunted, catching another look from the woman in front of him.

He didn't want to answer it, but then he got another text notification, then a phone call.

'Are you going to get that?' the woman asked with one thin eyebrow raised.

Angie was talking to the next customer as she helped pick out the wrapping paper for the gifts. She was distracted enough that he could answer his dad. He was the only person who emailed, texted, and called if Nick didn't answer his messages in seconds. Pop-ups for two more meetings appeared on his screen. Quinn wanted to confirm he had received them, but Nick knew his dad was spying. Nick texted back.

Got it

He started sifting through his email. So much for not going in the office today.

The woman in front of him had several boxes she needed wrapping, but the other male volunteer took her instead as Angie waved Nick over.

'Hey,' she said. 'What do you have there?'

Nick lifted the small box from the bag. It had no distinguishing marks to give her any hint of what was inside.

Angie stared at it as if she could see the gift. He wished she wouldn't guess. His hands tightened around the box.

'Which wrapping paper?' she asked.

'Whatever is your favorite.'

'I love this one. It's thick so that it doesn't rip easily.' She held up a red and white striped paper roll. 'I like to save this one for bigger packages, but I think it will be perfect for this one.

'You're the expert,' he said.

'I'd hate to agree with you for fear of sounding a bit self-absorbed.'

'Don't shy away from your talents. I can barely cut in a straight line.'

Angie locked eyes with him. 'I'm sure you'll be great. You signed up to help, right?'

'Yes. But I'll have to check the schedule.'

'You're up Monday.'

Nick blinked. 'You know my schedule now?'

She laughed. 'Only for this. I suppose that makes us a little more even.'

At least they could joke about him not telling her about his job right away. A prickle of heat nipped at his neck at the idea that she could have refused to speak with him again. He was happier with this outcome and would make it all up to her the best he could.

While Angie cut and folded, he was mesmerized by the way her hands moved over the gift. He knew what they felt like against his and couldn't wait for his next opportunity to hold her close to him.

'There you go,' she said, handing it over. Their fingers brushed over each other. This time, there weren't any gloves between them. 'Do you have anything else?'

He wished he had bought ten more gifts but hadn't thought ahead.

'Not right now.'

'That's a shame,' she said, glancing at the others behind her.

'Well, I should get going,' he said, staring at the gift. 'I'm headed to the office for a bit.'

'On a Saturday?'

'It doesn't really end until New Year's. But I'll see you later?'

'Definitely,' she said.

As he walked away, he placed the gift back into the bag. He couldn't wait until Christmas to give it to her.

Chapter 17

On Sunday morning, Angie and Maria packed up trays of cookies for Reese's baby shower. Angie's phone pinged from the other room, and she raced over to get it.

'Is it Nick?' her mom crooned from the kitchen.

'Ma,' Angie warned, but couldn't hide the smile in her voice. She paused when she saw it was from Emma.

Can you call me later? I think I have a job prospect for you.

Angie read the message a few more times before she heard Mom calling her. 'I can't carry all of these myself.'

On the way to Reese's house, Angie balanced the trays of cookies in her lap while unable to get Emma's message out of her mind. The booth and wrapping station had taken up so much of her time that she hadn't thought about the jobs rejecting her left and right. There was only one outstanding prospective position on her list, but she had concluded that no one was hiring. It was the busiest season, and most event planners wouldn't quit before New Year's Eve.

Angie wasn't sure what she wanted after that.

'Emma thinks there's a job I should apply for,' Angie said as they pulled into Reese's driveway.

'That's great, Angie. What is it?'

'I don't know. She wants me to call her.'

Maria patted Angie's knee. 'It's Sunday. That can wait.'

If it were up to her mom, Angie would live at home the rest of her life, job or not.

Maria got out of the car, and Angie grabbed her phone, promising Emma she would call her later. As much as Angie wanted to live in her bubble helping the homeless shelter and spending time with Nick, that wasn't reality. At least not past the holiday season.

***

After Angie rang the doorbell at Reese's house, her best friend answered the door within seconds. The moment she laid eyes on the trays, she grabbed them and ushered Angie and Maria inside.

'I'm starving.' Reese sneaked two cookies into her mouth sandwich-style.

Maria kissed Reese's cheek before entering the house.

'Oh, God, these are good,' Reese said. 'How long do you think can I play this pregnancy card? I need these cookies all the time.'

Angie laughed. 'Isn't there food here?'

Reese pulled Angie aside before closing the door. 'My mother-in-law isn't letting me touch any of it until everyone arrives. She wants the big wow factor. Besides, tiny sandwiches aren't going to fill me up. I feel like a garbage disposal.'

'You look great,' Angie said. Reese wore a billow navy blue dress. The high waist gave her plenty of room for her bump, but it seemed soft and comfortable.

'I feel like a blimp. But thanks.'

Angie hugged her friend and was surprised to find tears springing from her eyes. 'I'm so excited to meet the little one.'

'Me too.'

Reese took Angie's hand and brought her into the living room. It had been converted for the party from a modern style room to a winter wonderland. With the decorated tree as the focal point, paper snowflakes hung from the ceiling while twinkly lights swooped down from the walls. The tablecloths, napkins, paper plates, and food stands were varying shades of blues and whites. But the edging around the three tiers of the cake were pink for the baby's gender. Reese hadn't told Angie the name of the baby yet, but she was sure her friend already had it picked out.

Jeremy's mother, Elinor Tan, floated over to Angie. She was a shorter woman, barely reaching Angie's chin but with a strong disposition that even made Jeremy tremble in his shoes at times. She and Nonna would get along great. 'Angela. It's nice to have you home. Are you staying for good?'

'Not for good,' Angie said, careful to keep Reese out of earshot. She didn't want to upset her friend at the party.

'When are *you* going to tie the knot? I bet your mother is waiting for a grandchild of her own.'

Angie expected these questions. Most of her friends from high school were married with kids or on the way. She had been on track with Brett before his lies caught up with him. It appeared as if everyone under thirty who wasn't married was constantly bombarded with questions about their relationship status and fertility until they tied the knot and had kids.

'I ask her that every day,' Maria said, hugging Jeremy's mom.

Angie slipped away, letting the two moms plan their kids' lives out for them.

Reese insisted Angie sit next to her on the couch. Angie was the doting best friend, helping Reese rest her feet up on the ottoman. Reese complained that none of her shoes fit her, except for her winter boots which she only wore to get the newspaper from the driveway each morning.

Everyone in the room wanted to share baby advice with Reese. It seemed as if they all had a fun anecdote while Angie only listened. Reese was in her element, sharing the woes of pregnancy with the women who had been there before. She even learned a few stories about her mom when she was pregnant with Angie. Most of it was too much information, but the others laughed and commiserated with each other.

Then came the presents. Angie busied herself as the unmarried non-mother in the group and took care of writing down the list of gifts to help Reese write thank-you cards. She tried not to feel the pinching in her chest when everyone squealed at the cute clothes and toys.

Angie was so happy for Reese, so much that there were a few moments where she nearly cried herself. But the loss of Brett overwhelmed her. It wasn't exactly him. Her life was on track before he derailed her. She moved back home without a plan and wasn't sure where she would end up. Thanks to him, she had to start her life over. The distance to her own wedding, and starting a family stretched out of reach with each day she didn't make any forward decisions about her life.

While the others in the room talked about all the contraptions for infants she knew nothing about, Angie's thoughts drifted to Nick. He loved his nephews, she could see it through the sparkle in his eyes each time he talked about them. Would he want kids?

It was absolutely too soon to think of her and Nick together forever, but it was a nice segue from her thoughts of Brett. Her mood boosted even more with each second, and eventually her cheeks ached from smiling. Reese noticed Angie's change in attitude, and for once she didn't question her. Probably because she had some idea what made Angie grin.

When Angie left the house, the frigid air outside was a blessing against her heated cheeks. She checked her messages for contact from Nick, but Emma's unanswered text caught her attention.

Her delusions of staying in town flew out of her mind as she recalled the momentary choking cloud of doubt and angst she'd experienced at the party. Nick's presence was temporary. Her life had to come first. So, the moment she arrived home, she locked herself in her room and called Emma. If she was going to move forward with her life, she had to take the next step.

***

First thing Monday morning, Angie emailed her resume to the contact Emma gave her. Angie had a new sense of confidence as she drove toward the mall excited to see what opportunities awaited her around the corner.

Angie wasn't on the schedule until the afternoon shift, and the wrapping station was covered. She couldn't stay home and sulk about her life though. After the baby shower, it was as if the baby bug had bitten her mother and over dinner the night before it was all she could talk about.

With a little white lie about her schedule, Angie left home hours before she needed to be there. She wanted to feel accomplished for the day and help where she could.

When she drove by Kevin's Café, she spotted a familiar dog tied to the lamp post. Charlie stared at the café with her tail swishing over the sidewalk.

Without thinking, Angie pulled into the next available spot. Her chest tingled with anticipation of seeing Nick again. Their texts were enough when they were apart, but she yearned for the swirling lightness within her every time they were together.

Once she parked, she checked herself out in the rearview mirror before hustling down the sidewalk toward the café. Charlie spotted her, and her ears perked up before her tail lifted into the air. A wide grin spread across Angie's face as she patted Charlie's head. An older woman tutted at her, mumbling about petting strange dogs.

'You're not strange, are you?' Angie said, squatting to Charlie's level. She rubbed the soft fur of her face between her hands and Charlie preened.

A knock came from the window behind her. Nick stood there,

lifting a finger for her to stay. Angie unlatched Charlie from the lamp post and held the leash against her. Nick exited the café and wiped his mouth with a napkin before dropping it in the nearby trash can. He wore sneakers and track pants with only a vest. He had to be freezing. Though if he'd come from a run, then she bet the cold air was refreshing.

'You caught me,' he said, his eyes bright and warm.

'What did you eat?' A fluttering sensation settled in her chest as her gaze fell to the flaky crumb stuck to his lips.

Too bad he licked it away before she could tell him. 'A pastry. A bit of a contradiction to my run, but I haven't come down here in a few weeks.'

Angie's cheeks flushed at the memory of their first meeting. It seemed like years ago that she'd stood there unable to pay for her bagel.

'What are you doing here?' Nick asked.

Angie debated telling him how quickly her plans had changed the moment she knew Nick was nearby. 'I spotted Charlie and wanted to say hello.'

Nick unleashed a wide grin, which made Angie's heart skitter in her chest. 'So you're stalking me?'

'You wish,' Angie said, matching his smile. 'I told you, I'm here for Charlie.' Then the perfect excuse came to her. 'I thought I could take you up on that walk. Unless you have to be at work?'

Nick shook his head. 'I have a few meetings later. I wanted to give Charlie a little extra attention today. There's a park down that way if you want to walk with us?'

'Sure,' Angie said, tightening her grip around the leash.

Nick chuckled, forming a cloud around them. 'You can let it go. She'll stay by your side.'

'I'm not taking any chances,' Angie said, patting Charlie's head.

They walked down the street at a slower pace than Angie guessed they had come.

'I'm sorry I haven't been around much,' Nick said as they

166

turned the corner. The park was a small area of green directly across from the mall. It had a view of the massive Christmas tree from the lighting ceremony. If it wasn't for the cold, Angie could have enjoyed the view a little more. She had to keep moving to stay warm.

'I've been busy too,' she said.

'That's great,' he said. 'But, I didn't want you to think I'm avoiding you. Because that's not the case at all. There's a lot of stress at work, and my family issues seem to be cropping up a lot lately.'

'Is it about David and your father?'

Nick gave her a knowing nod.

They stopped by a stone fountain, devoid of water. 'You can talk to me about it. If you want.'

Nick let out a breath and opened and closed his mouth a few times before he spoke. 'It's harder around the holidays, especially after Dad saw David at the mall. It's been a while since they've seen each other face to face. I know as much as you saw from him, it's hard for my father too. He's not as open as David.'

'I can't imagine the pressure you must feel as they tear you in both directions.'

Nick sighed as if Angie shared the weight on his shoulders. 'I don't know if my father understands how difficult this is. He's so incredibly stubborn. His father was similar in that way where he could cut away people from his life like that.' He snapped his fingers for emphasis. 'My mother doesn't help because she ignores it, but I don't blame her. Living with him can be tough when he doesn't get his way. She makes excuses for him, but we're all tiptoeing around the real issue.'

Angie reached out and took his hand. 'I understand how hard that must be, Nick. I couldn't imagine cutting off a part of my family. It's unfair that your father expects that from you.'

'He's so black and white about everything. I wish I could convince him otherwise.'

'As long as you're the bridge between David and your parents, I think you're doing all you can.'

Nick swallowed. 'I appreciate that. I thought you were going to think the worst of me.'

'Why would I?' she asked.

Nick wiped a hand over his mouth. 'Your impression of my family wasn't the best.'

'You're not your dad,' Angie said, recalling the scowl on Mr Bower's face. She shivered thinking of it.

Nick squeezed her hand as easily as he had at the tree lighting. A warm, comforting feeling as if she were wrapped in a thick, fuzzy blanket enveloped her. His eyes widened in a silent question, and she walked with him, answering in her own way. She liked being with Nick. The thought terrified and excited her.

Walking with him in one hand and Charlie in the other, she saw a potential future. It was an option, but she wasn't sure how she could make it work. For a moment, she wanted to move her life in this direction to see what it would be like.

'There's a fenced-in dog area over here.' Nick headed toward that section of the park. Inside, two smaller dogs chased each other in circles.

A whine sounded from Charlie's throat, and Angie picked up her pace.

The moment they reached the gate, the two dogs inside sprinted in their direction. Angie held the leash closer to her.

'Charlie is good with other dogs,' Nick said, reaching for the leash. Angie let go as Nick unhooked Charlie and let her inside.

Charlie bounded into the area, stretching her legs.

'I think she's more human than dog. She has a sense of our lives. Her eyes are so knowing,' Nick said.

They leaned against the fence, watching the dogs play. Angie became aware of how close Nick stood next to her.

'She's amazing,' Angie said. 'You're lucky to have her.'

'I am.'

Angie's phone rang, and she tried to turn it off.

'You can answer it,' Nick said.

Angie didn't want anyone interrupting their time together, but it was Reese's ring tone. 'It's Reese. Every time she calls, I think the baby is coming.'

Nick walked over to Charlie, giving Angie her privacy. Reese was notorious for speaking loudly into the phone and Angie didn't want to talk about where she was, or who she was with, in front of Nick.

'Hey, are you going to the hospital?' Angie asked.

'I wish,' Reese said. 'I wanted to see when you were working today. The doctor said I need to walk around, even though my feet are the size of boats. I was going to visit you.'

The two smaller dogs started barking at Charlie, who kept one step ahead of them in a game of Tag.

'Where are you?'

'A park.'

'With dogs?'

'It's the park outside the mall.'

'You're not going into work until later.' Angie could almost see Reese digging her hand into her hip.

There was no use hiding it. 'I wanted to check on the booth. I was headed in when I saw Nick and Charlie.'

'Wait, back up. You're with Nick?'

'And Charlie. There's a small dog park here.'

'I don't care about the dog, Angie. I mean, I love dogs, but I want to talk about Nick.'

Angie bit down a smile. 'It's not a big deal. We're walking Charlie.'

'Since when is there a "we" with you two?'

'Since now, I guess.' Angie watched Nick, and as if their minds were linked, he turned to look at her. A lightness swooped through her middle and they grinned at each other.

'Are you now?'

When Nick turned away to walk toward Charlie, that familiar and uncomfortable tremor within her started up again. Her breathing quickened. 'He's great, but I don't want to mess it up again.'

'You can't mess up something that doesn't exist. You don't have any other job prospects. You're still young and can date people.'

'We're the same age.'

'But I'm married and pregnant. I live my adventures through you.'

For the first time, Angie admitted to herself she didn't want just to date Nick. If she was going to do this, she wanted to do it right.

'I need to meet this guy. Invite him to our house for the party.' Even though Reese was due the day after, she still insisted on hosting it. 'As long as the peanut is still in there, the festivities are still on,' she had said at the baby shower.

'Are you sure?' Angie didn't know if he would want to come. Was it a bigger step than she realized?

'Yes, I'm sure. Do it, Angie. You deserve a little fun.'

'Okay,' Angie said, a little breathless from the idea of asking him. She almost considered having Reese do it for her. She would have, but also Angie would have risked Reese telling him she didn't want her to.

Nick started walking back to her with Charlie by his side.

'I have to go,' Angie said before hanging up. She handed the leash back to Nick. Angie stifled the urge to twine her fingers with his again.

'I hate to cut this short, but I should probably head back to my apartment before work.'

'No problem,' Angie said, relieved that Nick hadn't overheard her conversation with Reese. On the way back through the park, Angie debated how she would ask him. There was no other way than just doing it. 'What are you doing Thursday night?'

'I don't have plans,' he said. 'Why?'

'Reese, my friend, is having a Christmas party. Do you want to come with me?'

'Sure,' he said as breezy as if she had asked him about getting coffee.

Angie's stomach swooped as Nick took her hand again, leading her from the park. She hadn't felt that comfortable with anyone for a long time. With Nick by her side, she couldn't recall a single moment from her past with any other man who made her feel as special as he did. She wanted to stay firmly in the present. With him.

Chapter 18

After meeting with Angie, Nick walked home with an extra spring in his step. Charlie trotted alongside him, affected by Angie's presence too. With her, it was easy and with no drama. Their future together was clearer than it had ever been with anyone else. Angie made him happier than he had ever been. It was strange and exciting to admit that to himself.

After showering and changing for work, Nick headed to the office. His good mood faltered when he spotted his dad, clearly on the warpath, making his way down the hallway toward Nick's door. He glanced over his shoulder at Nick and made a show of checking his watch and shook his head before storming into his office.

So much for the jolly man from the other night at the Christmas party.

Maya rounded the corner, glancing at Nick's father before walking to her desk. She raised her eyebrows and turned to her computer.

Nick didn't bother greeting him either. He had back-to-back meetings this morning and wanted a focused, clear head. His father's sour mood tended to pierce through Nick's good one. Using all his strength, Nick held onto the thought of Angie. He wouldn't allow anyone – not even his dad – to get in the way of that.

***

It wasn't until after the morning meetings that Quinn cornered Nick outside of the conference room. The rest of the employees were already off to their desks to continue working. So, unfortunately for Nick, they were alone.

'You were late this morning,' Quinn said.

'By ten minutes.' Spending time with Angie made it worth it. 'I was prepared,' Nick said in a low voice, careful in case anyone heard his dad chastising him at the office. He remembered that David had a lot less tolerance for those moods. But with Nick taking over his brother's responsibilities, and the fact that he liked working at the company, he often tried to diffuse the situation instead of inflating it.

'You're acting like your brother did before he left. Defiant. Rude. I'm still your boss.'

As if Nick didn't know that. He didn't need a reminder every day. But his problem was personal, not business. Though Nick was never sure Quinn knew the difference. 'I'm not defiant or rude. If this is about my *work* performance, talk to me. If this is about my personal life, we can go out to dinner as a family. Better yet, I bet David would love to have you and Mom over.'

His father's face turned a bright shade of red. If he were a cartoon, steam would have blown from his ears. 'Believe it or not, son, I have your best intentions in mind.'

'Do you?'

'I've been here through all of your breakups. Those women you dated left you a mess afterward. None of them had a solid job and wanted to spend your money on frivolous things. With Ivy, she has an excellent job and comes from a good family. I want you to be happy.'

173

Nick didn't realize his dad had paid much attention to his personal life until lately. He was a little taken aback by his father opening up about Nick's happiness. But that didn't change the fact that he wanted more control over Nick's life than he cared to give. Quinn knew nothing about Angie or his ex-girlfriends. It only seemed to matter when it suited or benefited him.

'I'm happy with Angie,' Nick said, pushing more of the relationship than what was on the table. Though they grew closer by the day.

'We'll see about that,' Quinn grumbled and left the conversation.

Nick watched his father leave, and his shoulders dropped. Now he knew a shred of what David felt like after any of their confrontations. He always had the last word and kept them wanting more.

***

There wasn't much left of Nick's good mood to get him through lunch. He wanted another burst of happiness from Angie, and he knew just where to get it. He was scheduled to help out with the wrapping station that afternoon, and it couldn't come any sooner. He didn't think anyone would mind if he arrived early to help.

With each step toward Angie, Nick tried to pound out his father's words as much as possible. Quinn's voice burned in his head. It was one thing to be disappointed in Nick's work performance, but his past girlfriends? None of them were bad people. They just didn't align with his life. For once, he was happy. Angie did that. All he could do was focus on his anger. If he stayed that way, he'd ruin the short amount of time he spent with her. That had to be his father's plan. If Nick wasn't going to break it off with Angie, he would play mind games instead.

It wasn't until Nick saw Angie that the thick cloud over his head lifted.

The line was about five customers deep. Since Nick wasn't the type who wrapped gifts for his family regularly, he hoped he wouldn't disappoint Angie. Ginger was working alongside her. Angie beamed as she finished off one of the gifts and handed it over to the customer. The lights above reflected the foil in the wrapping paper design. When she spotted Nick, her smile widened, and she waved him over.

Nick grinned at Angie and waved to Ginger as he circled the table. 'How goes it?'

'It's better now,' Angie said.

Her perfume enveloped him, and he leaned closer to commit it to memory.

'Well, my time is up,' Ginger said, stepping away from the table.

'See you later,' Angie said before Nick stepped in Ginger's place. 'Do you have any experience?'

'Not much.'

Angie lifted her eyes to his. 'Well, you can watch me for a few and then try yourself.'

Nick glanced at the line, and the customers eyed him with apprehensive stares. He wasn't about to disappoint them or Angie. While she wrapped a standard clothing box, he followed the way her hands pressed folds into the paper before taping down the smooth edges. Then, she wrapped a thin piece of ribbon around the box and tied it into a bow before using a pair of scissors to spiral the ends.

'Easy peasy,' she said, handing the present to the customer.

The next customer walked up, a woman who looked to be in her forties. Her pursed lips made Nick think Christmas wasn't her favorite time of year.

'Hi there,' Angie said, bumping Nick's arm. 'You ready to try?'

'Are you sure you can't do it?' Nick asked.

'Come on,' Angie said, taking the box from the woman. She had two other parcels in her bag.

He could do three boxes. Angie had made it seem so easy.

'First we pick out the paper,' Angie said.

She folded the edge of the package, showing him how to size it. 'Cut here.'

175

He started to cut the paper, but Angie didn't move away from him. She held the paper tight against the box, and Nick was aware of every breath she inhaled. When he reached the end of the paper, he realized he hadn't taken a breath himself. He sighed, and Angie giggled.

'It's not exactly diffusing a bomb.'

He laughed along with her as the woman in front of them checked her phone.

'Fold here,' Angie said, taking the two ends of the paper, and pressing them against the box. 'Then tape it.'

Nick reached over the box to get the tape. He turned his head and their lips nearly brushed. At that moment, the world collapsed around him, and it was just Angie and him. The longing in her eyes had to match his own. Angie licked her lips, and her gaze dropped to his.

The woman in front of them cleared her throat, and Nick broke away from Angie, unable to make eye contact with the woman.

'Cut a small piece,' Angie said, her voice softer than usual.

It pleased Nick to no end to know Angie reciprocated his feelings. They hadn't kissed since his apartment, but he wanted to be sure she was comfortable with him in the same way again. From the electricity between them, they were both ready to move forward again.

He cut the tape and Angie walked him through folding the paper against the sides of the box. It took him a few tries to get it right, but Angie smiled broadly at the final result.

'Nick, that's great. How about you work on the next two while I take another customer?'

Nick had the urge to ask her to show him again. Anything to keep them close. But they would never get through the line until he stepped up his wrapping skills.

Without waiting for an answer, Angie waved over the next customer and started to work. While he worked at a snail's pace on the next packages, confidence swelled within him as he worked alongside her. His schedule allowed only an hour of volunteering, and it passed too quickly for him. The tension between them heightened throughout the sixty minutes, and he felt dread when he saw Carrie walk toward him a few minutes before the end of his shift.

Angie caught her too and frowned slightly.

There was a slight break in customers after Nick and Angie finished with a young couple who had brought a dozen gifts between them. Angie's wrapping skills still far-surpassed his, but he was no longer a novice.

'Are you signed up for another spot?' she asked him.

'I can look at my schedule,' he said, wanting to continue working with her.

'Great,' she said with a beaming smile.

'I'll see you later?' he said.

'I hope so.'

Nick walked away from her, back toward reality. At least he didn't have any questions about how Angie felt for him. They were well outside the friend zone, and Nick wanted to keep it that way.

As he stepped in the elevator, a weight pressed on him. Without Angie's brilliant smile and infectious cheerfulness, he remembered the conversation with his father. Wrapping presents had been a welcome distraction, but he had no idea how to deal with his father's disapproval of who he chose to spend time with. The only other person he could talk to was David.

***

The next night, David and Nick sat together in the workshop. Nick invited himself over for dinner so he could get more time with his brother and family. Theresa was kind to add another place setting to her table and insisted he come over more often.

As much as Nick would have wanted to discuss his father with both David and Theresa, he didn't flaunt his father's name around David's family. It was a sore subject, and he didn't want to subject Theresa or the boys to that negativity. Nick needed to talk to his brother, who had lived with their father for a good part of their lives and understood him.

'I don't know how to change his mind,' Nick said to David.

'You can't,' David said.

Nick pulled a face.

'Listen, little brother. It was hard for me and Theresa to make it work before I transitioned out of the company. There was a lot of pressure from Dad and changing our lifestyle. Going from corporate to starting a business from home wasn't exactly easy.'

David made it seem effortless.

'I don't know why he's doing all of this now. During the busiest time of the year.'

'Maybe he's worried about you working with Angie. If something happens between you two, then it might be awkward.'

'She's staying for the holidays, and that's it.'

'Is it?'

'I don't want that to be it.'

'So, there is a relationship?'

'I think so,' Nick said. He'd never been so unsure about the start of one before. Angie liked his company as much as he did, but he sensed a sliver of hesitation between them. He guessed it was because of her previous relationship with her boss.

'You have to figure out what you want and go for it,' David said.

'I want to be with Angie,' Nick said, speaking his truth.

'That's great, little brother.'

'I never expected it to go this far. And I still feel like it's too soon to bring her into this drama with Dad.'

'It's too late for that. Angie experienced it firsthand and she's still around.' David stood from his stool, chuckling a low and hearty laugh. 'These things sneak up on you sometimes.'

They sure did. Angie was different to the other girls he'd dated. She had her own life and goals while genuinely caring about family. It was all he ever wanted. Nick would do whatever he could to keep her in his life.

Chapter 19

During the week, the wrapping station held a steady stream of customers. Somehow, Angie's stamina had snowballed. She spent more time at the mall than she did as a teenager. Outside of her schedule, she helped tally donations from the customers, while filling in during the volunteers' breaks. Her ability to multitask helped keep her job as an information specialist while wrapping for a worthy cause. It was the perfect storm, and it all would help Hazel and the others at the shelter.

The flow of the wrapping station varied with each shift, but she tried to keep the pace steady for the customers. Even though there was enough advertising for the station, Angie knew how important satisfied customers were for word-of-mouth recommendations.

She constantly checked the schedule to see if Nick's name popped up. It would be a miracle for him to fill in somewhere since all of the volunteer spots were full. Wrapping with him had changed their dynamic completely, at least in her eyes. Energy buzzed between them, and it had careened into her. All day, she searched the crowds for him but figured he was hard at work in his office. They were similar in that way. They threw themselves into work headfirst. Angie couldn't believe her luck in finding Nick. As much as she wanted to take a break from dating, she could see herself with him.

At least they would be together tonight at Reese's party. She had even treated herself to a new sweater for the occasion.

'I'll take you next,' Angie said to the next customer. Mr Bower stood in front of her, and she tried to keep calm. He wasn't scowling this time, but his expression was flat and eerily impassive. She put on her best welcoming smile and held out her hands. 'Who are we wrapping for today?'

'I'm not here for the station,' Mr Bower said.

'I'm not sure I understand.' Angie flashed back to the day of the confrontation between him and David. She wasn't sure what to expect when neither of his sons was present. Had he expected Nick to be at the station with her? At least without Nick or David there, she wasn't in too much trouble with him. Unless it had to do with her job, she didn't think she had done anything wrong.

Mr Bower rounded the table and stood at the corner closest to her. He tapped his knuckle against the table as if he were attempting to hammer it into the floor. There wasn't much between them other than inches of charged air. 'I wanted to tell you that you and Nick won't work out.'

'Excuse me?' Angie knew he had issues with David, but she thought everything was fine between Nick and his father.

'I thought you should know. He's with someone else.'

The world tilted around her. Nick wasn't with someone else. He couldn't be. 'I'm not sure what he's told you about us.'

'He hasn't said much, which is why I'm telling you. I can't have you wreck this for him. He doesn't need a distraction during his engagement.'

'Engagement?' Every smile, laugh, almost-kiss flew into Angie's mind at once, bombarding her. She had convinced herself that Nick wasn't Brett. Her gut instinct about him couldn't be wrong.

'Nick and Ivy have been sweethearts for years. They've finally come to a good place. You won't mess this up for him.

181

Understood?' Words escaped her mind as she shook her head. Mr Bower turned on his heel. 'You'll do the right thing, Angela.'

'Wow, that was intense,' Bernadette said from next to her. Angie jumped, not realizing the shift had changed already. It was Bernadette's third time volunteering. She worked at the makeup counter at Bloomfield's for as long as Angie remembered. The petite woman seemed as fragile as the powders she dabbed on customers.

'I know,' Angie said, unable to take a full breath. Nick couldn't be engaged to this Ivy woman.

'Hope you don't lose your job over this,' she said.

'Why would I lose my job? I didn't do anything wrong.'

'Other than dating his son,' she said, lowering her voice.

According to his father, she wasn't dating Nick. 'I mean we're not technically dating.' Or were they? Angie couldn't help the tension in her chest building until she could barely take a full breath.

The hurt she had felt from Brett's betrayal reared its ugly head. Nick had never said anything about another woman. But neither had Brett. Angie's life backpedaled to less than a month ago. It was the same situation. She was with her boss and the 'other woman'. Once again, she was the fool on the verge of getting kicked out of her job.

Bernadette frowned slightly before starting a new customer. No one was behind him, so Angie excused herself and jogged to the information booth. She needed a minute to herself. This wasn't right. Why would Nick bother with her if he was with someone else? It didn't make any sense.

Closing the door behind her, she raced over to the front of the booth and pulled down the front barrier for some privacy. She covered her face with her hands, choking back a ragged breath. Nick's charm had slipped under her skin. His lies burrowed within her, given with a false smile.

Angie grabbed her phone from her purse and pulled up Nick's texts. The tree, Charlie, their flirtation. It didn't make sense. Brett had moved their relationship along quickly after

182

they had met. The only step Nick took was holding hands and one kiss. If he was interested in a distraction from Ivy then wouldn't he have pushed for more from Angie? The thought made her stomach flip. She sat in the chair, running over every single one of their encounters in her head.

What was with Mr Bower's insistence on her not seeing Nick? If it were true, she wanted to hear it from him, no matter how hard it hurt. Angie wasn't going to make the same mistake again. She had found out about Brett when his lies caught up with him.

Angie's mind worked on overtime, going over every second she had spent with Nick. As much as she loved her wrapping station, her heart wasn't in it. It was as if it started to build a barrier to protect itself. Angie wanted to give Nick the benefit of the doubt, but the situation was too similar and too soon.

Angie had texted Nick to take a break with her, but he didn't message her back. They had plans to meet at Reese's house for the party so at least she would see him then. She had a few hours until then. Angie had kept the secret about Nick to herself, wanting to hear the truth from him first. If she confided in Reese, she doubted her friend would let Nick in the house to explain anything. Angie wondered if waiting for the party was the best idea, but she wasn't going to miss out because of a guy.

She wished it was all a misunderstanding. If not, Angie wasn't sure how she would come out on the other side. If that were the case, she might swear off men for good.

Throughout the rest of her shift, she kept an eye on the crowds moving past the information booth. With her luck, Nick would visit her, and she feared she might blow up at him. She never had the chance to do that with Brett since she had been too stunned to find out about his fiancée and then leaving her job. The move took up the conscious side of her brain while she had quieted the part who wanted to kick and scream at him.

***

Later that evening, a lump settled in her throat, preventing Angie from swallowing her nerves while she got ready for the party. Maria and Emilia were on the couch watching another classic Christmas movie, while Donato snored lightly from the recliner.

Maria glanced over her shoulder. 'You look great.'

Angie stood in front of the oval mirror in front of the door, putting in earrings.

'Where are you going?' Emilia asked.

'Reese's party,' Maria shouted loud enough to make Donato stir. Their hearing aids were spotty at times.

'Thank you,' Angie said, fluffing her hair. Since she returned home, she let it go in her natural waves instead of the iron-flat locks she did in California. She tugged at the hem of her sweater. It was a bright red with white trim around the cuffs of the sleeves. The color of the shirt accentuated the blush in her cheeks.

'Tell Reese we said hello, and to take it easy,' Maria said. 'She's going to be busy enough when the baby comes.'

Angie couldn't look at her mother, for fear of spilling all her emotions about Nick. She wasn't sure who to believe anymore, so she lifted the tray of cookies from the table by the door, said goodbye to her family and walked to the house. Which Angie would come home later that night? One with or without Nick Bower in her life?

The music from the Thompsons' display mocked her as she walked to the car. Angie watched the mechanical Santa move from side to side while waving his hand. Earlier that day, she smiled at the festive feeling. Now she knew how Dad felt each holiday season.

Christmas music blasted from the radio as she drove to Reese's. She couldn't be sad while singing about the red-nosed reindeer, but somehow heat moved behind her eyes with that familiar pinching sensation she always experienced before crying.

When she parked outside Reese's house, she sat in the silent car for a moment, psyching herself up for what was to come.

After several steadying breaths, she left the car, scanning the area for Nick. He wasn't there yet, but it was only a matter of time.

***

Angie distracted herself from checking the door every few seconds by helping Reese with anything she needed and mingling with people she hadn't seen in years. In high school, Jeremy had been the cheerful jock while Reese was the sullen outsider, which was why their party was more like a reunion than anything. At least it was for Angie. She hadn't seen a lot of those people since high school.

When Nick finally arrived, a new type of fluttering filled Angie's chest. One filled with nerves instead of anticipation. Now that the moment was here, she wasn't sure she could go through with it. Nick's brilliant smile weakened her knees as he walked over. He shrugged off his jacket revealing a tight-fitting black sweater and jeans. This was the Nick who went Christmas tree shopping with her, kissed her in his apartment, and held her hand the tree lighting. The secrets underneath were hard to see under the surface.

'Hey, Angie.' He leaned forward to kiss her on the cheek, but she stepped away from him. A flash of confusion crossed his face, but the turmoil inside of her was much worse. 'Where's Reese? I want to give her this.' He lifted a small box in his hands. The wrapping paper crinkled at the edges, but she could tell he had tried. 'They're not as good as you and your mom's cookies, but my sister-in-law swears by this bakery. And I've been looking for every opportunity to practice wrapping.'

Of course, he would bring her best friend a gift. Her heart softened to him, but not all the way. She scrutinized him, wondering if she had worried over nothing. Why would his dad lie about Ivy? 'She's over there.' Reese hadn't left the radius of the food table since Angie had arrived. Currently, she had her back

185

turned toward them while picking out the little hot dogs from their pastry bread blankets.

'Hey there,' Jeremy said from behind Angie. 'You must be Nick.'

Nick shook his hand and gave him the box of cookies. 'A little party gift.'

Jeremy inspected the box. 'Nice. Thanks, man. Help yourself to the food. It's nice to put a face to the name. Angie talks about you a lot.'

Angie's face flushed while Jeremy shot her a goofy grin.

'Wow, you talk about me a lot, huh?' Nick asked, grinning.

'Not a lot. I mean, sometimes.' Angie wanted to smile and flirt with him. She wanted to enjoy herself tonight. But she couldn't. Not yet. 'Nick, I wanted to talk to you about something.'

'Can I grab a bite first?' Nick asked. 'I had to skip lunch today.'

Angie lifted her untouched plate of food, not wanting him out of her sight again. 'I haven't eaten yet.'

'Thanks,' he said, dipping a cocktail shrimp into the sauce. 'What did you want to talk to me about?'

Angie opened her mouth, preparing to tell him everything which had plagued her all day. But before she could, the front door burst open and a couple walked into the living room blowing into party horns.

'The party is here!' the man said, tugging along the grinning woman on his arm.

Angie didn't recognize Maya at first. Since reconnecting with her, she hadn't seen a smile like that yet.

Everyone turned toward them, Angie and Nick included.

'Maya and Maddox are here,' Nick said.

Maya looked much different than the smart-suit woman who hired her. Skintight green leggings accentuated her muscular legs while a white belt cinched the waist of her red, billowy shirt. Mistletoe earrings dangled from her ears as she and her husband wove through the others in the room.

Maya's lips pursed around her party horn. She stalked over

186

to Angie with a small wave to Nick, plucking the horn from her mouth. 'Hey.'

'Hey,' Angie said. 'You look great.'

'Thanks. What are you doing here?'

Angie waited for Maya to laugh or tell her she was kidding. She didn't. 'You know Reese is my best friend. She has been since high school.'

Maya bobbed her head. 'Right. My husband, Maddox ...' she waved her hand toward him. He and Jeremy were shaking hands across the room. 'He started working at the dental practice earlier this year. I guess I never put two and two together.'

'Well, it's good to see you outside of work,' Angie said.

'Yeah,' Maya said, dragging the word out.

'I didn't know you would be here,' Maya said to Nick with a smile. Angie had the idea that this wasn't her first party of the night.

'It's like a work reunion,' Nick said.

'I'm going to get a drink. You two want anything?' Maya asked.

'I'm fine,' Angie said at the same time Nick said, 'Sure.'

'Hey, I know you,' Reese's voice floated over to them. Maya skirted away from them toward the table packed with drinks.

Angie turned to her, as her best friend narrowed her eyes at Nick. 'This is Nick. Reese, Nick.'

'This is Nick?' Reese asked, digging her hand into her hip. 'Lipstick guy?'

Nick's eyes widened, and Angie could have sworn his face paled. 'What are you talking about, Reese?' Angie wanted to ask Nick about what his father said, but she was more interested in what Nick had to do with lipstick. Her insides knotted, and she placed the paper plate on the table next to her.

'The other night, at Jer's holiday party, we were at the ice rink. I helped *Nick* get lipstick off his face from his date.' Angie hadn't seen Reese flash her teeth like that at anyone in a long time. She did it a lot in high school at bullies and guys who cat-called them in the hallway. No doubt she would have turned in Brett's direction if they had ever been in the same room.

Angie tried to keep the tremble from her voice. 'Your dad said you were engaged. Is that the same woman?'

'My dad said what?' Nick's mouth pressed in a hard line.

'He came to the booth today and told me about Ivy,' Angie said. 'What did he say about her?'

He almost sounded offended that she spoke of him. Was it all true? 'Are you seeing her?'

'No, Angie,' Nick said. 'We're friends. That's all.'

'Didn't look like it to me,' Reese said.

As if Jeremy had a gauge for Reese's moods, he walked over to them and placed a tentative hand on Reese's shoulder. 'Can I get you anything?'

'I think Nick has been lying to my best friend,' Reese said without taking her eyes off Nick.

'Angie,' Nick said, reaching for her hands again.

They went limp at her sides. With her suspicions confirmed, she didn't want to be near him, never mind have him touch her. 'Whatever my dad said was wrong. He shouldn't have told you anything about her.'

'You lied to me about your job, then about a woman you're seeing,' Angie said, wishing she had better control over her emotions. Tears sprung from her eyes as the rest of the party carried on around them. 'I can't trust you, Nick. There's nothing you can say to change that.'

'I thought we were over this,' Nick said. 'I'm sorry for not telling you about my job. But Ivy is not my fiancée. She's just a friend. We just met a few weeks ago.'

'Your dad said Ivy was close with your family.'

'Well, her dad is, I mean, it's complicated.'

Reese moved in front of Angie, blocking Nick with her body. 'You're not doing this to Angie. She's been through enough this last month. I think you should leave.'

Nick swallowed whatever he was going to say next before releasing a breath. 'If you just listen to me.'

Angie choked on a sob. 'I'm not sure I can trust anything you say right now, Nick.'

Jeremy cleared his throat. 'Reese is right. I think it's time for you to go, man.'

'Angie, please,' Nick said, reaching for her again. If he touched her, she wasn't sure if she could still be mad at him.

Instead of listening to more of his lies, she whirled around and stormed from the room. Charging into Reese's bedroom, she closed the door behind her and sunk onto the bed, wishing she could wake up months from now when all of this would be a distant memory.

After a few minutes, Reese came in to comfort Angie, but she wasn't about to ruin her friend's night. She wasn't going to allow Nick to have that power over anyone in that house.

When Angie returned to the party, Nick was gone. Reese said he had left quickly after Angie went into the bedroom. The rest of the night was an utter failure, but Angie used all her energy to push through and make it appear as if she was having a good time. Maya seemed oblivious to what had happened with her boss, but she wasn't going to talk about it with her anyway.

At the very least, letting go of Nick gave her the push to get out of her hometown as soon as possible.

Chapter 20

For the entire ride home from Reese's Christmas party, Nick debated on turning back. But Angie was so upset, he doubted anything he said would help the situation. Instead, he dialed his father's number on the phone. He had to know what he'd said to Angie before he could put a plan into place to get her back.

The line rang until it picked up on the last one. 'Nick, dear. It's late.'

'Hi Mom, is Dad there?' he asked through gritted teeth. His hands curled around the steering wheel. With each passing second, his anger grew, but that wasn't how he was going to get answers.

'One moment,' she said. 'Quinn!'

Nick inhaled several slow breaths before his father picked up.

'Nick, it's late. Is there a problem?'

'Yes, there is. What did you say to Angie?'

'What are you talking about? Is this work related?'

'She said you told her Ivy and I were together.' At least that was what he'd gathered from the conversation with Angie. Her crying in front of him broke his heart in two. As much as Quinn tried to force Nick into a relationship, he had overstepped a boundary by putting his nose where it didn't belong.

'It was for the best,' Quinn said. 'This relationship wasn't going anywhere.'

'That wasn't for you to decide, Dad.'

'Well, what's done is done.'

Nick jammed his finger against the screen to end the call with his father. He didn't realize his dad cared that much about Nick's personal life outside of his scheming to get him and Ivy together. He never expected his father to go this far.

Nick and Angie hadn't made an official statement about their relationship, but the memory of her hurt expression wounded him more than any other breakup. It was all his fault, and he had no idea how to fix it.

When he trudged into his apartment, Charlie trotted over to him. Her wet nose snuffled his clothes, and then she sneezed. He went her to the couch and collapsed on top. She curled up beside him, gently nudging his hand for a head scratch. Nick didn't have much energy to put into it, but she didn't seem to mind.

The tree stood there, unlit, adding to the depressed mood in the room. Lighting it wouldn't do much other than reminding him of Angie. He tried to remember the happiness he felt when he and Angie moved around the tree, filling it with ornaments. The way she felt in his arms …

An ache in his gut overpowered the surge of bliss as the memory of Angie running away from him at the party flew to his mind.

'What am I going to do?' he asked Charlie.

She looked up at him with those brown eyes, staring into his soul. If she spoke human, then she could tell him what to do. But Nick had to figure this out on his own. That involved momentous changes in his life. His dad had no right to mess with Nick's personal life, but he wasn't all to blame. If he told her about his job to start, then she might have believed him about Ivy. Knowing of her past, he shouldn't have ever been dishonest with her.

He tucked Charlie against him. She was the only one in his

191

life who wasn't upset or disappointed in him. He wanted to get Angie back, but he'd have to put the work in. He was dedicated and she was worth it. Nick only hoped that she would listen and forgive him.

**

The next morning, Nick logged onto his computer at work and located Angie's schedule for the day. He needed to talk to her, and all his texts from the night before had gone unanswered. She had to understand that what his father said wasn't true. Christmas was coming up next week, and he usually made a point of going into the office for the last two weekends of the year anyway.

He left his office, unable to even glance in the direction of his father's. Before he met with Angie, he made a stop first.

Angie was on the first shift, and he figured she wouldn't be in the best mood from the party the night before even though he burst at the seams to talk to her.

If she knew it had been his father who'd created this mess and not him, they could start over again like they did the first time. Nick wasn't sure if his plan would work, but he had to put everything on the table. Angie knowing the truth about him and Ivy was the only thing between them right now.

When he arrived at the information booth, he spotted Angie carrying several rolls of wrapping paper in her arms. She stopped a few times, adjusting her grip on the supplies. No one had shown up for the volunteer slot yet, so he had a few minutes alone with her.

Nick rushed over to help her right before one wrapping paper roll fell to the ground.

'Thanks, I'm all over the place today,' she said laughing, then their eyes met. Her smile flattened, and a guarded look hid her normally sparkling eyes. Angie dropped the rolls on the table and brushed by him into the booth.

Nick placed the roll on the table and waited for her. He wasn't going to corner her inside the small booth but backing down from talking to her would only make him look guilty.

'I don't want to get into this today, Nick,' Angie said when she came out with the tape dispenser in her hands. 'I'm not interested in repeating history.'

'Angie, I didn't lie.'

'You did about your job. How can you expect me to trust you? Did you give me this job because you felt bad for me? Is this all some game to you?'

Nick had known from the start that she would think that, which was why he didn't tell her about it right away. 'I had nothing to do with hiring you.'

Angie shook her head. 'I don't know what to believe, Nick.'

'Believe me,' he said, standing in front of her. 'My dad set Ivy and me up on a date a few weeks ago.'

Angie frowned, but he had to get it out.

'By the end of the dinner, I had made it clear that we were only ever going to be friends. You are the person I want to be with.'

'What about the park where Reese saw you?'

'She brought me there to talk about a real estate deal her firm is interested in.'

'And the kiss?'

Nick sighed. 'She kissed my cheek. Platonically.'

'This is all so complicated. I didn't even want to get in a relationship with someone so soon after coming home.'

'I know that, Angie. But it all changed after we decorated the tree. I thought we were in this together. I thought it all changed.'

She hesitated. Longer than he wanted. But if this was ending, he had to hear it from her. 'Listen, I want to finish this station because I think it's important. But I don't want to see you anymore outside of work. After the New Year, I'm not going to be here anymore. I'm moving on.'

'Everything else I told you was the truth,' he said, not caring about the desperation in his voice. It couldn't end like this.

'Nick, coming home was temporary for me. Even if I believed you, this – whatever this was – isn't meant to last. We should leave it alone.'

Nick's hands fell to his side as a weight settled on his shoulders. Angie's anger rolled off her in waves. 'I came here to apologize to you. I hope someday you will forgive me.'

Angie stared into his eyes but said nothing.

Nick took the hint and left. He thought she would have forgiven him after he explained himself. But she was right. She had no reason to trust him. The betrayal stung, just as much as his father's.

***

When he got back to work, Nick headed for his office with his shoulders forward and hands hidden in his pockets.

'Nick,' Maya said, standing up from her chair.

Nick stopped, but he wasn't going to talk about the night before. No doubt she had seen the confrontation with Angie and wanted to get all the juicy details.

'I'm sorry about last night.' Maya twisted her fingers together. A tic he had only seen once or twice when she was about to fire someone. She was nervous.

'You didn't do anything,' he said.

'I could have told them about Ivy,' she said. 'I've seen you two together. I know your father. I didn't—'

Nick raised a hand to cut her off. No one needed to blame themselves for his father's mistakes.

Maya leaned her arm on the edge of the cubicle. 'What are you going to do?'

'Honestly, I have no idea.'

'You told Angie about Ivy, right?'

'She doesn't believe me.'

Maya traced a finger over the top of the divider, avoiding

his eyes. 'From what I heard, some guy broke it off with her in California. What your father said probably didn't help.'

'I know,' Nick repeated as a crawling sensation moved up his neck.

'Give her time,' Maya said. 'If you like each other and are meant to be, it will work out.'

Nick wasn't so sure about that, but he appreciated the thought. He glanced at his father's closed door down the hallway.

'He's with Mr Kent right now,' Maya said.

'Thanks for letting me know.' Nick wasn't ready to see Jared again. No doubt Quinn would talk about Nick and Ivy's non-existent relationship and Nick didn't have the energy to protest.

For the rest of the day, Nick buried himself in work, dodging memories of him and Angie together. He didn't even want to go home and see the shadow of her in every inch of his decorated apartment. He wished he could prove to her that he was the same person she had fallen for. The Nick she knew had been there all along, yet she still didn't want him.

It wasn't until later that afternoon that Quinn and Jared left the confines of his office.

'This is all going to work out perfectly,' Jared said as they walked down the hallway together. 'Once Ivy secures all the permits, we will be well on our way.'

'It's what we planned all along,' Quinn said. 'Well, a little different but we're all ending up in the same place. Now if I could get Nick on board with Ivy, we can marry more than just our plans.'

The mention of Nick's name and the word 'marry' sent a blow to his chest, forcing him out of his chair.

Quinn spotted him, and his smile faltered. But he knew how to mask his emotions. He said goodbye to Jared and walked into Nick's office before closing the door behind him.

'What was that about?' Nick asked.

'Can't I spend time with an old friend?' Quinn asked, crossing his arms.

Nick wasn't a fool. Quinn wanted to know how much Nick had heard. He wasn't going to give up his hand, and neither was Nick.

'You're planning something with him.'

'I thought you weren't interested in the Kent family.'

'Don't play games with me. You were expecting me and Ivy to get married? That's not happening. There isn't a me and Ivy, Dad. There never was.'

'What are you talking about? You two are getting closer by the day.'

What reality did he live in? 'No, we're not.'

Quinn shoved his hands in his pockets. 'I can talk to her if you want.'

'Absolutely not. I'm done with you interfering in my personal life. I don't know what business deal you and Jared are cooking up, but I don't want any part of it.'

'Jared said you and Ivy discussed the development at the park,' Quinn said.

'Dad, we've been over this. She wanted to talk about business. It wasn't a date.' Though Reese had convinced Angie of the opposite.

'Well, maybe she wanted to wait until you called her back on a date. She probably saw you and Angela at the lighting ceremony and thought you were with her. That's over now, right?'

Thanks to him. 'This discussion is over. It's not going to happen.'

'If you give it a chance,' Quinn almost pleaded with him. It was as if everything he said about Ivy didn't sink in. When it came to business, his father wore horse blinders.

Nick wanted to prove to his father that he could be the man he wanted at work, but the rest of his life was off-limits. 'I'm heading to lunch.'

'Don't screw this up for us.'

Nick whirled around. 'I'm not doing anything, Dad. I wish you would let me fall in love with whoever I wanted. You don't want to lose two sons, do you?'

Quinn's frown pierced through him. Nick needed some time to think about his life, and he wasn't going to get that in the office. He was done arguing for the day and pushed past his father as he left the room. 'You can close the door on your way out.'

Chapter 21

Angie should have been sick of the limited options at the food court since she was there practically every day, but with a looming time limit on her employment at the mall she wanted to enjoy as much as she could of her hometown before she left again.

With Nick showing up to her shift unannounced the day before, her mood suffered. She found herself searching the crowd for him. Today, she had the urge to dig into a plate of greasy comfort food. Angie stared at the pile of chicken tenders over a mountain of French fries. Usually, she ordered two meals for herself in case she saw Hazel.

Angie was only a few bites into her meal when she spotted Hazel walking from the bathrooms. Edward was nowhere in sight, so she waved her over. Angie wasn't sure if Hazel knew that the wrapping station was to raise money for the shelter, but she wanted to share the news. Throughout the event, there weren't many times where people didn't show up to get their presents wrapped. They raised enough money to reach their goal and Angie wanted to tell Hazel all about it.

'I've been looking for you,' Angie said. 'How are you?'

Hazel carried a ripped backpack and a heavy winter coat. Both items had seen better days, but at least Edward wouldn't have an excuse to tell Hazel to leave if they shared lunch.

'I'm doing good,' Hazel said. 'This is my favorite season. I love all the lights and the feeling of warmth around this time of year.'

Angie raised an eyebrow.

Hazel laughed a low, raspy chuckle. 'Well, it's not so warm outside. But you know what I mean.'

'I do. Have you seen the flyers for the wrapping station?'

'I'm afraid I don't have any family to wrap presents for.'

Angie reached across the table to touch her hand. 'It's for charity. I set it up.'

'That's lovely dear.'

Angie smiled. 'The money is for your shelter.'

Hazel blinked. For a moment, Angie's world slowed as if time stopped altogether.

'All the money will go toward supplies and programs for the people staying there.'

Hazel's chin dropped to her chest, and her shoulders shook.

'Are you all right?' Angie had no idea if she had said something wrong.

Hazel looked at Angie with tears in her eyes. 'That is the nicest thing anyone has ever done for me.'

'I wanted to help somehow.'

'You have truly made a lot of people's Christmas, Angela.'

Angie wasn't sure what to say, so she slid her tray between them. 'I'm not sure I can eat all of this.'

'Oh, I'm not sure,' Hazel said, rubbing her midsection. 'I'm on a diet.'

'What?'

'Just kidding,' Hazel said, grinning. She reached for a fry and popped it in her mouth.

Angie sat back in her chair, letting Hazel take a few more pieces before she urged Angie to join in too.

As they talked, a swell of pride moved through her. The station was going to help Hazel and the others using the shelter. Angie couldn't have been prouder of taking a chance on a new venture. She didn't want Christmas to end.

'Tell me all about your holiday festivities. Did you see the tree lighting?' Hazel asked.

Angie told Hazel about the parties and events she went to, but left Nick completely out of it. Walls were already in place in her heart and she wasn't ready to break them down yet.

When there were only crumbs left on the plate, Angie sat back in her chair, wishing she could stay there for the rest of the day. She had work to do, though. Work that would get Hazel and others the resources they needed.

Hazel sat up straighter and waved across the space.

Angie turned around and locked eyes with Nick. He was in line at the Chinese food restaurant. He waggled his fingers at Hazel before stiffening at Angie's gaze. Her insides twisted while at the same time, fluttering. Her body was as confused as her mind.

'You know him?' Angie asked.

'Of course. That's Nick. He's the manager who allows me to use the facilities here. He's so kind. He's even bought me lunch a few times. That smile is hard to turn down.'

Angie knew all about his disarming smile and his charm. She wasn't sure why she didn't put them together. Of course Nick was the manager who allowed Hazel to stay at the mall during the day. The idea made it harder for her to stay mad at him.

Hazel gave her a knowing look. 'You two know each other?'

'We do.' If Nick was allowing homeless people to come into the mall for warmth and a place to wash up, how could he be the same man who lied to her about a fiancée? Angie had been so wrapped up in her own life that she'd missed all the signs once again. Angie briefly explained what had happened with Nick; she felt Hazel might be able to help offer some perspective.

'Well, I find around this time of year it's easier not to hold a grudge. He's a fine man, but everyone makes mistakes, am I right?'

She was more than right, but Angie didn't feel ready to admit it just yet. 'I need to get back to work.'

Hazel stood and hugged Angie. She had the same strong embrace as her mother. At that moment, it was what Angie needed. Her life had taken an unexpected turn in the last two days. All she wanted was to feel the warmth of someone.

'Do you feel better?' Hazel asked.

'A little.'

'It's the least I can give for everything you're doing for the shelter. I hope I will see you soon.'

'You will,' Angie promised before lifting her bag from the table.

'I'll take care of this,' Hazel said, indicating the tray. 'At least it will keep Edward off my back for a little while.'

'I'll tell him there are a group of kids on the other side of the mall causing trouble,' Angie said with a smile. 'That will keep him busy.'

Hazel let out another one of her cackles.

As Angie headed back to work, she looked for Nick in the food court, but he was gone.

The conversation with Hazel rolled over in Angie's mind as she fell into the soothing movement of wrapping presents. It was the last official day of the booth since Ginger planned to get the money to the shelter before Christmas so everyone could enjoy their holiday.

Angie helped make the mall patron's lives easier around Christmas, and it was for a good cause, but she couldn't muster the holiday cheer she had a few days ago. It was easier to close herself off from Nick than dig into her feelings about him. Their fledgling relationship had ended at a point where they could have flourished.

While she could have had one of the security guards or Stuart bring the money to the corporate office, Angie wanted to do it herself. As much as she told Nick she didn't want to talk to him, after the conversation with Hazel, she was willing to give him another chance to explain himself. The outcome was as ominous as the gray clouds outside, but Hazel's words about forgiveness around the holidays hit home with her.

After her last customer, Angie stacked the supplies into the corner of the information booth and closed the front window. The other stores were locking up for the night, so she wasn't going to bother with returning the supplies tonight. There were only a few rolls of wrapping paper left, but otherwise, they had used all the donated supplies. A rush of pride surged through her as she counted the money and shoved it into a plain white envelope before sealing it with extra tape.

At least as her personal life plummeted down a steep ravine, she was able to do some good.

On the way to the corporate offices, Angie checked her phone. A slew of emails came through, and she spotted one from Emma. The subject line was in all capital letters, and the words stopped Angie in her tracks.

JOB OFFER – READ ASAP – YOU GO, GIRL!

Angie hadn't set up any interviews with the potential hotels she'd applied to earlier in the month. But Emma had come through for her with a job which would use her skills. Her hands broke out in a sweat as she pressed the elevator button.

Responding to the email would have to wait. Distractions would only prevent her from saying what she wanted to Nick. At the very least, she wanted to remain friends with him. They had shared a lot over the last month. Even though it was a whirlwind friendship-almost-relationship, she couldn't let that go easily without getting all the information.

Angie crossed her fingers as she ascended to the offices. If Nick was there, would he have time to talk to her? She could have texted him, but surprising him as he had her might give her the best chance to know if he was lying or not. At some point in her life, she was a good judge of character. Now, she wasn't so sure.

The elevator doors opened, and Angie's heart pounded like

twelve drummers drumming. It wasn't the same fluttering feeling she'd had before the confrontation with Mr Bower, but it proved Nick still meant a lot to her. She wasn't sure if it was a good thing or not. At this point, could they even make a friendship work?

Angie took a deep breath to clear her mind and calm her nerves. She rounded the corner to Ginger's office and knocked on the door. The older woman looked at her over her glasses. 'Angela, come in.'

'I have the final amount for you,' Angie said, handing over the envelope.

'Everyone in the office is so proud of this event,' Ginger said. 'The higher ups want us to revisit it next year. We have big plans for bringing in members of the community to volunteer. It's all because of you. I hope you will be able to return and teach them your amazing wrapping methods.'

Angie glanced over her shoulder. She wasn't sure of the location of Nick's office, but she didn't want to miss him either. 'I'm sure the women at Bloomfield's would be happy to help. I'm not sure I'll be around next year.'

'Well, that's a shame. But you are always welcome back. You've made quite the impression on this place since you've been here.'

Angie hadn't intended to do anything other than breeze in and out of this town, but after years away, it did the same to her. It burrowed into her heart, just as Nick had.

'I appreciate that,' Angie said.

Ginger slid the envelope into her drawer. 'Have a good Christmas if I don't see you.'

'You too,' Angie said, slipping out of the room. She stood in the hallway, unsure where to go. Her phone blared from her bag, and several of the office workers peered over the tops of their cubicles to look at her.

Maya's eyes met hers.

'Sorry,' she said, silencing her phone. The screen lit up with Reese's face. She couldn't leave Reese hanging when she was so close to having the baby. But she was so close to Nick's office.

As she was about to answer a woman's voice floated out of the nearest office. 'Nick, what do you think about Peruvian food? There's this place nearby I'm dying to try.'

She stepped out of the office. The tall and lithe woman wore a fitted pant suit with spiked heels and glittering jewelry hanging from her ears and neck.

Ivy, Angie assumed. She looked like a female version of Nick; perfectly groomed and successful. Why wouldn't he choose her?

'Angie,' Maya hissed, waving her over.

Angie shook her head and fled toward the elevators. As if someone was looking down on her, the doors opened, and an older gentleman walked out dressed in a Santa suit completed with a white beard and mustache. A Christmas miracle.

'Thanks,' she muttered as she flung herself inside. She pressed the button for her floor, listening to the clicking heels coming her way. No way was she going to share an elevator with Nick and Ivy.

The door slid closed, and Angie held her breath as it started down. At least she'd got her answer about Nick's relationship status. He might have told the truth about them being friends. If they were going out, it was probably for the best. They probably deserved each other, and Angie needed to move on with her life too.

To distract herself, Angie wanted to look toward her future and inquire with Emma about the job offer. Instead, a voicemail from Reese lit up the screen. In her mad dash out of the office, she had forgotten about the call. She opened the voicemail and listened as her heart thudded in her chest.

'The baby is coming!' Then, Reese's cackling laughter sounded on the other end. 'Just kidding. Scared you, didn't I? That's what you get for not picking up for me. I'm currently polishing off a pint of ice cream and I have an extra spoon for you. Come by and we can eat our way through your feelings. Like I need an excuse.' More laughter then the call dropped.

Reese always seemed to know when Angie needed to talk. It

was as if she knew Ivy would be at the office, and Angie would almost confront Nick and her together.

Chills rolled up her arms, and she tried to rub them away. At least she avoided that confrontation. Angie texted Reese back to let her know she would be there soon. Nick was a part of her past, and she needed to move on with her life.

***

When Angie arrived at Reese's house, she pushed through the front door. She noticed a duffel bag resting by the couch.

'Our overnight bag,' Reese said, walking into the room. She wore a long-sleeved dress, her bump looking bigger than Angie remembered. Two pints of ice cream rested in her hands. 'Anytime now.'

'How do you feel?' Angie asked, plopping on the couch. The weight of the day settled over her, and her body buzzed with relaxation. She wasn't sure if she could move from her spot if she wanted to.

Reese handed over a fresh pint of ice cream, and Angie tore off the top. Reese tossed a spoon at her, and it landed in her lap. 'I'm okay. Waiting sucks, but I'm not going to force the kid out. She will come when she wants.'

'Like mother, like daughter,' Angie said. 'I'm not sure I could wait.'

'You do like to rush into things,' Reese said.

Angie pulled a face. 'You were the one to tell me to pursue something with Nick.'

'Oh good, a segue into him. I was wondering how we would get here.'

As if she didn't orchestrate it herself.

'Did you talk to him today? I assumed that was where you were when I called.'

Angie shrugged. 'He came to the booth this morning, but I didn't give him much of a chance. I went up to the office right before coming here, and Ivy was with him.'

Reese nearly choked on her ice cream. 'His supposed fiancée? This is better than a movie. What happened?'

Angie wasn't sure she wanted her life compared to a movie. At that moment, it was more of a tragedy than a spunky romance. 'They were getting dinner together. I practically sprinted away when I saw her. She's gorgeous.'

A cool hand brushed over Angie's cheek. 'You're gorgeous.'

'That doesn't matter anyway. He's with someone else. It's over.'

'Well, at least you got back on that horse. You would have to do it eventually. Now, you can move on.'

'Speaking of moving on,' Angie said, licking her spoon. She wanted to delay the inevitable if possible. Reese wasn't going to like what she had to say. 'I think I'm going to quit this job.'

'Because of Nick? No, you should keep going and make him feel awkward.'

'Emma emailed me today. About a job offer.'

'Oh,' Reese said, staring into her pint. 'Are you going to take it?'

Angie swallowed. In her rush to get to see Nick and going to Reese, she hadn't even looked at the email. 'It has to be better than working so close to Nick and there's not much of the season left anyway.'

'Don't abandon me again, okay? In a few weeks, you've made me get used to you being around. I don't want months to go by without you coming to visit my girl and me, but I completely understand. Nick made this super awkward, and if I see him again, he's going to get a piece of my mind. But I was happy to have you as long as I did.'

Angie leaned over and wrapped her arm around Reese's shoulder. 'I'll do better this time.'

It wasn't until Angie got into her car that she pulled out her phone. She opened the email app and began typing. *This is the right thing to do*, she tried to convince herself. Her heart hardened again as she took hold of her future.

Chapter 22

For most of the night, all Nick could think about was Angie running away from him at the office. After watching her enter the elevator, he'd had the urge to follow her. Had she come to talk to him and seen Ivy? Even though it was innocent, he knew what she saw. Once again, she mistook information as truth. He had his dear old dad to thank for that.

Ginger called his office number to let him know the final details for the shelter. Angie had dropped off the rest of the wrapping station money and then left without saying anything to him.

Nick absently dipped his spoon into his soup as the restaurant noise filled his ears. He had been lost in thought all evening.

'Nick?' Ivy asked.

'I'm sorry.' Nick placed his spoon on the table. They were in the Peruvian restaurant she had recommended. Since it was Saturday, the place was filled with people and the loud voices didn't do much to drown out his thoughts. 'What did you say?' Had she said something about snow? It hadn't snowed all season, and Nick was convinced there wouldn't be a white Christmas this year.

Ivy sipped from her water glass. 'You've been distracted. Are you all right?' She had asked him to dinner to share her ideas for the development by the ice rink, and he couldn't even get that right.

'Recently, I met a woman, Angie. I hurt her. Not on purpose. But I really screwed things up. I'm sure I ruined any relationship we could have had.'

Ivy patted her lips with a white cloth napkin. 'I had a feeling this had to do with another woman.'

'I don't want to monopolize your time with my relationships when we are supposed to be discussing your new business venture.'

'That's what friends are for, right?' she said, sipping from her glass. 'As much as I hate meshing my personal and professional lives, I tend to think of them similarly. If you want to grab an opportunity in life, you have to fight for it. Did you know that I wasn't the first choice for this project? Not even my father's reputation helped get me in the door, but I set up all the meetings with the right people and made the connections. It's the same with relationships. You have to try for it before you lose her for good. Then that will be on you.'

Nick blinked and cleared his throat. 'I see what you mean.'

Ivy laughed. 'From what you've said, you really like her. The worst thing you can do is let her go over a misunderstanding. You'll kick yourself for it later.'

'Is that what you've done with your boyfriend?'

'Actually, it was him. Which is why I can speak from personal experience. Even long-distance he created opportunities.' She stared off over Nick's shoulder and smiled as if she were remembering something. 'My father isn't happy with any of it. He never liked Trent, but you can't help who you love.'

She was right about that. If Ivy could go off on her own without an apology to her family, so could he.

Nick asked Ivy about Trent, and she carried on about him without pausing. The excitement in her eyes filled him with envy. He had seen that same sparkle in Angie's eyes before and he longed to have it back. He knew without a doubt, they had fallen for each other, and he had screwed it all up. He should have run after her at the office, but maybe it wasn't too late. He had to plan out what he wanted to say to Angie before he tried to see her again.

Ivy had survived a breakup, and she was well on her way to happiness. Nick and Angie could get over this bump in the road. Everything between them was out in the open, and her issue with Ivy wouldn't hold. They were just friends and their fathers wouldn't be able to push them together anymore.

Nick wasn't sure Angie would forgive him at all, but he was willing to work for it. For the rest of his life if necessary.

'Ivy, I wanted to ask about the development in the park.'

Ivy carved a piece of *tres leches* from the plate in front of her. 'What about it?'

'Our fathers seemed to think we were going to work on it together.'

'Well, they don't seem to know much about us, do they?'

'They don't.' This was why his father wanted him and Ivy together, and why both their fathers had discussed 'marrying' their businesses. Nick had no interest in working in real estate. Why had his father lied to Jared about it?

As much as things weren't settled between him and Angie, he had to find out what his dad's motivation was for pushing him into an agreement neither Ivy nor he knew anything about.

***

Monday morning, Nick texted David to meet to pick up the table from the booth. He hadn't been there when he had dropped it off and wondered if he could have avoided everything if he had. Their father wouldn't have shown up to derail Angie over his non-existent relationship with Ivy, and the drama with David. Nick could have cleared it all up in person. The sick feeling in his stomach kept him from dwelling on the past too long.

Angie worked the morning shift, so it was a perfect time.

With David as his wingman, he could gain the courage to convince her that they belonged together.

Nick's nerves spiked as he made his way to the booth. He hoped after this conversation, he wouldn't need an excuse to check in with her at work. They would be back to the place they'd been before. All his insecurities twisted in his gut. What if, after his explanation, she still wanted nothing to do with him? Nick tried to push away the negative thoughts and homed in on David standing next to the table with a rolling cart.

Darkness masked the inside of the booth, and Nick wondered which Angie he'd meet. Would he see forgiving Angie or angry Angie? He hoped for the very least indifference. His nerves wouldn't be able to take a twisted scowl or narrowed eyes in his direction.

What he didn't expect was an older man walking toward the front and plopping at the desk.

'Do you need help?' the man asked Nick.

'No, thank you,' Nick said, recalling the man's name – Gary. Apparently, Nick's face wasn't that recognizable.

'Morning,' David said from the other side of the booth.

'Hey.'

'If I didn't know any better, I'd have thought you were here to see me.'

'I am,' Nick said.

'The way you looked at that guy makes me believe you wished he would turn into a particular woman. Angie, perhaps.'

Nick shook his head. 'We're in a rough spot right now. She's pretty upset with me.'

'I'm sure you'll smooth it over.'

Nick wasn't sure about that.

'Theresa wanted me to let you know Christmas Eve dinner is at five-thirty. She wants the kids to go to bed early. Putting the presents out takes a lot of time, and the boys always get up earlier on Christmas Day.'

'Okay,' Nick said absently.

David waved a hand in front of him. 'Hello? Earth to Nick.'

'I did this. I should have fought harder. Now she's avoiding me.' Though, how would she have known he would stop by at that time to see her? She couldn't have switched her schedule that quickly. Maybe he was too predictable.

'Well, I've never known you to give up on anything. If you feel you're meant to be, it will work itself out.'

'Is that the motivational talk you're going to give me today? *It will work itself out?*'

'It worked for me. If you hurt Angie, she might need time apart. If you're meant to be, you'll find a way back to each other.'

Nick wasn't sure how much time he had before Angie found a new job. There was a time clock on their relationship, and he wasn't on the right side of it.

'You sure you want to help? You might mess up your fancy suit.'

'I remember a time when all you wore were fancy suits.'

David shuddered and managed to get a small smile from Nick.

Nick looked down at his clothes and then at David's jeans and button-down shirt. Since he'd started his workshop, his uniform consisted of flannel shirts and jeans. Nick liked his suits but wouldn't have minded the comfort. He helped David lift the table onto the cart, and together they wheeled it through the mall. He couldn't help checking the crowd of shoppers, thinking of the possibility of Angie running late for her shift. That would explain Gary being there during her scheduled time.

But when they made it to David's truck, Nick knew he wasn't going to see her today.

'I'll see you later?' David asked, clapping a hand on Nick's shoulder.

'Yeah.'

'Chin up, little brother. It will be fine.' David quirked his lips as a silent understanding settled between them.

As Nick walked away, his good mood plummeted. He had to

know what happened to Angie, and if he would get a chance to see her again.

***

When he returned to the office, Nick headed over to Maya's desk. She glanced at him before returning her attention to the computer screen. 'I need to tell you something.'

'What's going on?'

Maya glanced at the other cubicles next to her and waved him closer. 'Angie sent an email this weekend.'

'She did?' From Maya's expression, he had an idea of what it was before she said anything.

'She resigned. She thanked us for giving her the job, but I guess one of those hotels called her back.'

Nick's shoulders sagged. That was why Angie wasn't at the booth. She'd quit. He was happy for her getting a new job, but would she have stuck around for the holiday if he hadn't lied to her?

'Are you okay? You look pale. Sick, even.'

'I'm fine. It's fine.' He trudged into his office and closed the door. His confidence in talking to her before went out of the window. He checked his phone. There were no messages – just the string of texts he had sent after the party. The many apologies had gone unanswered. The last message from her was her telling him she was on her way to Reese's party.

Nick rubbed a hand over his forehead, shoving his hair aside. He wanted to try again, but her actions spoke volumes. Now, she would move on with her life, neither of them getting the closure they deserved. Though he didn't deserve much, and he didn't want it. There was more to their story, but it turned out someone had ripped out that half of their book. He turned in his chair to face the window. The clouds in the sky were thick and gray, adding to his already dark mood. It wasn't going to be what he had expected of a white and happy Christmas after all.

Chapter 23

Angie woke again to the sound of cabinets slamming in the kitchen. They were louder than normal, and so was her family. To anyone else, it sounded like arguing, but she knew better. Without Donato's hearing aids, the volume intensified.

The bright light from her phone blinded her for a moment. She had rolled down the shades to blanket the room in darkness since she didn't need to get up early again until after the holidays.

It was almost eleven in the morning. It had only been two days since she left the job at the mall, so there was no reason to set the alarm for herself.

There was no reason to quit the information booth until after New Year's for her new job, but she couldn't stand to be so close to Nick and she wanted the space to clear her head. A surge of guilt moved through her when she realized Gary would have to cover her shifts, but with the holidays slowing down, Maya assured her that it was fine.

Somehow, one of her family members managed to slam the refrigerator door, and Angie understood what was going on.

When she entered the kitchen, Mom put a hand on her chest in mock surprise. 'Angie, you're up. Now you can help with food prep.'

Angie let out a yawn. 'Let me make some coffee first.'

'Coffee is for the morning and after dinner,' Emilia said. 'We cook now.'

Angie curled her lip but didn't give her any backtalk. They had used their passive aggressive techniques to wake her and now she was going to work.

'Good to see you've joined the living,' Donato said, looking up from his crossword puzzle.

For the next hour, Angie busied herself with making food. Her hands moved on autopilot from years past, as if she jumped back onto a bicycle for cooking. As she rolled the meatballs, Nick's face didn't leave her mind. Somehow, the good times they had together were overshadowed by Ivy walking out of his office. Even if Nick had told the truth about Ivy, it was clear he moved on quickly.

Angie was about to do the same with her new position. So why didn't it give her the excitement she needed?

'Are you going to work today?' Donato asked as Angie stuffed the last meatball on the tray. She bent over to slide it into the oven.

'She quit!' Emilia said. 'I told you this.'

'It was a temporary job,' Angie said, unsure why her cheeks heated at the word 'quit'. She wasn't a quitter. Dad had taught her to carry through with anything she had signed up for. This was different. The possibility of seeing Nick at work couldn't happen. She wouldn't be able to get through the last few days of the season looking over her shoulder. It was bad enough to see him at the food court when she was eating with Hazel, especially after she told him what he had done for her.

'Nick is there too,' Maria said.

'Ma!' Angie shrieked.

Maria shrugged. 'You two aren't together anymore. Such a shame. But I understand why you wouldn't want to be at work.'

'He's not the reason.' Even though that wasn't the truth. If Dad were there, he would have shaken his head, disappointed with her

214

for quitting because of a guy. It was all too much, though. Two breakups in one month devastated her. She had to take control of her life, and this was how it would happen.

'Okay,' her mom said, giving Emilia a knowing look.

Angie groaned with frustration, stalking over to the sink to wash her hands. She needed a minute to process without her family interfering.

The landline rang from the wall behind her. Her mom apparently hadn't come out of the Eighties. The phone still had the long, coiled cord that Angie had stretched throughout the years of wanting a private conversation pre-cell phone.

'Can you get that?' her mom asked, holding up her flour-filled hands.

Angie wiped her hands on a towel and lifted the phone from the cradle. 'Martinelli residence.' It was Dad's go-to greeting for the house phone, and it was as much of a habit as rolling meatballs.

'Angie?' The panic in Jeremy's voice sliced through her.

'Yeah. Is Reese okay?'

'We're on our way to the hospital.'

A loud cry came through the other end of the phone. Reese's panting was louder than Jeremy's words.

'What was that?' Angie asked, plugging her other ear with her finger.

'The baby is coming,' Jeremy said.

'All right, I'm on my way.'

'It might take a while,' Jeremy said.

'You're going to be there,' Reese said.

Angie nodded as if either of them could see her. 'I will be there. Give me a few minutes.'

'Take your time,' Jeremy said.

'That's easy for you to say,' Reese groaned again as Angie hung up.

Maria and Emilia stared at Angie as a wide grin spread across her face. 'Reese is having the baby.'

Emilia clapped her hands together in a praying gesture. 'What a blessing.'

'Looks like you found your excuse to get out of cooking.' Maria pointed a wooden stirring spoon at Angie.

'Mama.' Angie wrapped her arms around her mother's waist and kissed her cheek.

'I know,' she said with a smile. 'Go. I want updates and pictures. It's your penance.'

Angie sprinted from the kitchen to change her clothes. She wasn't sure how long she would be at the hospital, but it didn't matter. Today was about Reese and her baby.

***

As Angie walked through the front doors of the hospital, her phone blew up with texts.

Are you here?

The baby is in distress. They're moving us to the operating room.

Angie shook her head. Distress? Operating room?

I'm here, Jer. Where do you want me to go?

She stood in the lobby for several minutes before texting him again. Angie waited. And waited. Her blood pressure spiked, and she sat on the nearest chair, staring at her phone.

'Come on,' she muttered to herself. She texted Jeremy again, reminding him that she was there. Though, if Reese were in distress, he would be by her side. The most important thing was keeping Reese and the baby safe.

Angie waited another ten minutes before approaching the front desk. An older woman in scrubs sat behind it, working at a computer.

'Hi,' Angie said.

'How can I help you?' the woman asked.

'My friend is having a baby. I guess there's a problem? I have no idea where to go.'

'There's a waiting room outside Labor and Delivery,' the woman said. 'Go through these double doors and follow the signs. It's on the other end of the building.'

'Thank you,' Angie said, clutching her phone against her chest.

Angie hustled down the hallways, keeping a sharp eye on the signs, so she didn't get lost. The cell reception disappeared a few times as she walked, passing holiday decorations hanging from the walls. Like at home, Angie couldn't feel festive when her life was so unpredictable.

She tried not to think about Reese and the baby in danger but could only manage short bursts before her breath caught in her throat again.

Angie pushed through the double doors into another waiting area. Most of the chairs were empty, but two families sat on either side of the room. One older couple, and a man with two kids on either side of him playing on tablets. She locked eyes with another nurse at the front desk. 'I'm here for Reese Tan.'

'Are you family?'

Angie almost said no, but she wasn't just a friend to Reese and Jeremy. To anyone who knew them, she *was* family.

'Yes,' she said. 'Jeremy Tan texted me, but I haven't heard from him. Do you have reception in there?'

The woman gave Angie a raised eyebrow before her gaze slid over her shoulder. 'You can take a seat. I'll inform them you're here.'

Angie gripped the edge of the desk, her knuckles turning white. The woman typed on her computer, signaling the conversation was over. She turned, trudging to the row of chairs in the middle of the room. The televisions in the corner of the room played the local news. She tried to distract herself with puff pieces about local holiday events but couldn't concentrate on anything but her phone.

I'm in the labor and delivery waiting room.

It was the only thing she could think of saying, without bothering Jeremy too much.

Angie texted her mom to let her know she was in the waiting room. With her preparations for the meals for the next two days, she wouldn't get to her phone right away. She couldn't even dig it out of her purse on a normal day.

The longer Angie sat there, the more anxious she became. She emptied her inbox filled with junk mail of holiday pricing and last-minute reminders for Christmas gifts. Angie had sent a box of gifts her apartment in California to her home before she left, including a pile of onesies for the baby's entire first year. She went a little crazy, but she was Aunt Angie.

The excitement within her never really went away though she'd suppressed it since coming home. When she was happy with Brett, she was bubbly and carefree. With the wintry weather and both Brett and Nick's betrayal fresh on her heart, she was a different person. She hoped she'd find happiness in her new job. It wasn't what she ever imagined for herself, but it was the start of something new. She would be able to see her family more often, and Reese too.

In a way, she was coming home, but still had the freedom she needed.

She sifted through her messages, and Nick's name lit up like a beacon several people from the top. His last message sat there, staring at her.

Angie, I'm sorry.

Her heart ached to talk to him even just for closure.

Angie glanced at the doors leading to the delivery unit. Snowflakes made from white paper were taped to the door. The other people waiting around her might spend Christmas in the hospital. Worse scenarios existed in the world, and she couldn't even accept Nick's apology. She slumped in her chair and clicked on his name. Maybe they could meet up for coffee before she started her new job. Not Kevin's Café. There were too many memories there. Somewhere else, perhaps.

As she began typing, her screen flashed with an unknown number on her phone. She had turned the volume of the ringer to the maximum, in case Jeremy called.

Everyone in the room turned to her, including the nurse at the desk.

Angie silenced the phone and skittered out of the room.

'Hello?' she said into the phone after she was in the hallway again.

'Angie, it's Maya.'

'Hey, Maya,' Angie dragged the words out, hoping she hadn't forgotten anything at the mall in her hasty exit.

'I wanted to give you the time to arrive at the press conference tomorrow to present the check,' she said.

'Oh, I thought Ginger was doing that.'

'Well, you ran the event. We're expecting you there around ten tomorrow. You might not work for us anymore, but you should finish what you started.'

Angie's hand gripped the phone harder than necessary. Even after knowing the issues between Angie and Nick, Maya still only cared about her job. But her original goal was to help the shelter, so she supposed she could be there to see it to the end. 'Yeah, I can make it.'

'Good, you can report to Mr Bower when you get there,' Maya said. 'I'm sure he will have you meet with the coordinator of the shelter.'

Angie wrinkled her nose. She didn't want to see Nick's rude father, but she supposed with her out of the way of his plans for his son's life, she could be civil. 'Thanks.'

'Good luck with the new job,' Maya said and then hung up.

Angie shuffled back into the waiting room and turned the volume on her phone to a reasonable level, placing it inside her purse. Jeremy and Reese were the only people she wanted to hear from, no matter how long it took.

It took another hour before Jeremy managed to send a message.

Mom and baby are good. Heading up to the maternity ward.
Reese is out of it, so don't come in here taking videos. I know
how you two are.

Angie smirked at her phone. Jeremy knew her so well. All she wanted was to see the baby, though. She stood up from her chair and headed toward the desk. Angie moved as if she were floating instead of walking. Reese and the baby were okay. All was right in her world.

'My fr – sister had a girl,' Angie said, unsure if the unit was for family only. 'Reese Tan?'

'Take the elevator to the second floor. You will have to check in with the desk to see if your *sister* allows visitors.'

Angie knew she was busted but smiled at the woman with the least amount of guilt possible. Nothing could shake her good mood as she strode to the elevator and pressed the button to go up. Angie lifted her phone from her purse and texted Mom the good news. She wasn't sure how long she could stay, but she wanted to be there for Reese for as long as she could.

***

There wasn't any trouble getting into Reese's room, but she had never seen her friend so pale in her entire life. Several pillows were propped behind her back to keep her upright. Angie hovered in the doorway. Sunlight streamed into the room. If she didn't know the temperatures had dropped, she would think it was a spring day.

Jeremy patted a cloth over Reese's forehead. Something stirred in Angie's chest as she saw the intimate moment between two brand new parents.

Angie tried to back out of the room, but Jeremy looked at her. 'Come in.'

Reese's eyes fluttered open. Her ashen face contorted into a crooked smile. 'You're here.'

'I've been here for some time,' Angie said, walking into the room as if there were mouse traps on the floor.

'Meet Grace,' she said.

Inside the bassinet, the baby was a wrapped-up little bundle of chubby cheeks and bow-like lips. Grace's eyes were closed, but she made tiny grunting sounds from her throat.

'I think I just died a little,' Angie said.

'Tell me about it,' Reese said, looking at her baby girl with wide-eyed amazement. 'I feel like I would jump in front of a bus for her. I've never felt that before.'

Jeremy raised his eyebrows.

'You're a close second, honey.'

'Gee, thanks,' he said.

'Tell me all about what happened,' Angie said, sitting in a nearby chair. She wanted to be near Grace, but not startle her awake.

Reese waved her hand at Angie. 'It wasn't a big deal.'

'You could barely breathe,' Jeremy said to her.

'She was worth it,' Reese said.

Jeremy pressed his lips together, shaking his head.

'You love me,' Reese said, color flooding her cheeks.

'I do.' Jeremy kissed her.

Angie peered into the bassinet again to look at Grace, partly to not stare at her friends but mostly because she wanted to see the miracle in front of her. She couldn't believe it. All the drama in her life meant nothing in front of that little girl. Grace would rule the world, and Angie wanted to watch it happen. It was a good thing her new job wouldn't take her too far away.

'Are you staying?' Reese asked.

'For as long as you want.'

Reese reached her hand to Angie, and they sat there for a while. Angie watched the most beautiful girl in the world dream about her future, and she planned to be there for every special moment.

Chapter 24

For most of his waking hours, Angie consumed Nick's thoughts. She even stepped into his dreams as a beautiful figure who stood before him with a blinding white light behind her. She was untouchable. No matter how hard he tried to tell how he felt about her, his mouth would never open. Eventually, she walked away from him into the darkness of his dream space.

The days leading up to Christmas should have been as happy and bright as they were when he and Angie were in each other's good graces. But that wasn't the case anymore, at least from her perspective.

Each time a sliver of a memory of her crept into his mind, Nick opened his drawer at work concealing the gift she had wrapped for him. It was the only physical memory of Angie's existence in his life. Without returning any of his texts, it was as if she were one of the ghosts of Christmas past. Eventually, he stopped trying to contact her.

Nick lifted the small gift in his hands. Angie had tied a bow around the box, and the ends were no longer springy and curled but limp and sad. He turned it over in his hands as he went over all the things that went wrong between them. Soon enough, it wouldn't matter. After Christmas, the meaning he wanted to convey from the gift would be lost.

Quinn appeared in the doorway. 'I need to speak with you.'

Without waiting for a response, he walked in the direction of his office.

Nick swiveled his chair to face the window. He needed a minute before talking to his father. Outside, thick white clouds filled the sky. If only it would snow, maybe then Nick could feel something other than sadness during this time of year. He inhaled a few deep breaths before peeling himself off his chair. He supposed dragging out the meeting wasn't going to make his father any less irritable to deal with.

When Nick reached the hallway, Maya waved him over.

'I'm about to go in with him,' Nick said.

'This will only take a second,' Maya said.

Nick shrugged and waved a hand for her to continue. Anything to delay the inevitable.

'I've asked Angie to attend the press conference.'

A sinking feeling of dread pooled in his gut. He and his father were going to the press conference. Angie would think it was a set-up. He wasn't sure if he was ready to see her so upset with him again. 'She doesn't need to be there.'

A sly grin crossed her lips. 'This entire event was her idea. She should be a part of it.'

Maya was right, but Nick never intended on forcing Angie to come. He had hoped she would come with him on her own, but that was before their relationship suffered from his father's lies.

'I thought it would be a nice way for you two to make up,' Maya said.

'I don't think that's what she wants.'

'It's Christmas. Everyone wants to feel good about their relationships this time of year. This could be your opportunity to tell her everything.'

'I already did that.'

'You haven't really,' she said. 'You've tried to tell her the same

223

things. Then she saw Ivy here. At least with this, you can plan what you're going to say. Show her how you feel.'

'At a press conference?'

'Why not? I can't force you two together outside of this event if she no longer works here. This is your last chance.'

'Angie made it clear she didn't want to speak with me again. I'm not going to force her into an uncomfortable situation.'

'Nick, you're not the type to give up on someone so easily. Especially someone this important.'

'This important?'

'Do you need me to say it aloud? You love her. Keep up, Nick.'

Love. Nick had thought he'd loved Molly, but he never felt this strongly about someone else before. In his past, he let go of his other girlfriends when he wasn't around for them. But with Angie, Nick had been available for her. Without her around, he was a mess.

'You're telling me you don't love her?'

'I didn't say that,' he said.

'Step one is admitting it to yourself.' Maya lifted her eyes to the ceiling and shook her head. 'No one thinks about love. It smacks into you like a train.' She clapped her hands together for emphasis, startling Carrie sipping from her coffee.

Maya's assistant tossed her an annoyed look as she mopped up the few spots from her desk with a napkin.

'I have a good feeling about this,' Maya said, turning back to Nick.

'Nick!' Quinn called from his office.

Nick winced. 'I'll let you know.'

'Don't think about it too much.' Her stern expression haunted him as he walked toward his father's office. She was counting on him to do the right thing. But other than what he had tried with Angie, what else could he do to convince her of his feelings?

'Close the door,' Quinn said the moment Nick arrived.

This was his opportunity for answers, but he couldn't get the idea of seeing Angie out of his mind. Would she think he had tricked her or was it best to leave it alone?

'Jared informed me that Ivy is seeing someone else. It's sad when your son doesn't even confide in you about something so important.'

'Her life isn't my business, and I doubt it's yours either.'

'It's because you were having a fling with that other woman.'

'It wasn't a fling. I care about her.' His chest filled with an emptiness he had only experienced when he was with Angie. He did still care about her, and he had to know if she felt the same too.

Quinn let out a grunt and shook his head. 'How can you care for her that much when you barely know her?'

'I know enough. I wanted to get to know her even more before you interfered.'

'I did what was best for you.'

'Best for me?' It was Nick's turn to scoff. 'You set up a scheme to get Ivy and me together to work on a development. This was never about a real relationship for you.'

Quinn blinked, caught in his own lie. He must not have expected Ivy to confide in Nick. Well, it was time to put him in his place. Quinn's arrogance only went so far with Nick. If they were going to work together long-term, he had to prove he wasn't a pushover.

'Why did you need me involved anyway?' Nick asked.

Quinn walked over to the windows and peered outside. Nick waited. It was all he could do until his father decided to speak.

When he finally spoke, his voice was low and filled with emotion. More than Nick had heard in a long time. 'I thought the project would entice you to stick around for the long haul.'

'I'm not leaving, Dad. Why did you think that?'

'David has been around a lot lately. You and I have been butting heads as well. I thought with Angie's influence you would leave too.'

'Dad, I'm not David. I like my job. You're difficult to work with at times, but I'm not leaving.'

225

Quinn swallowed and turned to him. 'You mean that?'

'Of course. But I don't want to butt heads with you. We were working together fine before you introduced me to Ivy. I appreciate her as a family friend, and that's all.'

Quinn shoved his hands in his pockets and stared at Nick as if he didn't believe him.

Nick sighed. 'As much as I love David, I'm not him. He never wanted this job. I do. It took me a while to realize it, but you need to trust me. No more schemes to keep me around.'

Quinn cleared his throat. Nick had never seen him so nervous. 'I know I work a lot. But it's a trait my father pushed for me. You're a great asset to the company with the way you handle the business, but it wouldn't hurt to see you settle with someone who thinks the same way.'

How could Dad care so much about Nick starting a life with Ivy, when he couldn't even bother to make peace with his eldest son and his family? He had two amazing grandsons and the kindest daughter-in-law. His judgment was off, and Nick was tired of it.

'There's an entire family on David's side. You could always make up with them.'

'This again?' Quinn let out a sardonic laugh. 'It's not happening.'

For a moment, Nick thought he had sliced through his father's rough exterior. He had what he wanted now, a promise from Nick he was going to stay. But he couldn't have all of Nick. Not when he treated David, Theresa, and the boys as outcasts.

'You can't have it all. I'm going to stay here, but you're never going to feel fulfilled unless you forgive David for living his own life. There's nothing wrong with that, and you're punishing his family for your own stubbornness.'

'Nick—'

'No,' Nick interrupted. 'You have the opportunity to make things right, and you're standing here in your ivory tower letting life pass you by.'

'It's too late anyway,' Quinn said, the tops of his ears reddening.

It reminded Nick of the last time he saw David and Quinn in the same room. The blowout had taken place in the office, after hours, and they all ended up changed.

'It's never too late.'

'You sound like David,' Quinn said. For once, his son's name didn't come out of his mouth like a curse.

'I have to go,' Nick said, realizing what he had to do. He had to make it right with Angie, the way his father would never do with David. When you cared about someone, you tried as hard as you could to keep them in your life. Nick understood her feelings about what he had done and how he should have been honest with her from the start.

Nick stormed down the hallway toward Maya's desk. 'I'll be there, tomorrow.'

Maya grinned at Nick. 'I knew you'd change your mind. You do love her.'

'Why do you care about this so much anyway? I thought you two weren't friends.'

'People change,' Maya said.

Anyone could change. Nick only wished his dad had received that memo. He had tried to get his father to see his mistakes with David, but he wasn't as enlightened as Maya. The best he could do was hope.

***

The next morning, Nick woke with a renewed sense of purpose. During his run with Charlie, she clung to his side as if giving him the confidence to push through his apology to Angie. Since it was Christmas Eve, the only meeting he had today was the press conference. He wasn't going to the office at all. He dressed in slacks and an olive-green sweater. It was a mix of professional and holiday attire. He wanted to look good for Angie and prove to her that he was serious about them. Butterflies flitted around his stomach, but he was more excited than nervous. His plan to get her back had to work. Opening himself up to her was a strange feeling, but he hoped it would pay off.

The conference would take place at a smaller events space across the street to the homeless shelter. When Nick reached the parking lot outside the shelter, he couldn't spot Angie's car. He wanted to wait for her, but also wasn't sure if she wanted to see him right away. No doubt she'd know he was coming to the press conference and would already regret her choice to be there.

Instead of forcing his side of the story again, he walked inside and hoped that inspiration would strike when he saw her.

A flash of movement caught his eye. Outside, Angie's grandparents' car pulled into the parking lot, and Nick's heart raced. Angie parked in the closest spot to the exit and stepped out.

He watched her cross the lot, and his breathing slowed. It had only been a few days since he saw her, but he realized at that moment how much he missed her. He couldn't let her go that easy. She had changed him, and he would never be the same.

Nick inhaled sharply, prepared to take on the challenge to fight for love.

Chapter 25

The morning of the press conference at the shelter, Angie dressed in one of her better planning outfits. Slipping on the black skirt and dress jacket over a white button-down shirt transported her back to her job in California. Over the last few weeks, she'd appreciated going to work at the mall dressing the way she wanted. She wasn't sure what was expected of her at the conference since Maya had been vague on the details. But if the camera panned in her direction, she wanted to look her best.

After meeting little Grace, Angie's excitement for the holidays had returned. She couldn't wait to get to the stores to buy more gifts for the new baby. She wasn't ready to go back to the mall yet, but she hoped after Christmas there were enough sales at other local shops that she could spoil her niece.

In the time Angie visited the hospital, Grace opened her eyes, cried, and filled Angie with the most incredible happiness. The highlight of her time was watching Jeremy figure out how to move the newborn while changing her diaper. Reese took many pictures, Angie assumed for blackmail. With the incision from the C-section, Reese couldn't move from the bed easily, and the nurses recommended they stay in the hospital through Christmas.

After the conference, Angie planned to head over there for

another visit. She was proud to be one of the few guests allowed at the hospital other than blood relatives.

When Angie came out of the guest room ready for the day, Maria waved her into the kitchen.

'You look great, Angela,' Maria said.

'Thank you. I'm a little nervous.'

'You shouldn't be,' Maria said. 'You did a wonderful thing. You should feel proud of your accomplishments.'

Angie was proud of making money for the shelter, but she was more nervous about seeing Nick. Ivy would probably be there by his side, making the situation even more awkward than the almost run-in at Nick's office. 'I hope it doesn't take too long.'

'Is Nick going?'

'I think so,' Angie said quickly, avoiding her Mom's watchful eyes. Any flicker of emotion would elicit a flurry of questions her way. 'I'm sure all the corporate people are. Well, at least his father.'

'That man who yelled at you? He deserves a talking to.'

Angie touched her mom's shoulder. 'Not by you.'

Maria waved her hands in the air as if dispelling steam from a boiling pot of water. 'Well, don't let that man lessen anything you've done for those people. He probably has that amount of money in his wallet, while they would appreciate it and put it to good use.'

Angie had no idea what Mr Bower's finances were like, but she knew she couldn't get into it with her mom, or she'd be there all day. 'I need to go. Love you.'

'Be sure to be back here for three,' Maria said. 'Nonno will probably pass out in the chair before dinner if we do it any later. You'd think he believed in Santa Claus from the early hour they go to bed.'

Angie's mouth fell open. 'There's no Santa?'

Maria shook her head, *tsk*ing her daughter. 'Bye, Angela.'

Outside, Angie shivered and zipped her coat to the top. The temperatures were supposed to drop significantly tonight. She still held out hope for a white Christmas. It was the one thing she wanted to make up for the most dramatic Christmas season of her life.

***

Downtown, the traffic was a mess. As much as Angie wanted to avoid the mall, it was the quickest route to the conference. She supposed it was a good thing there wasn't snow in the forecast to cause any accidents on the roads. The shelter was on the corner of the street next to a small lot. She parked across the street from the warehouse, which had been converted to a shelter almost a decade ago. Angie had passed the crumbling brick building many times in her visit without knowing what it represented for Hazel.

Since she had only seen Nick in David's truck, she had no idea if his car was there or not. But it was only a matter of time before she saw him. Through the front door of the building, Angie played with the hem of her jacket while she sauntered down a long hallway. She wasn't sure what to expect, but she followed the sounds of chattering people inside a room at the end.

There were already more than a dozen people inside the room. At the back corner there was a small stage with a blue curtain behind it. The podium and microphone sat in front of it. Official-looking men in suits stood toward the corner of the room, speaking to who she assumed were journalists.

A breath stole from Angie's chest when she spotted Nick and his father. Nick was the only one not in a suit, and he looked great as usual. Her insides quivered. At least she had dressed the part. She took off her jacket and folded it over a nearby folding chair.

As if he had a radar for her, Nick caught her eye and gave her a quick smile while continuing to speak to the journalist. He had work to do today. She understood that more than most. She scanned the room again and realized Ivy wasn't there. At least that was one small miracle.

Angie walked toward the table of coffee and bagels. She wasn't in the mood to eat, but she needed to do something with her hands. Ginger was there, spreading cream cheese on a bagel. Angie grabbed a cup to fill with coffee from the carafe. 'Morning.'

'Hi, Angie. It's good to see you. Maya told me about your resignation.'

'I got another job,' she said.

'That's great. We're going to miss you,' Ginger said, biting into her bagel. 'Hey, Nick.'

Angie stiffened and her entire body broke out in a wave of goose bumps as she turned to Nick. Ginger abandoned her by walking away with her breakfast toward the journalists.

'Hi, Angie,' Nick said. 'Thanks for coming.'

His voice struck her. Their nearness reminded her of their kiss and all the times they walked together hand-in-hand.

'No problem.' She inhaled sharply. Nick's scent overwhelmed her and brought back all the memories of their time together.

'Are you ready for this?' he asked.

Angie nodded. 'It's for a worthy cause.'

'I meant the speech,' he said.

Her hands tightened around the cup. 'I have to give a speech?'

Nick's lips quirked into a smile. 'No, I was trying to make a joke. To lighten the mood.'

She breathed a relieved sigh. 'Very funny.'

Nick pressed his lips together.

'What?' she asked.

'I've never seen you so nervous before.'

'I'm an event planner, remember? I don't like to be the center of attention.'

'I hope you didn't mind Maya calling you. I wouldn't have forced you to come if you didn't want to. She thought you should be here to see what you have done for all those people.'

'Maya set this up?' Angie couldn't believe Maya was still messing with her after all these years. As much as she wanted to be mad at her high school rival, Nick standing in front of her proved that her feelings hadn't gone away. Not even a little bit. But though she had told him she wanted to move on, she wondered if there was still any hope for them.

'I'm glad she called you,' he said.

Swirling hope surged through her. 'You are?'

'Mr Bower,' a tinkling woman's voice said from behind Nick. She wore a red and green sweater with dancing reindeer across the chest. 'Ms Martinelli. I'm so glad you're both here. I'm Katherine Banks. It's such a pleasure to meet you in person.' She was younger than Angie expected from their phone call, maybe in her late thirties. Curly brown hair stuck out from all angles around her loosely tied bun. Pink lipstick stained her smiling lips. This woman had dedicated her life to these people, and Angie was starstruck.

Angie felt the urge to talk to Nick more, but that wasn't what they were there for. 'I'm thrilled to have you here today,' Katherine said. 'We're so thankful for your support.'

'She's an excellent wrapper too,' Nick said. 'I used her services for my own gift.'

Angie recalled the small box she wrapped for him. At first, she'd thought it was for his mother or sister-in-law. But it was the perfect size for a bracelet or necklace for Ivy. Her smile wavered, but she was able to hold onto it for the rest of the conversation. It wasn't Katherine's fault that there was awkwardness between her and Nick.

'We're going to do it again next year,' Nick said. 'We would like to make this an annual event. We can branch out to the soup kitchen as well, as you have contacts there as we discussed.'

Angie tilted her head regarding him. She supposed making the wrapping station a yearly event made sense, but she had no idea of the planning Nick had done behind the scenes.

Katherine spoke animatedly to him about her work and the possibilities of a partnership.

Angie was painfully aware of his closeness. In their time

233

together, she hadn't seen Nick fully 'on' when it came to his job. He was as charismatic around Katherine as he had been the entire time she knew him. His smile was infectious, and with each passing minute, she returned to the conversation, unable to tear her eyes away from him.

Angie sensed the same heaviness in the air hovering over Nick as well. They hadn't finished their conversation, and she wondered if Nick would say he missed her or that he had moved on with Ivy. Imagining them together made Angie want to run out of the room and never look back. It was too hard, and she had quit for a reason. Maya had played one last trick on her, and she wasn't going to stay to let it play out longer than necessary.

Angie's feelings for Nick couldn't matter anymore if Ivy was involved. But if she wasn't, then it was Angie holding herself back. She wanted to forgive him, but most of all, push past her issues. Reese's insistence on Nick's betrayal made Angie believe she was falling into another trap with a guy too soon for her own good.

Katherine touched Nick's arm before pointing to the stage. 'I think we're getting started. Excuse me.'

Nick stepped closer to Angie. He opened his mouth to speak, but his father called him over. He tossed a glance at his dad and then back to Angie. 'I want to talk to you after this. Do you have time?'

'Sure,' she croaked out.

He brushed his hand over her arm before walking toward the stage.

Katherine and two other older men in suits flanked Nick and Mr Bower on either side. The men held the ceremonial check between them. Nick locked eyes with Angie and smiled. The camera people rushed in front of the stage and started taking pictures. Flashes of light lit up their faces. After a few moments, Nick's dad moved behind the podium.

'Ladies and gentlemen, it's an honor to be here today.' While he spoke, there was no sign of the man who had approached Angie at the information booth. He was professional and charming. Those were the touchstone qualities of a businessman. But in that, she saw a stark difference between Nick and his father. Nick's smile was sincere. He and Angie worked hard for the homeless shelter with the wrapping station and Nick helping Hazel find a place to get clean and warm. Nick might not be like his father, but Angie clamped onto her trust issues.

'I wanted to introduce my son, Nick Bower, who spearheaded this entire event,' Mr Bower said, clapping a hand on Nick's back.

Those in the room applauded for him as he took the podium. 'Thank you, everyone.' As the clapping died down, Nick took a breath and spoke into the microphone. 'Our local mall is a cornerstone of our community. We're constantly searching for ways to repay the people who support us. This year, a fine member of our community worked tirelessly to give as much as she could to the local homeless shelter. Her name is Angie Martinelli.'

Angie's breath hitched as everyone in the room turned to face her. But she only had eyes for Nick. He smiled and waved her toward him. Several of the journalists moved aside to let her by. She didn't want to be on camera, but for some reason, she knew with Nick by her side she would be fine.

Angie stepped up to the stage and stood next to Nick. While he spoke into the microphone, he didn't look at the cameras once.

'Angie has made me realize that this season isn't all about retail shopping. It's about experiences with those you love.'

He paused after the word love and Angie's stomach fluttered.

'And helping those who need it most,' he finished. 'I'm honored to know this incredible woman and I, for one, can't wait to see what she does next.'

The room erupted in applause, and Angie blinked, remembering she was on camera. She smiled, hoping it didn't look as shaky as it felt. The man next to her shoved the check in her hands while Nick took the other end. They stepped back, allowing Angie to stand close to Nick while the camera flashes filled her vision.

'Keep your eyes open and look above the camera,' Nick said under his breath.

With his voice, Angie relaxed. She no longer needed to force a smile as his presence and kind words overwhelmed her.

When Nick handed over the check to Katherine, a swell of pride moved Angie to tears. Katherine was close as well, and they laughed when they saw how emotional they were.

But Nick only had eyes for Angie, and along with her embarrassment over crying, her cheeks burned as well.

An overwhelming urge to flee the room took over, and once the cameras were off her, she stepped away from the stage and into the hallway. She glanced into the room, and it seemed as if no one missed her. They focused on Katherine, Nick, and Mr Bower.

'Angie.'

She turned to see Hazel shuffling over to her. She wore a jacket, and her backpack slung over her shoulder. Angie guessed it was time for her to head out for the day. She pulled on her own coat.

'I was hoping I would see you here. How lucky for me,' Hazel said.

'We delivered the check from the wrapping station,' Angie said. 'I was heading out to visit my friend in the hospital.'

'Did she have her baby?' Hazel asked.

'She did,' Angie said, grinning. 'A girl.'

'That's lovely.'

Nick entered the hallway and stopped abruptly when he saw the two of them talking. His eyes were wild at first and then filled with relief when they landed on Angie. She couldn't help wondering if he thought she had left without speaking to him. His fingers curled over his jacket slung over his arm.

'There are the two lovebirds.' Hazel preened at them. 'Angie, you know Nick talks about you a lot.'

Even though Nick grimaced, he looked more handsome than ever. Probably because Angie couldn't have him. 'Hi, Hazel.'

'Good morning, Nick.'

'Angie,' he said. 'I thought we could continue our conversation?'

'I'll leave you to it,' Hazel said, heading for the back door.

'I'm on my way to visit Reese and the baby.' At least she would have an out if she needed one.

They headed for the front door together. There was no one else in the hallway to interrupt them from this conversation.

'I wanted to ask about you quitting,' Nick said, holding the front door for her. The frigid air swirled around her, and she tightened her jacket over her chest. 'I hope it wasn't because of what happened between us.'

'I got a job offer.'

'That's great,' he said. The ends of his words clipped as if he were holding back. 'So, you're leaving?'

Angie nodded. She remained guarded, keeping the information to herself and protecting her heart. Without knowing for certain what their relationship meant, she couldn't open herself up again just yet.

'I wanted to tell you how sorry I am about what happened. I never intended to lie to you.'

She had to know. 'What about Ivy?'

'Me and Ivy, we're friends. You, Angie, are the most important person to me.'

Nick told his truth so many times. Now she was the only person standing in their way.

'It seems like I'm too late though,' he said.

Angie released a breath.

'I understand,' Nick said, shoving his hands into his jacket pockets. 'Merry Christmas, Angie.'

He walked toward the lot, but her feet froze against the concrete. He got into his car. A sleek gray Lexus.

Angie looked up at the sky filled with thick clouds. She waited for a sign. Her heart tugged in his direction while her practical mind kept her in place. Could she love again so soon? Or were they never meant to be?

It wasn't until he drove away that she could finally move toward an uncertain future where her heart was as empty as it was when she had arrived home a month ago.

Chapter 26

Nick gave Angie the opportunity to forgive him, yet she didn't. As he walked to his car, his feet were like bricks of ice. He kept a slow pace, expecting to hear Angie calling out to come back to talk to him. They could go out for coffee or lunch and dig into the possibility of a future between them.

But she didn't.

There was also her new job. It seemed as if she'd forgiven him enough to say hello to each other if they happened to pass on the street. He still couldn't believe it was all over for them. And this was how they ended their holiday season after getting so close over the last few weeks.

The day stretched out before him. Charlie was already with Mrs Watson until later that night, and Nick wasn't going to go home to stare at the tree he and Angie decorated together. He deserved to feel terrible about the events between them, but he wasn't going to wallow in it.

There was also the matter of returning the ornaments. He supposed he could contact Angie after the holiday with that as an excuse to check in. If she was already off to her new job, he supposed he could drop them off on the porch. A sick feeling welled in his stomach at the idea of slinking away from contact with her family. That wasn't like him. He wasn't sure what she had told them, but at the very least he owed them a thank you for allowing him to share the season with them.

As he drove from the lot, he spotted Angie outside the shelter. The light was red, so he stopped almost in front of her. She stared off into the sky as if she were puzzling out the meaning of life. She had no idea he was watching her, and when the light turned green, he slowly drove away.

Nick wasn't proud enough to think he had something to do with her somber expression, but it gave him a little hope that Angie wasn't as over him as much as she wanted to appear.

***

Other than needing to pick up supplies to wrap gifts, Nick wanted to be at the mall. It was the one place he could melt into the crowd and mull over his thoughts. He wasn't going to bother David with his problems so early in the day. They had a meal to prepare for tonight and Nick didn't want to get in the way of their holiday celebrations. No doubt Theresa would want to dig into what happened between him and Angie over dinner anyway.

The mall closed early due to Christmas Eve and wouldn't open again until the day after Christmas. He couldn't help moving toward the information booth more than once. He wasn't sure why he thought Angie would pop up there, but it was as if she left an imprint on the place and him.

Nick wondered if he would ever be able to come down to this place and not think of her. She'd left enough of an impression on his life that he wasn't sure if that were possible. He wished he would have thought about gift shopping sooner. Then, he could have come to the wrapping booth and spent even more time with Angie, instead of the one special gift.

When Nick finished shopping, he went to the apartment, unable to look at the tree for more than a few seconds. He set up his own wrapping station on the dining room table with his back facing the tree. Thinking of his family's expressions while they opened his gifts distracted him enough to get him through the next few hours.

Every year, Nick tossed his gifts into bags with tissue paper, but it seemed a disservice to his family to do that this year. With each gift, he put the same love and care into the folds of the paper that Angie had. His heart had hardened to the fact that he had lost her for good, but at least she still influenced him. He would never regret meeting her and hoped that he had become a person worth loving for all of his faults.

Even with all the decorations, music, and lights surrounding him as he and Charlie left the building, his mood was as dark as the night sky. He wasn't sure a flurry of snow would help either, but it couldn't make things worse.

***

Seconds after Nick rang the doorbell at David's house, the door flung open. The boys – clad in their matching red and white Christmas sweaters – wrapped their arms around Charlie's midsection. She kissed them to a chorus of 'gross' and 'eww' before she bounded into the house.

'Merry Christmas to you too,' Nick deadpanned to the boys as they ran off.

'We're in here,' Theresa called from the kitchen.

David walked into the living room, rubbing his hands under a towel while giving a pointed glance at the gifts. 'Wow. You went all out.'

'I learned a lot this year.'

'Seems like it,' David said.

Nick placed the gifts under the tree. It was smaller than the one Angie picked out, but all the homemade ornaments made from yarn and sticks made it that much more special.

'Merry Christmas,' David said, drawing Nick into a hug. His sweater was the same as the boys. Every year since the boys were born, the family had matching outfits. It was corny in the best way possible.

'You too,' Nick said, clapping his hand against his brother's back.

'Theresa is requesting you cut the Christmas ham,' David said.

'She's requesting?'

David chuckled, holding up two bandaged fingers. 'My hands have been through enough this week with new projects. How about you help me out a little?'

'Only because it's Christmas.'

Theresa and David outdid themselves. Nick noticed the change in furniture in the dining room. The table from the mall held the platter of ham, with steaming vegetables in bowls, and home-made bread among mouth-watering sides. The scent of the food was enough to calm his rolling stomach. The food and family reminded him of a simpler time in his past and wished his parents could complete the picture in his mind.

'It looks better with some use,' David said when Nick asked about it.

'How did the press conference go this morning?' Theresa asked Nick as everyone sat down.

Nick took his place next to the ham and grabbed the carving knives. 'Did you watch it?'

'We did,' Theresa said. 'You and Angie looked great together.'

Nick cut a look at his brother. 'That's not exactly how it is anymore.' Nick concentrated on his task hoping he wouldn't have to answer too many more questions right away.

Someone knocked at the front door. David looked around the table. 'Who could that be?'

Theresa stared at her plate. 'Why don't you go and see?'

David narrowed his eyes at her, but she said nothing. They were at a standoff until a knock sounded again.

'Or I'll get it,' Theresa said, getting up from her chair. She muttered something to herself that David somehow heard and he responded with his own mutterings as he rushed after her.

'Is it Santa?' Evan asked.

'He comes down the chimney,' James said.

Charlie barked from under the table and started pacing around the room before she fled toward the door.

'You know Santa doesn't appear to kids,' Nick said.

'Who's at the door then, Uncle Nick?' James asked.

Nick turned in his seat. Everyone was with their families tonight. The only person missing from the table was Angie. Nick had intended on being with her for at least one holiday feast. Had she wanted to make a final grand entrance before telling him she was going to stay in Brookside to be with him? He shoved the chair away and flew into the other room.

In his heart, he knew it was too good to be true. Nick's ears pricked to hear his parents' voices in the hallway.

'Grammy!' Evan said, bouncing up and down.

Nick's mother appeared in the doorway. A glittery hair piece tied back one side of her hair, exposing the collar of her white turtleneck.

David and Quinn stood near each other but didn't speak. Any time he saw his father and David, it never ended up well. His father held wrapped packages in his arms. He must have found the wrapping paper fascinating because he didn't look at David once.

The boys rushed over and hugged Nick's mother. Nick didn't recall the last time he'd seen his mom with the boys. It should have surprised him more to see her there on Christmas Eve when they hadn't invited her. Or had they?

Theresa kissed his mom on the cheek. 'Thank you for coming, Yvette. Merry Christmas.' Then they whispered to each other low enough that Nick didn't hear a word.

He started to suspect this wasn't as much of a surprise as he'd initially thought.

243

Quinn stood by the door as if he was ready to flee at a moment's notice.

Charlie blocked the exit, panting and expecting a scratch from the newcomer. Quinn hadn't come to his apartment since Charlie was a puppy.

'What are you doing here?' Nick asked.

David folded his arms over his chest. 'Funny, I asked him the same thing. I still have yet to get an answer.'

Usually, Quinn had the upper hand. But in David's home, the tables had turned. He wasn't going to allow any of the drama to unfold in his house on a holiday.

Nick stood next to his brother, showing his loyalty. After the mess he had stirred up with Angie – and he'd barely apologized for it – Nick wasn't sure if he was ready to forgive their father yet. Showing up didn't automatically excuse everything he had ever done to David.

'Someone reminded me that I'm the only one who can make things right with our family,' Quinn said, glancing at Nick.

David's shoulders slumped. 'You want to make things right? What does that mean, Dad?'

Quinn cleared his throat. 'I've missed a lot. I'm sorry it took me so long to realize. I want to see my grandkids. Go to soccer games. Spend holidays together. This season isn't quite right without it.'

Quinn's gaze fell to the boys, and his eyes widened. Nick could have sworn they started to tear up too.

'Boys,' David said, clearing his throat and emotion from his voice. 'This is your grandfather.'

James and Evan glanced at each other before walking toward Quinn.

'Are those presents for us?' Evan asked.

Yvette laughed, and Quinn blinked a few times before he smiled.

'Of course,' Quinn said, squatting in front of the boys. 'But how about we eat first? Your Grammy told me all about your mom's cooking.'

Theresa wrung her hands together, while David stood stock-still next to her. It wasn't the picture-perfect family reunion, but it was enough for now.

'Let's eat before it gets cold,' Theresa said, leading everyone into the dining room.

'Nick, help me with these chairs?' David asked.

Nick followed him to the front closet. David pulled two folding chairs from behind the thick coats.

'Did you set this up?' David asked, whirling on Nick. Redness lined his eyes. David had always been the more emotional brother. But it was much more than that. Their father had taken the first step toward repairing their relationship. It was more than any of them expected.

'No,' Nick said.

'I knew it was Theresa. I mean, I suspected, but I had to ask.'

'Why would she do that?'

'She's been talking to Mom on the phone a lot. Since the discussion with Dad at the mall, she's been pushing me to talk to him. I think she took the initiative this time.'

'Are you okay with this?'

'Do I have a choice?'

'You can kick him out. No one would blame you.'

David shook his head. 'The kids need both grandparents. This will be good for everyone. I'll handle Dad.'

'Do you think he's willing to change?'

'He wouldn't be here if he wasn't. He said someone told him to make things right. It's a Christmas miracle if I ever asked for one.'

They went into the dining room. Theresa had already set up two more place settings. Yvette and Quinn were on either side of the kids, and Nick's dad seemed entranced by James' story about how he set traps for Santa around the house.

The conversation bordered on polite, and Quinn didn't talk much, but it was a start. Everyone in the same room was the biggest step forward their family had taken in a long time.

Quinn's smile widened even more after dessert when the kids opened their one Christmas Eve gift. It didn't surprise Nick that they went for his mom's gift. They were bigger than the toys Nick purchased for them. And her wrapping skills far surpassed his. In each of the boxes were a new set of Christmas-themed pajamas, a movie, and popcorn. The boys argued which movie to watch that night and begged Theresa to allow them one more snack.

David set the limits of one popcorn package to share and refereed three rounds of Rock, Paper, Scissors to determine which movie to watch.

Nick yawned, wanting to get home. The day had exhausted him enough that he wasn't sure he could last an entire movie. He doubted the boys would either, but Christmas Eve was special for David and his family. His sulking about Angie would ruin it.

'I should go,' Nick said, standing from the couch.

Yvette headed outside, and Theresa hugged him before helping the boys to their room to change into their elf pajamas before the movie.

Quinn sat comfortably in the reclining chair, grinning wider than Nick had seen in a long time. He hoped the change in heart from his father would bring about a new chapter in their family. Nick wished he could have been part of the change, but he was happy David had someone so special in his life to push for more. He said goodbye to his family before clicking his tongue for Charlie. She peeled herself off the floor and trotted over to him with heavy feet and sleepy eyes.

Outside, Nick spotted his mother on the front stoop. She stared upward at the clear night sky, her expression hopeful. She had a lot to hope for since their family was on their way to starting over again.

'Good night,' Nick said.

Yvette shivered and turned to him. 'Goodnight, Nicholas.' She kissed his cheek. 'I'll see you tomorrow for dinner?'

'Yes,' he said.

'You know, Theresa did all this tonight.'

'We figured that,' Nick said. 'You two are sneaky.'

'Your father is stubborn,' she said with a smile. 'I guess even though it took a while, everything fell into place.'

On the way to his car, a realization struck him. The way his mother looked at the sky as if it held a secret Nick couldn't quite figure out. Had Nick mistaken the final look from Angie? He thought her staring at the sky meant she didn't want to see him, but what if it was the opposite? Did she want him to come back for *her*? He could have gone to her and demanded she listen to what was inside his heart. Running away from relationships when they were hard wasn't going to get him anywhere. Angie had challenged him from the start, and she had to know everything he felt for her before she made her final decision.

Nick wasn't sure where her future headed, but he would work with it if she wanted to be together.

If David could forgive his father, was it a stretch for Nick to believe that Angie could do the same? There wasn't history as there was between his family members, but neither of them could deny their connection. If it couldn't happen around Christmas, then when could it?

Hope swelled within him as he drove home that night. It was too late to see her tonight, but was there one more Christmas miracle in the world for him?

Chapter 27

Armed with three packages balanced in her hands, Angie walked into the hospital for the third time that week. After a massively carb-loaded dinner from the night before and an equally heavy breakfast, she could have slept for days. After all the arrangements for the holiday, Reese and Jeremy made it seem a waste not to let them have a semblance of a Christmas. Their gifts were at home, and Reese refused to bring their things to the hospital when they were leaving in a few days. Instead, Angie brought her gifts for the Tans in the hope that she could jump-start her own holiday cheer.

Meeting Nick yesterday hadn't gone the way she had wanted. Their unfinished business hovered over her head like the cloud-filled sky. She had judged him too harshly. He had apologized and explained his side of the story. It was everything she needed to forgive him, but still held back. She couldn't forget how kind he was to Hazel, how loving of a relationship he had with his brother, and what a good dog-dad he was to Charlie. He wasn't a cruel person who hid secrets from her. Nick had made a mistake.

Even more, she had made the biggest one by not forgiving him. Nick was going to do a lot of good for the community, and

248

it was because of her idea. He never claimed it as his own, yet Angie couldn't get over it. What was wrong with her? Maybe she didn't deserve him at all.

When Angie walked into Reese's hospital room, Grace and Jeremy were missing.

'I can come back if you want to sleep,' Angie said, placing the gifts on the small table.

'No,' Reese said, wincing as she adjusted herself in the bed. Angie wished she could take away her friend's pain. 'Are those all for me?'

'One of them.'

Reese frowned, and Angie laughed. At least Reese hadn't lost her sense of humor through her ordeal. Dark bags sagged under her eyes, and Angie could tell she hadn't slept much. 'Where is Jer?'

'At a bathing class with Grace,' Reese said. 'I needed a little break.'

'From Grace?'

'No way – from Jer. He's amazing, but he's more neurotic than me. He's making me nuts checking in on her every few seconds.'

As the door to the room opened again, Angie covered a laugh with her fist.

Jeremy wheeled the portable crib into the room. 'Merry Christmas, Angie.'

'You too,' Angie said, craning her neck to see Grace. 'Good swaddle.'

Jeremy puffed out his chest proudly.

'Don't say it—'

'I'm the Swaddle King,' Jeremy said, cutting off Reese.

'You've done it now,' Reese said.

'I mean, Gracie doesn't move at all,' Jeremy tried to explain. 'It's textbook.'

Reese groaned and leaned against her pillows. Her eyes drifted closed before snapping open again.

Angie made her way over to Grace and watched her sleep. Soon enough, Reese faded out.

Jeremy walked over. 'I'm going to bring her the nursery for a bit.'

When he left, Angie tried to be as quiet as possible to let her friend sleep. Once Jeremy returned, she'd make her way home to let them relax together.

Her phone pinged from her bag, and she dug through to silence it. Reese didn't stir, but Angie wasn't going to give her a reason to wake up.

Angie, I need to see you.

The text from Nick sent a whoosh of air out of her.

I know it's Christmas, but can we meet for a few minutes?

'Don't leave him hanging,' Reese said.

Angie glanced at her friend. 'What are you talking about?'

'I know it's Nick. You always get that goofy grin on your face. As much as you pretend you don't want to be with him, I know the truth. I see through you.'

Angie hated being that transparent, but Reese spoke the truth.

'I'm starting to believe what he said was the truth.'

'I know it is,' Angie said. 'But can I do this again? You were the one who said I should take time to myself.'

'If you hadn't met him, I think you should have. But with him insisting there was nothing between Ivy and him, I believe him. You should too.'

'But Brett—'

'Brett never told you the truth. That snake put the blame on you. He's off with his fiancée without a brain cell of his caring enough to apologize. He threw money at you to leave.'

Angie sniffed as the corners of her vision blurred.

'He was a horrible man. But Nick isn't. I told you I'm clairvoyant.'

Angie choked out a sound between a sob and laugh.

'I need to get some sleep anyway. Did you know that these amazing nurses come home with you? Trust me, I asked.'

250

Angie glanced at her phone before typing the words spoken from her heart.

When and where?

***

Twenty minutes later, Angie arrived at the park near the mall. It was the same place where she and Nick had walked Charlie the day she'd spotted them at the café. Memories rushed over her, but she wanted to hear what he had to say before she allowed her hopes to soar. She spotted both Nick and Charlie by the large fountain closer to the center of the park. They were the only ones there since most people were at home spending time with their families. That had been her plan, but she couldn't pass up the need to know what he wanted.

Nick turned to her, and a breath stole from her lips. The temperatures had dropped from that morning as the clouds hid the sun from view.

Charlie's leash slipped from his grasp, and she bounded over to her. Angie grabbed onto the end of it and allowed Charlie to shower her with kisses. Her heart swelled with happiness. But when she met Nick's eyes, her stomach sunk. His serious expression wasn't what she expected.

'The mall isn't the same without you,' he said. 'Are you sure you can't stay longer?'

'I told you I have another job.'

'I know,' he said softly.

Clouded air rolled up from Charlie's panting mouth. She dutifully sat next to Angie, peering up at them. Angie handed the leash to Nick. Even between their gloved hands, a spark snapped at his touch.

'Okay, I lied,' he said.

Angie's mouth fell open.

'When I said mall, I meant me,' he said. 'My life isn't the same without you, Angie. When you turned to me that day in the café, everything changed. I want to be a better version of myself when I'm around you. For years, I took advantage of the holiday season as a time to make money. Now I know there's more to it. What is the point of holidays and special occasions when you don't have someone to share them with?'

'Nick—'

'Please, let me get this out,' he said, holding his hands up between them. 'I know you're leaving because of your new job, but I wasn't sure if this could work out. I'm willing to try with you.'

Angie smiled as her entire body buzzed to be closer to him. 'You want us to work out?'

'Of course I do,' he said. 'If I could go back to the first day we met, I would have told you about my job regardless. It was a mistake to keep that from you. It was ridiculous and selfish. But even then, I wanted you to have everything you needed at the time. I always believed in you.'

Angie opened her mouth to speak, but Nick held up a hand to stop her.

'I have no excuse for my father either. He shouldn't have meddled in my life, or yours. I don't want you to walk out of my life because of that.'

'I'm not leaving.' If she learned anything from the last few weeks, honesty was key. Especially because she agreed with everything he said.

'What are you talking about? You said you had a new job.'

'It's in the city, just a short train ride each morning and evening. I'm staying in Brookside.'

'You are?'

She nodded. 'For a long time, I wanted to escape this place. It started as an adventure to see where I wanted to be, then the memories of Dad kept me away. I've been away from home for so long that I didn't realize how much I missed all these years. I love my family, Reese, Jer, Grace …' Her words swallowed the last name she wanted to say. Was it too soon to tell him the truth of her heart? 'My friend, Emma, informed me of a fundraising event planner position at her company. The wrapping station unlocked a feeling inside of me that I'm not ready to let go of just yet.'

'I'm sorry about everything,' he said.

'Me too. But I want to see what happens with us.'

'I'll do anything to make it up to you.'

'Good,' she said.

Nick sighed. 'I can't believe this.'

She took his hand in hers. 'Believe it.'

Nick moved closer to her until they were inches apart. She lifted on her toes and pressed her lips against his. They were warm and soft. Her eyes fluttered closed as his hand wrapped around her waist, pulling her closer. The world fell away from them as they kissed. Memories flooded her mind, specifically when they were alone at his apartment. The same excitement coursed through her at his touch. *This is right*. Nick was always right for her. Hardening her heart had only prevented them from being together. Now, it softened and opened to the man in front of her.

Nick slowly broke the kiss, and Angie lowered herself to the ground again. Charlie's nose bumped her hand before letting out an excited yelp.

Angie laughed as the sensation of Nick's lips faded from hers. She wanted more, but he looked as if he wanted to say something.

'I have a gift for you,' he said, pulling out a familiar wrapped box from his jacket.

'You made me wrap my own gift?' She laughed – she hadn't expected the gift to be for her. He had tricked her in the best way.

'I wanted to see you that day. It was my excuse and I wanted to surprise you. I was a terrible wrapper, so I needed the help.'

'You have some talent.' Angie weighed the box in her hand. The wrapping paper reminded her of the good she had done since she came home. Gently, she shoved a finger under the seam and opened the gift. She glanced at Nick. His eyes sparkled with anticipation. Angie let out a small gasp when she realized what was inside the box. She lifted the string of the glass snowflake ornament she had picked out the day they went Christmas tree shopping.

'You said it reminded you of family,' he said. 'Neither of us had much between us other than family heirlooms. I thought we needed a new tradition.'

'We?' Angie asked a little breathless.

Nick smiled, and her knees wobbled. His hands wrapped around her waist, and he pulled her close. 'I don't intend to let you out of my life again. That is if you'll have me.'

'Of course,' she said.

Nick leaned closer, and Angie lifted her chin, waiting for another kiss.

Instead, something wet peppered her cheeks.

Nick tilted his head back and laughed.

'What is it?' she asked, wiping away what she thought was Nick's tear. They had been through a lot the last few days, but she didn't think he was the overly emotional type.

'It's snowing,' he said.

The clouds opened, and thick flakes cascaded from the sky. Angie grinned so hard her cheeks hurt. 'Finally.'

Nick's expression softened as he looked into her eyes. 'Finally.'

Then, they kissed again – one of many more to come.

Acknowledgements

As always, I want to thank the HQ Digital team for making my stories come to life. Thanks to Belinda for believing in Nick and Angie's story. It's been a pleasure working with you again. Thank you for finding the story and challenging me and these characters.

As always, TSAG – you are the support system that I've always wanted and will forever appreciate all of you.

Thanks to Laurie, Kierney, Jessi, and Carla for helping me during the early stages of this book. Your input has made this book into something amazing, and to Matt and Joanna, for helping me make this story as accurate as possible!

Thanks again to my readers, Mom and Leigh, for being my best cheerleaders and not being afraid to call me out on the little things. <3

And last but certainly not least, my readers. Thank you for supporting me through my writing career, and I love you lots and appreciate you!

A Letter from the Author

Merry Christmas!
I hope you enjoyed falling in love with Angie and Nick as I have. This story began as my love letter to Hallmark Christmas movies, as they have been my November/December obsession for years. Angie and her wrapping station popped into my mind years ago as if she were plucked from the Christmas universe and wouldn't let go until I told her own festive romance story.

I'm humbled and honored that you've chosen to add *Wrapped Up for Christmas* to your shelf, and I hope you got all the Christmas feels from this story.

If you enjoyed this book, I would be forever grateful if you left a review. Reviews are how readers find books, so even one or two sentences helps immensely in getting Angie and Nick's story into more hands.

I love being in touch with my readers, so feel free to contact me on Facebook, Twitter, or Instagram to chat about the story or books in general.

Thanks for reading and happy holidays,
Katlyn

Dear Reader,

Thank you so much for taking the time to read this book – we hope you enjoyed it! If you did, we'd be so appreciative if you left a review.

Here at HQ Digital we are dedicated to publishing fiction that will keep you turning the pages into the early hours. We publish a variety of genres, from heartwarming romance, to thrilling crime and sweeping historical fiction.

To find out more about our books, enter competitions and discover exclusive content, please join our community of readers by following us at:

@HQDigitalUK

facebook.com/HQDigitalUK

Are you a budding writer? We're also looking for authors to join the HQ Digital family! Please submit your manuscript to:

HQDigital@harpercollins.co.uk.

Hope to hear from you soon!

If you enjoyed *Wrapped Up for Christmas*, then why not try another delightfully uplifting festive romance from HQ Digital?

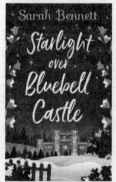